Dark Biology

Bonnie Doran

I0674195

DARK BIOLOGY

Contact Information: titleadmin@pelicanbookgroup.com

All scripture quotations, unless otherwise indicated, are taken from the Holy Bible, New International Version[(R),] NIV[(R),] Copyright 1973, 1978, 1984 by Biblica, Inc.™ Used by permission of Zondervan. All rights reserved worldwide. www.zondervan.com

Cover Art by *Nicola Martinez*

Harbourlight Books, a division of Pelican Ventures, LLC
www.pelicanbookgroup.com PO Box 1738 *Aztec, NM * 87410

Harbourlight Books sail and mast logo is a trademark of Pelican Ventures, LLC

Publishing History
First Harbourlight Edition, 2013
Paperback Edition ISBN 978-1-61116-277-6
Electronic Edition ISBN 978-1-61116-276-9
Published in the United States of America

Dedication

To my husband.

Praise for Bonnie Doran

First Place, 2005 East Texas Writers Association Contest (young adult novel)

Second Place, 2006 Inspirational Writers Alive! Contest (young adult novel)

1

Infection Minus Ten Months

Hildi's nose itched.

She ignored it. While she waited for her lab partner to emerge from the airlock, she checked the seals of her blue biocontainment suit again. Good habits could save her life.

Hildi pulled a coiled yellow air hose suspended from the ceiling and plugged it into a socket near her waist. The deflated suit expanded as air roared past her face. The familiar ballooning sensation saddened her for a moment. She'd miss her work here.

Then she grinned. She'd be wearing a pressure suit in her new job and performing similar cutting-edge work in an even stranger environment.

Her practiced eyes appraised Biosafety Level 4, the Centers for Disease Control and Prevention's most dangerous lab. Everything down and cold. But an adjoining room held liquid-nitrogen freezers filled with hot agents, the deadliest diseases known to man. Francine stepped from the airlock. Hildi's college friend had never worked in Level 4, but she moved with confidence. Hildi stared into Francine's faceplate and noted her calm expression. She'd do fine.

Hildi maneuvered past the stainless-steel tables dominating the room. She pulled two-inch test tubes, a push-button micropipette, and other tools from drawers and placed them in the biosafety cabinet, a glorified box with a fume hood and clear front that rested on the work counter. She detached her hose, inhaling the reserved air in her suit.

Humming to herself, she walked into the adjoining room and attached her suit to another hose. Every time Hildi moved in the lab, she repeated the procedure, a necessary inconvenience if she wanted to continue breathing.

She punched a code into the lock of one of the stainless-steel freezers and extracted a vial of the latest X virus that may or may not have killed John Doe.

Returning to the biosafety hood, she slipped her yellow-gloved hands under the clear protective shield, a sneeze guard at a toxic salad bar. She withdrew a tiny sample of the unknown and released it into one of the tubes. After Hildi repeated the protocol many times, she keyed the information into the computer.

Hildi glanced at Francine just as she straightened from a hunched position over a microscope. Francine turned, her movements jerky like a marionette's. Her suit's chest zipper gaped, exposing her blue scrubs underneath. She seemed to shrink as her biosuit deflated.

Hildi froze.

"I've got a problem here!" Francine yelled, her voice quavering. The rush of air in their ears turned conversations in Level 4 into a shouting match. Francine fumbled for the zipper with trembling fingers.

Hildi's heart skipped several beats, then she zipped the suit shut in one smooth motion. "Zippers get worn. They can pop open."

Francine's white-rimmed, dark-chocolate eyes returned to normal. "How bad was that?" Her voice still quavered.

"Your suit had positive pressure the whole time. A hot agent couldn't get in. You OK?"

Francine gave a nervous chuckle. "Sure gave me the jumpy jitters." She turned back to the scope.

Hildi released the breath she'd been holding. Risk was part of the job. Zippers failed. Gloves failed. Usually it wasn't life threatening.

She placed the rack of tubes in the incubator cabinet maintained at the ominous temperature of warm blood, and then returned the original sample of hot agent to the freezer. Her mood descended into a gray chasm. She already missed the challenge of Level 4. But she had a job offer that would take her research to a whole new level. She could smell that Nobel Prize. Her brother Chet would never catch up to her now.

Hildi exhaled a heavy sigh that fogged her faceplate. "Done," she yelled. "Finally I can get out of here and scratch my nose."

"Thought you'd be used to it after three years."

"Never. Right now it's driving me nuts."

Francine chuckled and headed for the airlock.

Hildi followed. She inhaled the chemical smell as the decontamination shower sprayed disinfectant over her suit. The two of them scrambled out of their blue suits as soon as they reached the changing room. Hildi scratched her tingling nose with ferocity.

Francine grinned at her and walked to the regular showers which contained detergent for washing and a bath of ultraviolet light.

Hildi hung her short suit next to Francine's long one. She reached up to caress a sleeve of the guardian that protected her against infection. "Thanks for keeping me safe. I'll be back."

Hildi stripped and marched naked to the shower. No modesty in this job. Afterward, she tugged on jeans and a mauve T-shirt.

Her lab partner's perfect complexion glistened as she toweled off. Hildi's pale skin and red curls contrasted with Francine's coffee coloring and corn-rowed black hair. Not exactly twins separated at birth.

"When do you get in to Houston?" Francine pulled on black leggings and a flowered tunic then grabbed her tiny purse.

"Around four." Hildi grimaced. "Rush hour. My favorite time." She longed for the feel of the afternoon sun on her face, but she wouldn't enjoy it today.

"I'm surprised Director Hunt gave you such a long leave of absence."

"It's a fantastic opportunity." Her spirits bounced like an acrobat on a trampoline. "But it's not like I won't be working." She grunted as she wrenched her holds-anything-and-hides-everything handbag from her locker.

Francine smiled. "You know, I might just lock you in one of the labs until after your flight leaves."

Hildi laughed. "You wouldn't dare."

"Don't try me. I'm missing you already." Francine hugged her. "I can't believe you'll be gone for over a year."

Hildi swallowed to keep her voice from cracking. "I *will* be back for visits, you know."

"You'd better be."

They walked through another airlock into a corridor and less-lethal safety levels. The burning, moist smell of giant autoclaves bid a pungent farewell.

"You just don't want to work with Chet." Hildi baited her friend.

"Don't rub it in." Francine lowered her voice. "Did you hear? Your brother's in big trouble." Francine sounded like she relished the thought.

Hildi groaned. "What did he do this time?"

"Chet worked on that new anthrax sample from England without authorization. Director Hunt turned three shades of purple."

"Hunt's a bit paranoid about the paperwork, that's all."

Francine shook her head. "Your brother has an attitude."

"I know." Hildi frowned. "It's hard to work in the same building with him when he avoids me like—well—the plague."

"He's done a good job at alienating *everyone* around here, so don't feel special."

They drove directly to the airport in Francine's tired green Altima. The Atlanta traffic, abysmal at any time of the day, choked Hildi with exhaust fumes. She turned up the AC. "Sure you don't mind caring for my cat?"

"Whiskers will be just fine."

Francine pulled up to departures, opened the trunk, and hefted the bulky suitcases. "What do you have in here, moon rocks?"

Hildi grabbed her carry-on. They chatted until a security officer ordered, "Clear the lane, please."

Hildi fished in her purse for a tissue and gave Francine one more tight hug. "Thanks for everything."

"*Vaya con Dios.*"

Hildi wheeled her suitcases to the nearest door, her stomach fluttering as if she'd just won the lottery.

Maybe she had.

****

Hildi deplaned in Houston after an unremarkable flight. She heaved her suitcases onto their wheels and stepped outside. A tanned man in a polo shirt and jeans held a sign. *Dr. Hildebra.* Someone hadn't quite fit her name on the cardboard. Situation normal.

"Evangeline?" He smiled.

"Please call me Hildi."

"Larry Gomez."

Hildi stifled a gasp and flung her starstruck feelings aside as she wiped sweaty palms on her jeans. Larry's exploits in space were the stuff of legend. She shook his hand.

He loaded her luggage into the trunk of his silver Jaguar convertible. More diesel exhaust assaulted Hildi as they headed south on I-45. She'd expected oil fields and cowboy hats when she first came here but instead found apartments, shopping centers, and malls. Same humidity as Atlanta, same traffic. He chattered nonstop.

Hildi interrupted. "So tell me about the rest of the team."

"You'll like them. Jasper Reingold and Frank Schotenheimer."

Hildi nearly jolted out of her seat. "Frank?" If she'd known, would she have volunteered for this assignment?

In a heartbeat.

Larry's face held a puzzled frown. "You know him?"

She hesitated. How had Larry missed knowing

about her relationship with Frank? Would it jeopardize her chance to work in space? No way to hide it now. "We were engaged."

"Well, things are about to get interesting." Larry's mouth quirked. "The director moved him up from a later mission when our pilot shattered his leg yesterday."

She stared at the scenery. Frank? On her team? Scenes flashed in her mind. Their first kiss that had warmed her to her toes. Her growing suspicions. The night she confronted him about his gotta-work-late excuses, and he confessed his affairs. Trampled dreams.

Lord, I could use a little help here.

Larry must have sensed her mood. He didn't say a word for the rest of the trip.

An hour later, they pulled up to the employee entrance of a sprawling facility, the salty tang of the Gulf of Mexico perceptible even this far from the ocean. Shimmers of heat rose from the pavement. After the security guard examined their badges, he beamed. "Dr. Hildebrandt? Welcome. Let me page Dan Stockton for you. He asked me to notify him when you arrived."

Hildi's mind whirled. First Frank and now Dan? Last time they'd talked, Dan had been training in Alabama. Probably his idea of a romantic surprise. She tried to submerge a surfacing smile. She wanted to jump into his arms when Dan arrived. Instead, she forced herself into neutral pose. He wore a periwinkle silk shirt with coordinating tie. Always a tie, as if he could never relax.

Larry whispered in Hildi's ear, "Now you know why he's earned the nickname Dandy Dan."

"Hildi." Dan stepped toward her with an eager grin, glanced at Larry, and stopped in mid-stride.

"You know him, too?" Larry's glance bounced back and forth between them like a hyperactive tennis ball.

Dan hesitated. "Uh, yes. We've met."

An uncomfortable silence descended. Hildi stared at the polished floor, counting the squares. She didn't want to tell the mission commander about another relationship, especially when she couldn't explain it herself. An on-again, off-again, long-distance relationship that was going nowhere.

Larry cleared his throat and turned to Hildi. "Another fiancé? Have *we* ever been engaged?"

Hildi laughed, relieved he didn't ask any more questions.

Dan smiled. "Would you rather go to your quarters first or eat?"

Her stomach rumbled in response.

"Perry's Steakhouse?" Larry still eyed them with suspicion.

"Yes, sir." Dan spread his arms and planted his feet on the emblem emblazoned on the floor, like a barker at the circus. "Welcome to the Johnson Space Center and phase two of astronaut training."

2

"I" Minus Nine Months

Chet's nose itched.

He scowled as he waited forever for his new lab partner to emerge from the airlock. Hildi's leftovers again. Francine wasn't his idea of a perfect coworker, but the boss hadn't given him a choice.

"What took you so long?" he yelled as she finally entered Level 4.

"Keep your pants on." She glared at him through her faceplate, muttering under her breath.

Chet clenched his jaw. Francine's hostility could ruin a perfect morning. Must have gotten it from his sister. Well, two could play at that game. "Set up the microscope and slides in the hood," he snapped. "I'll get the virus."

"Yes, *sir.*"

Chet ignored her as he maneuvered past the counters to the incubator. He extracted a rack of tiny plastic flasks containing an unknown procured by a British epidemiologist in the Congo. They contained living cells from a monkey's kidney, tiny drops of blood from an unnamed human victim, and a nutrient bath. If John Doe died from a virus, the monkey cells would shrivel up and burst. Chet could be holding one of the deadliest diseases known to man. And it was the

9

deadly diseases that fascinated him.

He carried the rack and set it beside the microscope. He placed one of the flasks under the scope, leaving the cap in place, then stared into the eyepieces until he got a clear look at the living cells. The virus itself, of course, would be too small to see.

Francine took test tubes to another safety hood.

"Careful with that. And handle those slides with tweezers."

"I know the protocol." Her back blocked Chet's view of her work. Probably deliberate. His blood pressure rose. If she did her job, she'd extract droplets of the unknown with a pipette and place them on slides. But he couldn't do *his* job of supervision with her antagonism.

Chet performed a day's detective work with no conclusive evidence that John Doe died from a virus. He huffed. Most viruses came, mutated, and went. Sometimes they killed people. But most of them were small potatoes compared to Ebola. Get exposed to that, and you could kiss the world good-bye in hours, not days. And no one knew where it came from. Now *that* was a mystery worth solving, not this stupid name-that-virus game.

He stood and stretched, checking the chest zipper of his suit again. He'd heard through the grapevine about Francine's zipper episode. He glanced at her to check her suit seals, but she bent over her work, still not finished. What a slug. He had better things to do than supervise a minion.

Time to check the monkeys.

Chet stepped down a corridor into another room lined floor to ceiling with stainless-steel wire cages. Most were empty, but a few contained rhesus monkeys, their screeching muted by the rush of air in Chet's ears. The monkeys raced back and forth in their cages, eyes staring at him from furless pink faces. They recognized him even through his faceplate. Eager paws reached through the bars for treats. The dominant male displayed his boredom and yawned, exposing wicked canine fangs.

Chet grinned as he grabbed fruit-flavored cereal bits from a box and held out his hand to the male. The monkey plucked the bits from his open palm, crammed them into his mouth, and held out his paw for more.

Keeping his palm flat, Chet distributed the treats. None of the lab animals ever bit him, but their sharp teeth could easily puncture his gloves. Bad idea.

Chet lingered at the cage of his favorite primate, a brown rhesus weighing twelve pounds. Minnie's eyes were solemn as she took the cereal. She'd survived the Ebola virus. All of them were survivors. They should be allowed to live the rest of their days in peace, but they would never leave Level 4 except in body bags destined for the autoclave.

Francine came in and offered treats as well. When she turned to face Chet, she raised an eyebrow and smirked. Chet fumed. Everyone in the lab got attached to the monkeys. So did he. Why was it such a big surprise?

"Did you finish the slides?" He slammed the cereal box on the counter.

"Yes." She spat the word.

Francine should be fired for her sullenness. He hoped he never worked with her again.

"I'm leaving." Chet beat her to the airlock. He cycled through and entered the men's suiting area.

After he finished the decontamination procedure and pulled on jeans and a T-shirt, he strode through the final doors of the level. Francine's back retreated ahead of him in the hallway. She must have dressed in record time.

Chet passed his badge in front of the security scanner, nodded at the guard, and left the building. A cool April day greeted him outside, and he donned his jacket for the short walk home. He pounded toward Shepherd's Lane, his stomach tightening as he seethed about the unfairness of it all. While he'd been sweating in Sierra Leone, working to identify and contain an unknown virus, perfect little Hildi nabbed the opportunity of a lifetime—experimenting with viruses in space. He usually ignored her ambition as long as it didn't trample his own objectives, but enough was enough. She'd mirrored his every professional move. They even looked alike.

Their work on vital vaccines—Hildi with Lassa fever, Chet with Ebola—could revolutionize the African continent already ravaged by AIDS. Whoever won the race would get all the accolades. Last one in was a rotten egg. And he'd never win if the director kept giving him such stupid assignments.

That Nobel Prize is mine, dear sister.

He stopped as his elderly neighbor shuffled out her front door. "Hi, Edna. Let me get your paper for you." The news carrier had tossed it on the roof of her aging Cadillac, the jerk. Edna nodded her thanks and shuffled back.

Chet stepped into the sparseness of his house—gray blinds, modern couch and chair in red, a large-screen television in basic black, a small dinette. A metal-and-glass display case showed off his origami creations, with his beloved full-rigged sailing ship in a prominent place. Baker's racks in the kitchen sagged under the weight of appliances and alphabetized gourmet ingredients.

He set his briefcase near the door and strode to the kitchen. Peering into the refrigerator, he pulled out a bottle of Riesling and poured a glass into stemmed crystal. A perfect pairing with his Szechuan chicken.

He marinated the chicken and chopped vegetables. Waiting for the brown rice to finish steaming, he sat in the chair, sipped his wine, and read a bit from his e-reader.

A blinking light on the phone near his elbow indicated a voice mail. He punched the button.

"Hi, honey. It's your mom. Hope you're having a good day. We're praying—"

He erased the message. He should switch to cell phone only. She didn't know the number.

When the timer chimed, Chet pulled himself out of the chair, heated his wok, and stir fried his dinner. The dish needed more crushed red pepper but otherwise was perfect. He ate it with ivory chopsticks and chased his meal with another glass of wine.

After cleaning up, he turned on the news and pulled his latest origami project toward him. Events hadn't changed since yesterday—war, economic woes, tsunami damage. Someday they'd announce real news like a vaccine for AIDS, and he wanted to be a part of it.

The anchor paused, apparently waiting for the teleprompter to switch to another story. His dark hair had just the right touch of gray to lend him authority. "In Houston's Johnson Space Center, the crew of the first manned Rigel capsule is training for its mission to the International Space Station. Among the astronauts returning America to space is Dr. Evangeline Hildi Hildebrandt, a renowned vaccinologist with the Centers for Disease Control and Prevention. She'll be testing her theory that microgravity, which causes certain microbes to flourish, can also aid in the development of vaccines. For more, we switch to Gary Nelson. Gary?"

Gary the reporter appeared with Chet's sister standing by his side. "So Dr. Hildebrandt, any Nobel Prizes in the works?"

Heat surged through Chet's body. He slammed the off button on his remote but not before Hildi's laugh penetrated the airwaves.

Spoiled brat.

He'd show her. He'd show everyone.

3

"I" Minus Five Months

Hildi took a deep breath. The McDonnell Douglas C9B Skytrain II mocked her from the tarmac of Ellington Field. She and the other astronauts waited to board the infamous Vomit Comet. They all wore blue jumpsuits with their names embroidered above their left pocket and the Rigel patch on their short sleeves. The members of her crew were there: Larry the commander, Jasper the mission specialist, and Frank the pilot. Her mouth tightened. She could be civil with Frank, couldn't she? She was a professional. She breathed a prayer she'd act like one.

The crew of the next mission joined them—Dave, Jim, Shorty, and Dan, her...what? Boyfriend, friend, Frank's ex-best-bud? Or just a casual no-commitment date? She wished she knew.

"Beautiful plane, isn't it?" Larry planted his hands on his hips. "Until it climbs over the hill."

"You're right about that." Dan grimaced. "I'm glad we don't ride the thing often."

Over the hill. Astronaut-speak for the high point of the parabolic flight path, when she'd experience weightlessness for the first time. Hildi had heard the stories. She hoped they were the result of astronaut bravado. It couldn't be that bad.

They boarded and sat in the main compartment. A faint, sour odor clung to the padded walls.

"I think it'll be a giggle." Hildi had enjoyed every other practice session thrown at her. Why should this be any different? She buckled herself into a seat against the wall.

Dan winked at her.

Frank stared at him briefly before turning his attention to Larry. "Piece of cake."

Shorty laughed. "I hear the other astronauts loved it. For the first few dips, that is."

"At least we won't have this roller coaster on the space station." Larry shook his head. "Hard to believe the actors and film crew for *Apollo 13* did it voluntarily just to make a movie."

"You mean we don't have to volunteer?" Jasper slapped his forehead with Oscar-winning melodrama. "Why didn't anyone tell me?"

Dan glanced at Frank. Frank scowled back at him.

Hildi examined her cuticles. She hoped someday the men would give up their infantile behavior and act like friends again.

Small talk dominated the cabin as the plane taxied. It seemed like any other plane at takeoff. Then it started climbing at a forty-five-degree angle, weighing them down with twice the force of gravity. Hildi's stomach twisted her light breakfast into knots.

Her body leaned toward the tail of the plane. Her memory intruded. She was spinning on an amusement-park ride, sliding into her brother as they got dizzy together. The memory faded with a pang.

The jet accelerated and leveled off. Just before it went over the hill, Hildi started floating in the induced weightlessness. "Whee!"

Jasper grinned as he somersaulted in the air. "Yahoo!"

"Enjoy it while you can, kids." Larry propelled himself from one wall to the other.

Ten seconds of microgravity…Twenty…Thirty…

Hildi floated down to the padded floor as the plane dove at a thirty-degree angle, leveled off, and started another steep ascent. Two g's returned as the plane followed a precise parabola to counteract gravity, thirty seconds at a time.

Weightless returned. Hildi floated up and drifted down.

Dive, climb, over the hill, dive, climb…

On the eighth parabolic cycle, Dan retreated to his seat, looking a bit green and clutching a sick bag. By the tenth cycle, Jasper and Shorty joined him. By the twelfth, Dan retched.

Hildi wrinkled her nose. The smell and sounds of vomiting created a chain reaction. She survived until cycle thirty. When the plane finished the fiftieth parabola and descended for landing, she could only groan in relief. Her tummy would never be the same.

Frank alone remained unscathed. He'd always bragged about his cast-iron stomach. Handy thing to have in space. He turned to her and flashed a lopsided grin.

Her insides lurched, but it wasn't due to excess stomach acid. Was he thinking she could forget about his indiscretions and resume their relationship?

Buddy, that rocket launched a long time ago. Get over it.

4

"I" Minus Four Months

Whee!

Hildi hovered like a seagull on an air current. She hung suspended underwater in the Neutral Buoyancy Laboratory at the space center. Divers surrounded her for safety, their bubbles racing each other to the surface. Two hundred feet long and forty feet deep, the training pool was an exotic playpen.

"Still doing OK?" The crew trainer's voice sounded tinny in her helmet.

"Sure. I've scuba-dived at twice this depth."

"Yeah, but I bet you weren't wearing an Extra Vehicular Activity suit."

She snorted. The bulky outfit didn't feel much different than a biosuit.

Hildi's mind wandered to her first scuba dive with Frank. A blue-and-green queen angelfish had swum just inches from her mask. She seized that pleasant memory as less pleasant ones intruded.

A six-inch flash of gray zipped past her. Hildi gasped. What was that? The theme music to *Jaws* played in her headset just as she noticed the wind-up invader's tail movements. She chuckled. "Hey, who let the shark out?"

"Wasn't me," the trainer said, all innocence.

Practical jokes ran rampant at NASA. Humor helped to ease the tension from intense training, so the brass ignored most of the antics. She suspected Jasper.

Hildi sank toward a mockup of the space capsule. Jasper followed.

Larry hovered near the capsule with a tool in his hand. "Ready to bolt a few panels into place?"

Jasper signaled OK. "Sure, Larry. Are we using oak or pine panels?"

Hildi rolled her eyes. "Where's Frank?" With another bimbo? If only she could believe he'd given up his indiscretions.

"Pilot training," Larry said.

Fine. Hildi's conscience said her attitude wasn't fine. The dagger of Frank's betrayal had sliced deep, but God had healed those wounds.

Hadn't He?

She wanted to treat Frank as a friend.

Didn't she?

Now NASA had thrown them together for ten months of training and a flight to the station. Determination filled her. So be it. She'd act like a professional. It disturbed her, however, that he seemed to trail her like a bloodhound. She was through with romance. At least with him.

Hildi concentrated on the job at hand. She wouldn't let Frank ruin her fun.

****

Dan surveyed the three stepped levels inside Mission Control and stared at the fifteen curved desks with their clusters of computer monitors. In just a few months, the place would be alive with controllers—flight director, mission operations director, flight surgeon, and his own position as CAPCOM.

A smile rose to his lips as he anticipated the job as capsule communicator. He took pride in his work as the only one who talked directly with the spacecraft.

The flight director entered the room. Dan had never met anyone more intense. With Steve Walters's unruly blond hair and the kind of looks that attracted women like children to ice cream, people often underestimated the man. Dan would never do that again.

"Reminiscing?" Steve's blue eyes pierced through Dan's thoughts.

"Yeah, boss." Dan touched his own station in the row of desks. "I enjoyed being CAPCOM for the shuttle missions. This will be a lot different."

"Not so different. You know the Rigel's instruments just as well as the shuttle's. The equipment's changed, but astronauts stay the same, eh?" Steve winked.

Dan grimaced at the old joke. "Not exactly."

"See you here at takeoff minus ninety-six hours." The director left.

Dan saluted his retreating back, thankful Steve would be flight director during his own shift. Only a fellow astronaut knew the subtleties of space flight, and Steve had logged enough missions to fill bookshelves.

The public affairs officer, Barry Stokes, hurried past the desk, and Dan shook his head. Dealing with the press wasn't his idea of fun, although the media would pay little attention except for the occasional human-interest story. Even with the first-flight status of the Rigel series, space was too ho-hum.

Unless something went terribly wrong.

He thought about Hildi's work today in the pool, the closest thing on Earth to a weightless environment except for the Vomit Comet. If he knew Hildi, she'd love the launch. She was a born adrenaline junkie.

His jaw clenched. Working in space with all its dangers had never bothered him. Now someone he cared about deeply would be at risk. He gnawed his lower lip. His real concern should be Hildi's work in Biosafety Level 4 here on Earth. The constant threat of exposure to lethal bugs gave him the willies.

He shrugged at his overactive worry gland. The other astronauts were all veterans, and he knew she'd be in good hands. He just wished he could enjoy Hildi's reaction to space. And monitor Frank's behavior. His old friend still pined for her.

Hands off, buddy. She's mine now.

Or was she? He enjoyed being with her. He respected her, liked her, cherished her. But was that all?

He took a comb out of his pocket and tamed his dark hair, grateful he had an appointment with the barber.

Hildi met him in the hallway, her curls still damp from a shower. Beautiful, with or without makeup. "Hi."

"Hi yourself." He smiled when her stomach grumbled. "Ready to eat?"

"I'm ready to eat a Texas longhorn, tail and all."

****

Frank eased up on the controls and peered at the

full-color, flat-panel display, a startling improvement over the old shuttle's instrument panel. Just a little more thrust...He shut down the attitude jets as the Rigel spacecraft's nose slipped into the docking ring of the International Space Station.

"Capture complete. Nothing but net." He grinned. He'd slam-dunked the docking simulation again.

"Third time in a row, hotshot."

"Roger." Frank reset the capsule for another training session. He could fly this critter blindfolded, even with the manufactured emergencies thrown at him by the guys in charge. An autopilot was always available to take over the tricky docking procedure, but no one trusted the software. He ran his fingers over his blond crew cut. "Let's try the landing procedure, Flight. Mix it up a little."

"Roger."

As he waited for the computer download, Frank chewed an energy bar and chugged water from a bottle. Once more, he wished for a shuttle-style landing. Flying the shuttle had been *real* flying, even if it was a powerless glide to the Kennedy Space Center. For the new Rigel series, a pilot only had to point the spacecraft into the proper trajectory and deploy a parachute. Big deal.

When the simulator showed reset, he followed memorized instructions to maneuver the capsule into a tightly defined angle of descent, critical if the crew wanted to survive. When the instruments displayed a pre-calculated altitude, he pressed a button, feeling imitation yanks of the drogue parachute and then the main ones. Finally, he hit the virtual ground. The impact jolted every joint in his body. He was home. He much preferred a water landing, but the spacecraft could handle either scenario, dependent on the whims of NASA.

"Landing complete." Frank finished his final act— readying *Reconciliation* for egress. *Reconciliation.* What a name for the first manned flight in the series. But he didn't have a voice in the matter. Rumors said it had something to do with the new treaty with North Korea.

Larry was all right, the kind of man everybody liked on sight. Jasper, too. Hildi...His thoughts tumbled into self-blame. Sure, he and Hildi were on amicable speaking terms, but their polite interaction didn't assuage his unrelenting guilt. He'd really blown it, and busted balloons were impossible to patch.

When he'd gotten the new assignment, the flight director had grilled him on whether he'd have a problem working with his former fiancée. Frank assured him he could handle it. After all, he'd just be piloting a space ferry. He and Larry would drop off Hildi and Jasper then pick up Leonid and Joe. Two days together on *Reconciliation* and a few days on the station before heading back. He didn't understand NASA's concern.

Wrenching his thoughts back to the gauges, he concentrated on the next test.

After several more hours, he'd had enough. "Hey, Tom, can I call it quits for the day? I'm ready to get out of this can and grab some grub."

"Roger that. Got a hot date tonight?" He could hear the grin in Tom's voice.

I wish.

Frank popped the hatch and climbed out of the capsule that NASA claimed was designed to hold four people. Four little people. His knees always brushed the edge of the instrument panel as he trained. At least

Hildi wouldn't feel cramped.

He wondered about Hildi and Dan. He'd watched them during the last few months as they trained together for their mission. There was something between them, but he wasn't sure what.

His childhood friend and rival had been cool toward him ever since the breakup. Frank didn't know how to act around Dan, either. And Dan was the new golden boy in the eyes of NASA. He would pilot the next mission, another test of the new Rigel series. After that, a dress rehearsal for the moon launch. In low Earth orbit, the pilot would extract the lunar lander module and dock with it, a maneuver as awkward as shooting hoops while encased in Jell-O. The flight after that would be to the moon itself if Congress ever approved the funding. NASA had already been forced to reduce ISS personnel to three, a skeleton crew trying to do the work of six. Frank shook his head at the never-ending politics.

His stomach complained that a mere energy bar didn't substitute for dinner. A thick rib eye sounded good, medium rare with a baked potato. He hailed Jasper, who needed no coaxing to join him at Perry's Steakhouse.

Walking out, Frank spotted Hildi and Dan on their way to the parking lot, holding hands.

Ouch.

5

"I" Minus Three Months

Hildi'd taken Atlanta's transit system from the airport. As soon as she emerged from a MARTA station, she enveloped her friend in a bear hug.

Francine squealed. "I can't believe it's been seven months."

Hildi grinned. "Time's fun when you're having flies."

"*Ribbit.*" Francine shook her finger. "Don't ever do this again."

They stowed Hildi's carry-on and drove into gridlock. Typical Atlanta traffic.

"So how's astronaut training?" Francine thumbed her steering wheel as she not-so-patiently waited through another cycle of the traffic light.

"Grueling. They let me off for good behavior this weekend, but I usually don't get any farther than Perry's Steakhouse." Hildi smiled. "Last week I went to the beach with Dan. That was nice."

"And?"

"And what?"

Francine grabbed Hildi's left wrist. "No engagement ring?"

Hildi snatched her hand out of Francine's grasp. "No. He hasn't asked me. Yet."

"What's wrong with that man?"

Hildi sighed. "I don't know."

Francine raised an eyebrow but said nothing more until they pulled up to their favorite Chinese restaurant. "Is this OK for lunch?"

"Perfect. You can't imagine how tired I am of steaks and the Johnson Center's food."

As they walked in, Francine eyed her up and down. "Yep. We need to put some meat on those bones."

Hildi sighed again after they ordered their usual choices—hot-and-sour soup, Mongolian beef, and garlic chicken. "Dan and I have run into a bit of a snag. Our careers."

"I don't understand."

"It's simple. We both love our work, and neither one of us wants to give it up."

"You've got to be kidding. Why should you let your jobs interfere with love?"

Dipping a spoon into her soup, Hildi twirled it before answering. "I know. It's stupid, but there it is. He's so stubborn—"

"Oh, and you're not?"

"Don't you start." Hildi immediately regretted her sharp tone. "Sorry. Things have been a bit tense with Dan lately, and the training's wearing me out."

Francine sipped her tea, apparently weighing her next words. "You're not thinking of breaking it off, are you?"

Hildi ignored the sudden lurch in her stomach. "Perish the thought." *Or not.*

Francine dropped the subject.

Hildi described the practical jokes she'd endured at the hands of fellow astronauts. "And then *someone* put a slide rule in a glass case inside the simulator, with a note saying, 'In case of computer malfunction, break glass.'"

Her friend guffawed, wiping her eyes with a tissue. "Was Jasper the culprit?"

"I think so. He and Frank are nose to nose in practical jokes."

"How is Frank, anyway?"

Distant. Hildi huffed out a breath. "He's been acting a bit weird. One day he's Mr. Eager-to-Please, the next he's avoiding me."

"Do you think he suspects? About you and Dan?"

Hildi propped her elbow on the table. "He might. We've tried to keep it quiet so NASA doesn't know. They wouldn't like it."

"Good grief." Francine cracked open a fortune cookie that crumbled with the force of her grip. "Do they expect you to turn into automatons while training? Can we say *human*?" She rescued the slip of paper and read it aloud. "'Money and fools are soon parted.' Well, no one said these things were infallible."

Hildi broke open her own cookie. "'Love will find you in the oddest place.'"

"Ha."

Hildi tried to smile, but her heart wouldn't cooperate. Love itself was odd. "As a matter of fact, they don't expect us to be human. Just astronauts. But enough about me. How're you?"

"Same-o, same-o." Francine signaled their young Chinese waitress for a fresh pot of tea and poured another round.

The scent of jasmine and the hot brew did little to calm Hildi's worry. Her nerves tightened every time she thought of Dan. Romance and Dan didn't belong in the same sentence. Where did that leave her?

Francine described the latest Level 4 work in general terms, since the CDC insisted on confidentiality. "Oh, by the way, I'm sorry to tell you Nellie died."

"Oh, no." Hildi's emotions descended to a gray place. She loved that rhesus monkey.

"Yeah. She was a sweetie. The last virus we gave her was just too much."

Hildi sipped her tea, cradling the warm cup. "How's Chet? You ever see him?"

"You mean, speaking of microbes?" Francine wrinkled her nose. "Not since I worked with him that one time. I begged Director Hunt not to do that to me again. Chet's reckless, irresponsible—"

"I know."

Their server brought the bill. Francine grabbed it. "My treat." She lowered her voice. "Scuttlebutt is that he's still in trouble with Hunt."

"You mean you didn't have a calming influence on him?" Hildi loved pulling her friend's chain anytime they talked about her brother.

Francine harrumphed. "Hey, let's get out of here and do something fun. Are you up for a movie? We can check the computer listings when we drop off your stuff."

"Anything but space opera."

"Done."

Hildi's heart hummed with the simple pleasure of hanging out with a friend. And an uncomplicated relationship.

6

"I" Minus Ten Days

Carol Hardesty smelled burnt bacon as she sat at the dining table and thumbed through a lingerie catalog. *Oh no.* She ran to the stove and tonged stiff slices onto a paper towel. At least she hadn't ruined the scrambled eggs. She divided them between two plates, added the bacon and blackened wheat toast, and carried breakfast to the table. Mike folded the Saturday paper and attacked his meal without grace or a thank you, his eyes still glued to the news.

Carol sighed and ate in silence. Again. She tried being a model housekeeper, but Mike preferred to do the cleaning. She aspired to be a perfect cook, but all it got her was dry chicken. Tantrums to get her husband's attention didn't help. Coaxing Mike to take a walk together—or to do anything together—resulted in a blank stare. Even the silent treatment hadn't worked.

She thought she'd have a fairytale life. They'd met in college, fallen in love, and married a week after graduation. Mike climbed the corporate ladder. She started a website design business. But now, five years later, their love was stale and so was their marriage.

Carol pushed away her plate, finger-combed her ragged brown bangs, and turned her attention to the mail. Junk, bills, magazines. A brochure caught her eye. She read it and re-read it, hope growing. Could this be the answer to her prayers?

She slid it across the table to her husband. "Honey, look at this."

Mike grunted as he glanced up from the paper, eyeglasses perched on the end of his nose. He picked up the brochure and read the title. "A marriage seminar? Why would we want to go to that?" He tossed it on the table and returned to his reading. His blond hair peeked over the top of the paper as if asking what her problem was.

She shook her head. He still didn't get it. "Please. It's important to me. Besides, it's Worthington Hildebrandt."

"Is that the crackpot who was drummed out of his denomination?"

"He's not a crackpot." Carol grabbed the brochure and scanned it. "I've always wanted to hear him speak. And he's doing a seminar here in Denver. Listen to this. 'Worth and Laura have experienced firsthand what can hurt a marriage. They will teach the principles needed for a strong relationship. What they reveal can make a difference in emotional, spiritual, and physical intimacy.'" Carol cleared the dishes from the table, half a slice of bacon leering at her. She snatched it before her diet noticed. "It's only a hundred dollars a couple," she spoke around her chewing. "We can afford that."

"A hundred bucks for a seminar? I bet they insist you stay in the hotel, too." Disgust etched his face.

"It does include lunch." Carol hated the little-girl pleading in her voice.

"What's the matter with you? We don't need

anything like that."

"Yes, we do!" Carol slammed the egg skillet into the sink, adding scalding water and tears. "You always have your head in the paper. We never talk anymore."

"I keep telling you to join some clubs." Mike's calm voice infuriated her. "You need to branch out a bit, make new friends."

Carol continued her tirade. "You're never home, and when you are, you never acknowledge my presence. Monday is our fifth anniversary, and you'll be working late. Again." Bitterness edged her voice.

Mike gave her a puzzled frown. "I thought we agreed to go out on Tuesday."

"You'll forget. You always do." She loaded the dishwasher, determined to tamp her temper.

Mike put down the paper and sighed in apparent defeat. "When's the seminar?"

Carol picked up the brochure and checked the dates. "Uh, the weekend after next, Friday and Saturday. Monday is the last day to register."

"I wanted to work on the yard that weekend. It's the only chance I'll have with the overtime at the office." He crossed his arms in an I-won't-budge-from-my-plans gesture. "Tell you what. I'll attend this thing, but I'll have to skip church on Sunday to trim the hedges. Do you mind?"

Carol controlled her impulse to hurl the dish sponge at his face. He always tried to manipulate her, especially when it came to Sundays. She drummed her fingers on the counter. She hated going to church alone. Everyone would talk. But if the seminar would make a difference in their marriage…

"Deal."

7

"I" Minus Five Days

C. Worthington Hildebrandt raised his eyebrows as he turned to his wife. "No luck, I take it?" He glanced toward the mantel to the framed photograph of their son in happier days. Chet and Worth had identical hair back then. Now gray strands sprouted among Worth's red curls like weeds in a lawn. Age and the price of his betrayal had taken their toll.

Laura wrinkled her nose as she returned the cordless phone to its cradle. She plopped into the blue armchair, propping her feet on the ottoman. "I had to leave a message. I don't know if Chester screens his calls or just wasn't home. Evie says he often works late." She flipped a strand of brown hair behind her ears.

Their daughter, who preferred the nickname Hildi these days, always made excuses for Chet. Worth was tired of excuses. She wanted to spare her mother's feelings, he supposed, but Laura was too smart for that. "Well, you tried." His lopsided smile was an attempt to reassure Laura, but his heart dropped to his toes. He fought his decidedly unchristian desire to let Chet stew in his own angry juices. His son had never forgiven him. Worth had a hard time forgiving himself for nearly tearing apart his family. One rip remained.

"I can't imagine what this is doing to you, Worth." Laura sighed. "Maybe it would be better if I didn't call him."

Worth responded with what little enthusiasm he could muster. He owed her that much. He walked over to the window and gazed into the backyard. The bushes needed trimming. He turned to her. "No, I think you should keep trying, at least for his sake."

"For *his* sake?" Laura's voice raised a notch, the loudest the soft-spoken woman ever got. "I hit a brick wall every time I invite him for the holidays. He hung up on me the only time he picked up the phone. He's our *son*."

Worth sat on the loveseat and raised his arm.

She slid next to her husband and cuddled into his embrace. "Why can't he be more like Evie?"

He stroked her hand as if he could stroke away the hurt. Her question was one Worth had asked God many times, and he'd never been satisfied with the answer. "Chet is still filled with rage. Until he comes to terms with his anger..." He stood again and paced, thoughts of estrangement with their son churning in his mind. "I'm glad forgiveness won out with Evie. Only the Lord can turn Chet around."

"If you ask me, he's taking this too far. Soon he'll be nothing but a bitter old man."

"He hurts himself as much as he hurts us." Worth said the words, but the old pain persisted.

"It's getting harder and harder for me to reach out." She straightened the coasters on the coffee table, apparently skewed one degree off center. "So...are you looking forward to this conference?"

Worth chuckled at Laura's usual tactic—an abrupt change of subject. Chet's behavior poured boiling water on her heart. She'd come back to the issue after she calmed down. "Yeah, I am. I've always liked Seattle. The office tells me we should have the best turnout ever." Worth returned to Laura's side and pecked her cheek. "You did a great job of choosing the luncheon menu for Saturday."

"Chicken is always a safe choice."

"What would I do without you?" Worth closed his eyes. "There are so many broken marriages out there. If we can help just one couple, it'll be worth it."

"Well, I for one will be glad when the Seattle trip next weekend is over, we're done with the conference here in Denver, and we can spend time at home." Laura stood and wrapped her arms around herself. "We need some 'us' time, and right now I'm exhausted. Especially after that woman in Detroit." She huffed. "I hate the ones who ask for advice but are really looking for permission to blame their husbands. I don't know how you stand it, teaching these couples and knowing full well some will fall over the brink of divorce no matter what you say."

"All we can do is speak the truth and leave it to God. Like we do with Chet."

Her eyes filled with tears.

Thankfully, Worth also knew when to change the subject. "Heard anything lately from our astronaut daughter?"

She smiled and wiped her cheeks. "She sent us an e-mail. Evie jokes that the training is killing her, but I know she loves it. She always did love being the daredevil." Laura's tone turned serious. "Only this time it's not jumping from a ten-foot wall with a homemade parachute. This *could* get her killed."

"She'll be fine." *I hope.* "You know how careful

NASA is these days. She'll be with veteran astronauts and have plenty of training herself." He grinned. "We take our life in our hands every time we get on the freeway."

"I know." Laura's eyes took on that faraway look. "Our daughter the astronaut."

"Hard to believe."

"I worry about her."

"Of course you do. She'll be going into space. You don't know what alien race might be lurking behind Mars, just waiting—"

She grasped his hand. "Oh, stop it." A frown wrinkled her forehead. "I was thinking about Frank and Dan."

"She's forgiven Frank, and Dan…well, I like Dan."

"So do I, but she'll be spending a lot of time with Frank." Laura turned to Worth. "I know how hard forgiveness is. It's easy to say the words but harder to live it."

Worth winced.

Laura knew from experience what a man's unfaithfulness could do to a relationship. She had taken him back, but not without tears and fears. His heart ached for Hildi as much as it ached for his wife. Hugging her again, he cocked his head. "What did she say about Dan?"

"They're still dating, if that's what you mean. It's been a year. I'm glad she's taking it slow, but—"

"They should be engaged by now?"

She folded her arms and glared at him.

Worth stared at his watch and gasped. "It's been two whole hours since we talked about this."

Chuckling, she fell back into his arms. He loved to make her smile.

"We need to pack." She pulled another gear change.

He shrugged. "I'll do it in the morning."

"I don't know how you speed-pack. Me, I like a list."

"That's because you're organized."

Laura took a deep breath. "Well, if we're going to make it to the plane on time through the morning rush hour, I'd rather start now. Should I take the aqua pants or the red dress?"

"Love, you look wonderful whatever you wear." His usually confident wife must feel vulnerable, or she wouldn't ask. He vowed to enjoy some time together without the usual overbooking of counseling appointments. "The dress, of course. It's always been my favorite. But let's pray before you disappear into the bedroom."

They asked God's blessing for the conference, the attendees, and the message. But Worth's thoughts were with his children.

8

"I" Minus Three Days

Hildi sighed and then cuddled into Dan's shoulder. Warm sand tickled her toes as they sat on a beach towel, admiring a pumpkin-colored moon as it rose out of the sea. Stars twinkled their welcome. The surf *shooshed* in a comforting rhythm. Ahh...

Picnic on the beach with her favorite person. The perfect setting for that special question. God must have ordered this romantic moment especially for them.

Dan wrapped a protective arm around her. He gazed into her eyes and...pointed at the moon. "Full moon."

"Nice." *And...?*

"See that large spot in the center? That's the Sea of Tranquility. That's where Apollo 11 landed."

"Uh-huh." Right now she was not interested in a history lesson.

"That's right where I'll land."

Hildi crossed her arms against her chest. Not again.

"C'mon, you know how much the moon shot means to me." He squeezed her closer. "You can wait that long, can't you?"

"You've got to be kidding."

Dan leaned forward. "I'm worth waiting for."

Hildi jumped up and paced in the sand. Of all the pigheaded, egotistical...She turned and plastered an I'm-so-confused expression on her face. "Waiting? For what?"

"You know."

Planting her hands on her hips, she glared at him. "I don't know. You've never asked me, Mr. Astronaut. You might own the stars, but you don't own me."

Dan's mouth dropped open, but no sound came out.

Mission aborted. Again.

She spun on her heel and strode up the beach, fists clenched. His sputtering and the snap of his flip-flops behind her made her run. She had a good head start.

Hildi raced through the parking lot with her tote bag banging against her calf, reached her Smart Car, and slammed the door. The grinding noise from her overactive attempt to start the engine ratcheted her frustration level another notch. No sense taking it out on an inanimate object. After a deep breath, she turned the ignition key more gently, and the vehicle purred to life. As she roared away, her rearview mirror showed a waving, shouting bacterium at the edge of the asphalt. Hildi left her *ex*-boyfriend to find his own way home. Served him right.

****

Dan stood in the parking lot, his mouth still open. He clamped it shut. What had he said this time?

He shook his head at Hildi's outburst. It wasn't like her. He racked his brain to figure out what had set her off. They were talking on Galveston Beach...

He slapped his forehead. Of course. She'd

expected him to propose. He hadn't actually asked her to marry him, but she should have known he intended to. He probably would have, too, until she threw a temper tantrum. What was her problem? Did he have to spell out everything for her like a procedural manual? He just didn't get it.

Dan chewed his lip as he retrieved the towels, anticipating a forty-mile walk to the apartment complex in Clear Lake unless he flagged down a fellow astronaut. He could pound on her door and settle things. No. He should let her cool off. He started the trek as determination hardened.

He'd win her back.

****

In the drive to her apartment, Hildi's anger turned inward. She'd lost her temper. That was happening a lot lately when she and Dan had a few moments alone. Why were they always arguing? Was he the pigheaded one, or were they mutually obstinate? Maybe *she* was the problem.

She sighed as she pulled into her parking space. Another possibility jarred her. Was this an indication they weren't made for each other? Or was his apparent cluelessness something else altogether? She'd just assumed they had an understanding, but what if he was attracted to those women who always hung around space boys? In the year they'd dated, he'd never said he wasn't dating others. If he went out with one of those…those sirens, she'd feel betrayed. The way she felt when Frank had cheated on her.

As she trudged up her walkway, Frank nearly bumped into her, dropping his mailbox key. She had once thought his freckles and dimples were cute. "Sorry." Speak of the devil. The *last* person she wanted to see. Or, maybe the second to last.

"You startled me." Frank bent to retrieve the key. He cocked his head. "You seem a bit preoccupied."

"Oh, you know how it is." Hildi didn't want launch into a long explanation. She faked a smile and hid behind small talk. "Any more emergencies like that last simulation and I'll just get out and walk."

Frank laughed. He had a nice laugh. Too bad he'd tainted it by his infidelity.

"You want to come in for coffee?"

After the spat with Dan, Hildi was sorely tempted to accept kindness, even from him. Exhaustion answered for her. "Thanks, but I'm beat."

"I'm buying." He stepped closer, a pleasant whiff of his cologne reminding her of better days in their relationship. He seemed eager, attentive.

She hesitated then shook her head. "Maybe next time."

"Catch you in the salt mines, then." Frank walked past her.

****

Frank glanced at Hildi out of the corner of his eye as she entered her apartment. He ground his teeth. Anger simmered underneath her light words. Another argument with Dan?

He knew the signs in their secret smiles. Dating, with all its dancing emotions. His anger festered to think his old childhood friend had hurt her, although their disagreement gave Frank the opening he needed. Perhaps he could still salvage their relationship. If they could only talk...He shook his head. After he'd wantonly disregarded their engagement, would she ever give him a second chance?

Frank entered his own apartment as resolve enveloped him.

He'd win her back.

****

Hildi entered her apartment, feeling oddly relieved. She tossed her tote bag on the easy chair and rummaged through it. She retrieved a half-eaten sandwich—ham and Swiss on rye. Still edible. Funny how arguments made her hungry.

After polishing off the sandwich with a good-for-you salad and a can of soda, she indulged in a piece of dark chocolate—her ration for the day. A warm shower helped ease tense shoulders. She pulled on shorts and a NASA T-shirt then flopped into the chair. She dumped the remaining contents of her tote bag on the coffee table. A women's magazine fell out, the kind filled with photos of all-glamour-no-blemish models. She'd picked it up out of idle curiosity, the cover promising an article on the space program. The article stank almost as much as the perfume sample buried inside. Tossing the magazine aside, she reached for her novel.

The lingering scent of the scratch-and-sniff card plunged her heart down a painful path. She'd smelled women's cologne on Frank that day. Sensual, seductive...

"I thought you said you were training late." She could no longer deny her doubts, especially when he smelled like Chanel No. 5. Hildi didn't wear perfume.

"I was! Do I have to check with you every minute?" Frank stomped into her kitchen and pulled a cola from the refrigerator.

She followed him, short fingernails gouging the palms of her clenched fists. "Don't lie to me. I can smell somebody's eau de stench." She plucked a long strand of blonde hair from his shirt. "This isn't mine."

He swigged his soda. "I went out for a drink with a coworker. That's all."

Disbelief squeezed her heart. She advanced on him. At least he had the decency to retreat, although decent didn't describe his behavior. "We're engaged, Frank. It means exclusive. Or didn't you understand that when you proposed?"

He held up his hands. "I didn't do anything."

Knots formed in Hildi's stomach. She stared at him as comprehension twisted the rope tighter. If only she could strangle him with it. "This isn't the first time, is it? Is it?" Her voice quavered. "Did you sleep with her? With them?"

"No."

"Don't lie to me."

"OK, maybe I slept with some of them. It's no big deal."

Hildi's jaw dropped along with her heart. He was actually making excuses for his behavior. Anger replaced her disbelief. "No big deal? Whatever happened to that no-sex-before-marriage commitment? What happened to your commitment to God, to me?"

Frank lowered his gaze.

Busted.

He huffed a breath. "You have no idea how these women come on to me. All the astronauts have groupies."

"No, they don't." But they make themselves available. Her fists clenched, begging for a chance to deck him. "So that's the way it is? You see absolutely nothing wrong with sleeping around before the wedding. Our wedding."

"I guess I wasn't thinking. I'm sorry I hurt you." He reached for her, cradled her face with both hands, and caressed her cheeks with his thumbs. "C'mon, honey. Those were just flings. You're the one I want."

She stepped back. Pain sliced through her. She yanked the engagement ring from her finger. At least she had summoned the dignity to place it in his palm instead of throwing it out the window. "I won't marry you. Now get out."

Hildi startled out of the dark memory, still rubbing her ring finger. She exhaled. At least she'd had the good sense to end the relationship. Frank was ancient history. Dan was a different problem, but at least he wouldn't cheat on her. Would he?

She reached again for her novel. On second thought...

Hildi checked her watch, pulled out her cell phone, and speed dialed Francine's number.

"Hello?" A sleepy voice answered.

"Did I wake you?"

"Hildi!" Francine's excitement reached ear-splitting level. Hildi held the phone at arm's length.

"Glad I caught you at home."

Francine chuckled. "Well, I had a hot date with a virus, but the microbe canceled at the last minute. What's up? Has a certain someone popped the question?"

Hildi snorted.

"He didn't?"

"No, he didn't. It was a perfect evening at the beach. We watched the stars come out. The moon rose…then he pulled his moon-mission mantra." She pounded the armchair.

"Do you want me to strangle him for you?"

"Nah. That's my job." Hildi huffed out a breath. "Tonight's quarrel really makes me wonder if God plans for us to be together. I want Dan, not a sparring partner."

"It'll pass. Just think how much fun it'll be to kiss and make up."

Francine's suggestive tone made Hildi smile in spite of herself. It was short-lived. "I don't know, Francine. I just don't know."

"Maybe Dan's right. Maybe you should wait until he comes back to Earth. Until he gets the moon out of his system."

"Hey, I thought you were on my side. That'll be two years."

"I'm on both of your sides."

Hildi inhaled a huge breath, clamping her teeth on a sharp answer as Francine continued.

"Look, all I'm saying is maybe you guys shouldn't have the wedding right after your stint on the space station. Let him have his moon mission. Then you can launch your marriage."

"Our relationship *is* a launch, delayed for months due to technical difficulties. At the rate we're going, it could be scrubbed."

"Well, I for one know you'll blast off. You just need to get past this."

Hildi shook her head. "Every time I think he's going to propose, he talks about the moon. I'm tired of playing second fiddle to another stupid NASA program." A yawn escaped her.

"Glad I'm so entertaining."

"Sorry. I'm a little sleep deprived. I'd like to think you're right, but I'm bone tired of waiting."

"Maybe you're just bone tired. Get some sleep."

"Yes, Mommy."

"I'll pray for you. Everything will work out."

Francine, the ultimate optimist. Hildi smiled in spite of her heart's protests. "I'd keep a stiff upper lip, but I'd get a sprain. Thanks for letting me unload on you."

"Anytime."

"How are things at the lab?"

"Same old thing. The scenery never changes. And your brother's still in trouble."

"Figures."

Hildi turned off the phone, prepared her coffeemaker for the morning brew, and yawned again. She headed for the bedroom.

As she fought for sleep and lost, sadness wrapped around her. *Lord, I said I forgave Frank, but have I really?*

Another thought intruded. *And does Dan really love me?*

9

"I" Minus Two Days

"So you're telling me I'm fired?" Chet stood before a polished walnut desk in the administration building, his jaw clenched.

Director Hunt peered over his horn-rimmed glasses. "You're a good worker, Chet, but we don't feel your skills are best served in Level 4."

"Oh, so you're *demoting* me." He glanced behind Hunt at his reflection in the glass protecting the U.S. President's photo. The shower Chet had taken after his blue-suit work had plastered his red hair to his scalp. He could have at least used a comb before facing his boss, not that he had any respect for the man.

"There are plenty of opportunities in Levels 2 and 3," Hunt said. "Some of our most vital research is performed there."

Chet stifled a smirk. The man was begging. Chet was irreplaceable, and the boss knew it. "Ebola is the real challenge, and that's Level 4 work."

Hunt stood and waddled around his desk, bending his neck to maintain eye contact. "Your team members have become concerned about your mindset." He seemed to pick his words like a politician. "We can't allow a flippant attitude in the lab. I warned you after that stunt with the English virus, but you continue to perform unauthorized work. I can no longer tolerate such behavior." Hunt crossed his arms. "Well?"

Chet's nostrils flared. His teammates were spreading lies about him. "I'm not flippant."

The corners of the director's mouth turned upward in that smile again. He should run for Congress. "Look, you've been overworking yourself for months on this latest research. Maybe you need a break. Take a week or two. Relax. Get some perspective on this. Then we'll talk." He put his hand on Chet's shoulder, a gesture that autoclaved Chet's blood.

"Is that an order?"

Hunt peered over the rim of his glasses. "Just consider it a strong suggestion."

Chet spoke through clenched teeth. He wasn't going to tolerate Hunt's treatment one second longer. "In that case, my vacation starts now." He stomped out of the office and slammed the door.

Grabbing his laptop case from his cubicle, he stuffed it with the few things he wanted for a forced leave of absence and stalked out. He spotted a few of the other scientists, but they suddenly seemed absorbed in their work. He didn't want to talk with them, either. Francine passed him in the hallway and scowled at him. Big surprise. She was buddy-buddy with his dear sister, who obviously had filled her head with lies.

Traitors.

He walked past a coworker's desk and spied the keys she'd tossed on it. Sloppy. Hmmm. She had access to the Infectious Diseases Lab, Level 3. Something clicked in his brain. He snatched the keys and strode to the lab in a nearby building. No one around. A scrawled note over the eye of the security camera indicated a malfunction. So much the better. He unlocked the door, slipped inside, and set down his case.

Chest freezers lined the walls of the room, with stainless steel worktables in the center. Snapping on a pair of gloves, he opened a freezer and plucked a vial at random. He squinted at the label. H1N2—a pretty run-of-the-mill flu strain. Good enough. He pulled off his gloves inside out, encased the tiny container in one, and stowed it in his briefcase. That should mess up Hunt's precious paperwork royally, and they'd never trace it to him.

He returned to the office building and replaced the keys on his coworker's desk, careful to leave them in just the right position. She had a habit of taking long lunches, which worked to his advantage today. He smirked.

Satisfied, he clocked out. He experienced a momentary worry when a security guard checked his laptop case, but as usual, the guard did only a cursory inspection. He waved Chet through.

He marched to his house, strangling the handle of the case. Wisdom told him he should toe the line at work, but no way was he going to kowtow to his arrogant boss.

Inside his modest home, he plopped on the couch and retrieved the vial of colorless liquid from its latex-glove package. He held it up to the light and studied it. Amazing how much misery could be contained in such a small package. The theft had been an impulse, just to mess up paperwork and pull Hunt's bureaucratic chain, but releasing it in a public place—or, say, the boss's office—might be educational.

A slow smile spread across his face. Perfect. He stroked the vial like a treasured pet.

The blinking light on the phone caught Chet's attention. Frowning, he set down the vial and pressed the play button. He groaned as he heard a familiar voice.

"Hi, hon, it's your mom." Her voice had a high pitch as if she'd plastered a fake cheeriness to it, though it was hard to tell on a recording. "Say, your father and I will be teaching a marriage seminar in two weeks in Atlanta. Why don't you join us for dinner afterwards on Saturday night? Our treat." She hesitated. "I know you're still angry, but we miss you. We want our son back." When she continued, her voice sounded strained. "Well, anyway, we'd like to see you. By the way, we're home in Denver this weekend for another seminar, and the trees are just starting to bud. We especially love the aspens in the yard. We wish—"

Chet slammed his finger on the delete button. When would she learn? She called every week, filling his machine with her stupid pleas. Always the clueless peacemaker. He never wanted to talk to her or his father again. Ever.

He hung his jacket in the coat closet and removed his tie. Not in the mood to cook lunch, he ordered Chinese takeout with egg rolls and crab cheese wontons. Sweet and sour sauce in packets was abysmal, so Chet decided to prepare his own. He set a copper-clad pan on the stove and gathered ingredients. By the time his meal arrived twenty minutes later, his sauce had thickened to the perfect consistency.

As he munched on Kung Pao chicken and fried rice, an idea coalesced in his mind. Setting his ivory chopsticks aside, he called Cruise Adventures and asked for Tony.

"Hey, Tony, it's Chet Hildebrandt." He crunched into an overdone egg roll after drowning it in his sauce.

"Well, long time no see. Or hear. Ready to book another cruise?"

"Yes, and a long one this time. Europe, or maybe the Mediterranean. I've had enough of my job for a while."

Tony chuckled. "Hasn't everybody? Let me see what I can do. When do you want to leave?"

"ASAP."

"Can I call you back this afternoon?"

"Sure. I'll be home all day. Catch ya later."

Chet shoveled the remaining fried rice into his mouth. As he ate, he glanced past the otherwise bare dining room wall to the corkboard jammed with newspaper articles—"Ebola Wipes Out Village," "West Nile Virus Strikes Colorado," and "Influenza Will Hit Early This Year." He cleaned the kitchen while listening to a Bach fugue on his top-of-the-line stereo system.

The phone rang. He ignored it. The answering machine clicked on.

"Hey, Chet, it's Tony from Cruise Adventures. I found a deal for you. It's a transatlantic cruise, leaving Fort Lauderdale for fifteen days total. But—"

Chet plucked the handset from its base. "Across the Atlantic? You must be nuts. How long does that take?"

"Seven days, but you'll love it. The ports of call include the Bahamas, Bermuda, Portugal, Spain, and England among others. The cruise line's running a last-minute special. I can even get you into a London hotel if you want, but that's extra, and only the ritzy ones are still available."

"Hang on." Chet grabbed a pen and scribbled on a note pad. "So what are the dates?"

Tony hesitated. "The thing is, they do this route only in April, and the ship sails in two days. Can you be ready that soon?"

"I was born ready."

"So do you want me to book the cruise?"

"Sure. I appreciate your work on this."

"No problem." Tony gave him additional details, including the price, and told Chet he could pick up the tickets the next morning. Chet declined Tony's offer to book airline flights, preferring to make his own arrangements.

After hanging up, Chet smiled. Although the trip was a bit more expensive than he expected, he deserved it after Hunt's treatment. He hadn't had a vacation in, what, two years? Long overdue. Now if he could only charge it to his expense account...He shook his head. He knew better than to risk that kind of trouble with the boss.

Glancing again at the vial next to the phone, Chet frowned. What should he do with it? He could infect his boss, or return it to the lab, or destroy it, or...He cradled his chin in his hand. An idea formed. Of course. He'd add a little detour to his itinerary.

Chet pulled out his laptop and set it on the dining room table. He browsed for an online travel service and booked a one-way trip from Atlanta to Denver, leaving tomorrow afternoon, and another from Denver to Fort Lauderdale. He didn't reserve a return flight from London, uncertain how long he would want to stay. He always wanted to keep his options open.

Chet slid his laptop into its case and tucked the vial inside. He threw in a packet of origami papers and his e-reader, loaded with medical thrillers. Then he stepped into his bedroom to finish packing.

His parents would get a little surprise.

10

"I" Minus One Day

Carol fingered a wisp of her overgrown bangs as she waited for the seminar to start. When she'd signed up, reservations told her the weekend was nearly sold out, but she still hadn't anticipated the hotel's cavernous conference center to be so packed. The straight-backed chairs in once-popular burgundy made her fidget.

She glanced at her husband, eyeglasses perched on his nose, head buried in a science fiction novel. Mike claimed he had to keep his mind occupied, but it looked like an escape tactic to her. Escape real conversation. Escape intimacy.

Escape marriage?

Carol shifted in the uncomfortable chair. She'd gone the last two years with a silent partner. At least he'd agreed to attend the seminar. Her lips curled into a not-quite smile. Desperately she clung to the prayer the seminar would improve their relationship, but hope had faded to a murky gray. What would it take to reignite their love? She clutched a dog-eared copy of her favorite women's novel, identifying with the heroine's desire for an affair—with her husband.

Carol shivered and shrugged on her sweater. She had forgotten how chilly a hotel's conference room could be. "It sure is cold in here."

"Hmmm?" Mike's eyes didn't leave his book.

"I said, it's cold."

He lifted his head, inserting a sales receipt as a bookmark. "I like it. Better than roasting to death. By the way, that roast was good last night."

Was he being sarcastic? "I thought it was a bit tough."

"Maybe a little. You should buy it from that organic place. A coworker raves about their meat."

Carol crossed her arms. "It was on sale."

"Honey, we can afford better beef."

Heat rose up her neck. She tried so hard to make a dinner that would impress him, but she always overcooked it or undercooked it or something. She could be nominated for the world's worst cook. Now he was starting an argument right before a marriage seminar. She blocked the lava flow of anger before she told him what she *really* thought.

As Mike left to stretch his legs, Carol tamped down her emotions and turned on a pleasant smile for the couple sitting next to her. They'd introduced themselves earlier, but she couldn't remember names in spite of her attempt at mnemonics. George the Jolly? Betty the Beatific? They seemed the least likely to need a marriage seminar. They were the kind of elderly couple that had grown to resemble each other—same eyeglasses, silver hair, and sweet expressions. They were holding hands.

"Have you attended this conference before?" Betty's gentle smile included Mike as he returned to his seat.

"Nope." Mike's terse response rankled Carol. Then he added, "But you seem like veterans."

"Worth and Laura are dear friends. We seldom get to attend their seminars. We're so glad they decided to hold one in their hometown." Betty glanced at the still-empty stage then turned her attention back to Carol. "We live in Centennial."

"We're from Littleton." Carol found herself warming to this kind woman with wise eyes.

"Oh, you're so close. Maybe we can get together after this is over. We've met so many new friends through these seminars."

"Maybe," Mike said.

"We've formed an ongoing group with some of the attendees. You know, to focus on relationships." She leaned over to whisper in Carol's ear. "Have to keep the home fires burning."

"I resemble that remark." George gave a mock-angry snarl.

Betty reached into her voluminous purse, pulled a business card from its depths, and handed it to Carol. "If you're interested, e-mail me."

Carol glanced at the card. "You sell cosmetics."

"Yes, dear. Now that the kids are grown and moved away, I wanted to do something fun."

Cosmetics. Carol had to admit her makeup could use an update. And her wardrobe. And her waistline. "Maybe you could help me with makeup colors sometime."

"I'd love to."

"Fun?" Mike raised an eyebrow. "Sounds like as much fun as a root canal."

Betty's laugh tinkled like a delightful wind chime. "Men. Even George doesn't get it, but at least he tolerates my enthusiasm. Most of my sales are to established customers, but it took years of hard work to build up my clientele. George is my biggest cheerleader."

"It helps support her habit." George dead-panned his words.

Betty lightly slapped his forearm. "Honestly. Just because I enjoy bridge with the girls—"

"Bridge?" Carol's interest went up a notch. "You play bridge?"

"Yes, dear. Would you like to join us? We meet every Tuesday evening. We can always use new players."

"Or victims." George winked.

"I'd like that, but I'm not a very good player."

Betty patted Carol's arm. "Oh, don't worry. We play, drink tea, and talk. We do it just for fun."

"For fun and the teacups," George said.

"Teacups?" A confused frown crossed Mike's face.

George rolled his eyes. "Yeah, they play for teacups. They keep track of their scores for the month, and the girl with the best overall score wins a cup and saucer. My wife has enough to start her own tea shop."

"So what do *you* do when they're playing for teacups?" Mike actually sounded interested.

"Bowling with the guys." George's eyes twinkled. "Had to do something in self-defense. Beats listening to the hens cackle, though I love to sneak a scone or two when they're not looking."

"Well, I never." Betty struck a faux-offended pose, nose in the air, and turned away.

"I like to bowl," Mike said. "Carol and I were in a league once, but that was before her surgery. I've missed it."

Carol raised an eyebrow at her husband. "I never knew you were so disappointed." *You never told me.*

"I didn't want to rub it in, since you can't swing a ball anymore." Mike turned to the elderly couple. "Carpal tunnel."

Carol sighed. "The surgery was months ago. It didn't help much."

Betty patted her hand. "You poor dear."

Carol wondered at the sudden lump in her throat. Betty seemed to radiate compassion. Carol barely listened to the rest of the conversation. So, Mike really missed bowling? Had she given the impression she didn't want him to bowl alone? She couldn't remember ever discussing it.

Mike glanced at the podium as the speaker finally mounted the steps. Carol lassoed her stray thoughts. She'd sort out cosmetics, bridge, and bowling later. The four of them sat and turned their attention to the front as someone introduced Worth Hildebrandt.

****

Showtime.

Worth scrutinized his image in the mirror as he struggled with his red tie and checked his makeup. He grimaced. He hated the greasepaint but knew it was necessary. A film crew was videotaping for a future DVD, and his ruddy face would glow in the camera lights without a little powder.

"Ready, Worth?" Laura sparkled in her red dress, its simple lines emphasizing her trim figure.

"Yes, except for this blasted tie." He blew out his breath as he yanked it apart for the third time.

Laura untangled it and reached on tiptoe to create a perfect Windsor knot. "I always liked this tie on you. Makes you look distinguished with your salt-and-cayenne hair."

He huffed. "And chokes me half to death."

Laura smiled. "Not as much as I will if you don't behave."

"It's getting a little frayed. Do you really think I should wear it for the taping today?"

"Just tell them why this particular tie is so important. It's the best way to get their attention."

Worth nodded. He never wore any other tie. Taking her hand, he led her out of their room.

They stepped onto the stage as the audience applauded. Worth inwardly chuckled when he realized he and Laura were waving almost in sync.

"Thank you, thank you." Worth raised his hands to quiet the crowd. "I'm so glad you've made the effort to come. Let's open our meeting with prayer."

The room hushed.

"Heavenly Father, thank You for gathering us here. You know each of us and why we've come. Some are expecting more excitement from their marriage, some more peace. For some, it's a last-ditch effort to save their relationship. Regardless of our circumstances, Lord, we pray You will stir us to put You first in our lives. Challenge us, encourage us, rebuke us for Your name's sake. In Jesus' name we pray. Amen."

The participants remained expectant. A few coughed and sneezed. It wasn't cold and flu season, but Worth's own allergies always kicked up in the spring. The room was especially frigid. Worth usually removed his suit coat but was glad the cameramen insisted he leave it on.

"Now, you may be asking yourself why you should listen to what I say. I can't know your individual struggles as I might if I were counseling you. But I can empathize with you and give you practical tools to help in your marriage. The only reason I can do that is because I've walked where some of you are walking now. I know what it is to go to bed and wonder if your spouse would be there in the morning. I've been both the spouse wondering whether my wife would stay, and the one who didn't come home.

"Laura and I are here for one thing. To help you with your marriage the way God helped us. You've heard the rumors. The media can be, shall we say, overenthusiastic in reporting flagrant sin in prominent Christian leaders. Let me set those rumors to rest."

Worth took a deep breath. As many times as he'd said the words, they always twisted the guilt thorn a little deeper. "I committed adultery. With multiple partners. Many of you have heard of my indiscretions and my being drummed out of the pastorate. I deserved it. It wasn't any fault of my wife's. I was prideful, lustful, unfaithful."

He glanced at Laura, whose eyes filled with tears. Worth swallowed. Hard.

As he continued his confession, he spotted a young man with a television camera in the back of the room. He wasn't part of the film crew. Worth recognized the network logo. Figures. He'd been unable to escape the media since he'd started his ministry several years ago. *Tape away, son. You'll only get an earful of grace.*

"In spite of that"—he stopped as he waited for the lump in his throat to shrink—"in spite of that, God restored our marriage. We love each other more than ever. Tomorrow will be our thirty-fifth anniversary."

The audience erupted in a standing ovation. A few yelled congratulations.

Laura picked up the thread of their opening remarks. "The road back was a rocky one. We're not going to sugarcoat it. We both shed a lot of tears. There were times I wondered if it was worth the effort. I can tell you it was. How many of you read those sweet, inspirational romance novels?"

The response of the audience always amused Worth. Most of the women raised their hands, along with a smattering of brave men.

"We're here to tell you that in real life, it doesn't happen that way." A few chuckled at Laura's statement. Some rolled their eyes in a "duh" gesture. Worth surveyed the crowd, noting the reactions were typical.

Laura continued. "Marriage is not a 'happily ever after' tale or a story of 'I love you, and you love me, so that's the way it will always be.' It requires blood, sweat, and tears. Tears of repentance, sweat of emotional effort, and blood—the blood of our Savior who died so we may live."

Worthington cleared his throat. "Let me tell you a story. It's about this red tie I'm wearing..."

11

"I" Minus One Day

Chet boarded the crowded plane and fought his way to an aisle seat in the back. No room to stow his carry-on. He grumbled as he surrendered it to a flight attendant for checking. Situation normal. He preferred first class, but that wasn't an option this afternoon.

He slid into his row and placed his laptop on the middle seat.

"Hey, 'scuse me, please."

Chet stepped out to let a Goth with fluorescent pink streaks in her hair slip past him. He resumed his seat and fiddled with the overhead light and vent before buckling in.

The girl turned to him. "Hi. Going to Denver?"

Duh. Chet nodded.

"I'm headed to Golden, actually. I'm going to School of Mines. Majoring in electrical engineering. Do you live in Denver?" The words tumbled out in one breath.

"No." He opened his case, extracted a package of origami papers, and lowered his tray table.

"I really like Colorado. I'm in my third year now. School's tough, but I learned to ski last winter. I like spring skiing. Did you come here to ski?"

*Let's see...*Chet extracted a piece of black paper and

started folding.

"You do origami? Cool."

He continued folding and handed the finished product to the girl. "Here. An Egyptian Slit-Faced Bat. It suits you."

Her eyes narrowed. She threw his masterpiece on the floor, made a rude remark, and turned her back on him.

Mission accomplished.

A few stragglers still boarded. One man whose head nearly scraped the ceiling pointed at the middle seat next to Chet. Chet returned the table to its locked position and stepped into the aisle again.

"Whew!" The man pulled his leather attaché to his lap and drew his knees to his chest. "Just made it. Glad I got the priority line at security." He dabbed sweat from his forehead. His eyes flitted from Chet to the Goth to the window as the plane pulled away from the gate. "I'm an accountant. Holmes and Company. What do you do?"

Great. Another gabby. Chet flashed a winning smile. "I study maggots in decomposing bodies."

The man paled. He fumbled in his case for a small bottle, shook out two pills, and chewed them. "Dramamine," he squeaked.

Chet smirked. He lowered the armrests, stowed the origami papers in his case, and retrieved his e-reader.

An unremarkable flight.

****

Chet rode the packed terminal train to baggage claim and retrieved the rest of his luggage. He stood at the counter of the rental car agency, burying his face in the e-reader. The check-in process always took forever. He selected a luxury sedan and drove directly to the event's hotel, located in the middle of the Denver Tech Center.

He waited in line at the registration desk as a high school basketball team checked in—all seven hundred of them. He'd watched them file in from buses. If he'd only been two minutes earlier…

When his turn finally came after an eternity and a half, he asked for the penthouse suite. Might as well treat himself. Leaving his heavy suitcases in the trunk, Chet retrieved his overnight bag and took the elevator to the top floor. He quickly changed into sweat pants, T-shirt, nylon jacket, and running shoes. He pulled a baseball cap low over his eyes, hidden behind a pair of grocery-store glasses. He admired the disguise then used the elevator to descend nine floors to the lobby for his reconnaissance mission.

He found the inner workings of the hotel by entering the double doors marked "Employees Only." No one challenged him. The narrow passageways led to laundry, housekeeping, and back doors to meeting rooms.

He snagged a busboy uniform from the laundry hamper. Wrinkled but relatively clean. Stuffing it under his jacket, he left. He meant to return to his room but made a wrong turn and ended up in the kitchen.

"What are you doing here?" a voice demanded. Chet turned to see a man in a white jacket and chef's toque glaring at him. Chet assumed he was the sous chef since it was late in the day.

"Oh, hi. I'm new here. I start tomorrow as a busboy and wanted to check out the place. Been working here long?"

"Too long." The chef narrowed his eyes. "Awfully old for a busboy."

"Reversal of fortune."

"Be on time tomorrow. You'll help set up lunch in the Mt. Evans room for a big conference."

"Oh, that marriage thing? I saw it on the schedule."

The chef only nodded.

"OK. Thanks."

Chet left, faking nonchalance. He had just poised his finger over the elevator button when the doors opened and his parents strolled out. He ducked into the stairway, but they never glanced his way. Relief and smugness fought for supremacy in his brain. He climbed the nine flights rather than risk being seen by anyone else he knew. George and Betty always hung around his parents like remoras on sharks. He had a stitch in his side when he card-keyed into his suite.

The mission had taken him past dinnertime. The room service menu offered the typical semi-exotic choices. No Chinese? Chicken Alfredo would have to do. He considered a split of wine but dismissed it. He needed a clear head for tomorrow.

He smiled as he anticipated the newspapers' report of an early flu season. They'd soon discover a new outbreak unresponsive to the annual vaccine. How long would it take the CDC to trace it to the hotel? A few days maybe, if the virus spread as fast as he suspected. He'd be at sea by then, but he could check the news through the cruise ship's Internet service.

He changed his mind on the drink and perused the mini-bar refrigerator for champagne. Not his favorite, but he'd cope.

Good thing he wasn't a criminal, just a guy pulling a big practical joke at a marriage conference led by the two people who should be the last ones to give advice. He had to admit sneaking around like an international spy thrilled him. James Bond and all that.

He accepted his meal from room service and tipped the server generously. He'd worked in a hotel in his college days, much to his disgust, and knew the job had little to recommend it salary-wise. He earned a smile and hopefully a bit of extra service. And privacy.

Arranging his napkin, he savored the Alfredo, which was actually very good, and then turned in. Tomorrow would come way too early.

****

Chet ate a light breakfast in his room. He ironed his busboy uniform, put it on, and studied his reflection in a mirror. A close-enough fit. He then dug into his bag for the vial, disposable gloves, a paper face mask, and a cheap plastic spray bottle. He added water to the bottle, dumped the vial's contents into it, and screwed on the cap. No need for a biohazard suit with such a mild virus, but a little extra protection couldn't hurt. He exited his room with the bottle hidden in a deep pants pocket.

After running down seventeen hundred flights of stairs, he emerged near the elevators out of breath. Got to get more exercise.

He pretended to be extremely interested in the indoor pool as an entourage of people passed him. Were his parents among them? The uniform rendered him invisible, but he waited until their reflections in the window disappeared, then found the door to the labyrinth of corridors in the service area. Showing up on time was critical to blending in. The chef he talked to earlier looked up from his sauces and scowled at him. "You are here for the luncheon?"

"Yes, sir."

The chef pointed to a closet. "The silverware is there."

"I was told to fold napkins."

Mr. Toque shrugged. "The napkins are there. I assume you can fold a Bird of Paradise?"

"Of course." Chet put his hands in his pockets so his clenched fists wouldn't show.

"Why the face mask?"

"Cold."

"All right, then. We need four hundred napkins on those tables before noon. Put one in the center of each plate with the head facing out. Understand?"

Chet seethed. Of all the arrogant busybodies. He never got along with chefs.

The man turned and headed back to the kitchen.

Chet relaxed. So far, so good. Now to get to work.

Grabbing stacks of cloth napkins from the closet, Chet piled them on a cart and wheeled it into the banquet room. Other staff members were busy spreading tablecloths and arranging condiments, but they ignored him. He found a corner in the room, pulled out the bottle, and quickly sprayed the napkins.

"Why are you doing that? Spraying the napkins, I mean?" The young Asian busboy spoke perfect English.

Chet searched the files of his brain to come up with a plausible answer. "Adding a little water makes them easier to fold. Watch." He folded one into a Bird of Paradise, grateful for his hobby of origami. "See?"

"Huh. I never heard of that trick, but it seems to work." The boy flashed a quick smile and returned to his duties.

After he finished spraying the napkins and folding them, Chet placed a virus-laden bird on each plate and grinned. How appropriate. He'd worked on a new strain of bird flu last week.

His hands cramped, and his back ached before he was done. Other servers had napkin duty as well, but his creations looked much better. No surprise there. He crackled the kinks out of his back and left the room. After trudging up the nine floors to his suite, Chet peeked out the stairway door to check if the coast was clear then card-keyed inside. He shed his clothes and showered. After changing into a business suit, he repacked and tucked the vial into a pocket of his overnight bag.

Wadding the uniform into a ball, Chet buried it in the bottom of a dirty linens bag on the first housekeeping cart he saw. He tossed the spray bottle and gloves in the cart's trash. The maid's vacuum droned from a nearby room. Carrying his overnight bag and laptop, he risked the elevator and, once on the lobby level, blended into a group of businessman taking a break from a seminar. One of the men motioned for him to join in a discussion. He smiled and nodded, understanding nothing of the conversation about software. He glanced at his watch, excused himself, and strode to the hotel lobby. Still ahead of the noon check-out time and the basketball slugs. He sailed through the revolving doors, hurried to his rental car, and drove off.

Operation completed.

12

"I"

"That was delicious." Carol wiped her lips with her napkin, folded it carefully, and placed it next to her demolished dessert. Give her chocolate, and her diet went out the window. The scalloped potatoes were too salty, but far better than her usual burned, greasy effort.

"Yeah, not a bad lunch for hotel food with four hundred mouths to feed." Mike finished his chocolate cake with a flourish, scrubbed his mouth with the napkin, and threw it in a heap on the table.

Carol scowled but resisted the urge to scold. She wasn't going to start an argument here, and she was trying to respond to her husband in a positive way. Rev. Hildebrandt's words stung—or was it God's conviction? He'd encouraged the attendees to really listen to their spouses. It had been harder than she expected during the assigned exercises. Mike was better at it, a fact that surprised her.

"Worth always picks out the most marvelous menu." Betty savored two bites of her cake and put down her fork. Carol admired the woman's self-control.

The older couple had apparently adopted her and Mike. Carol welcomed their friendship and example of marital give-and-take. Even Mike seemed impressed. At least he wasn't hiding behind a façade of indifference.

George leaned over to him. "I have it on good authority that Laura's the one who does the details like menu planning. You and I both know the gentler sex is better at that kind of thing than us macho types. We're too busy fighting the mastodons."

Mike cracked up. Carol couldn't remember the last time she'd heard even a chuckle from him. How she had missed it.

The thought disturbed her. How long had he walked around with a scowl on his face? Three months? Six months? Ever since her carpal tunnel surgery? Probably. What a witch she'd been. No matter what Mike did, he couldn't cook well enough, though he'd attended cooking school, or clean well enough in spite of his obsessive-compulsive tendency when it came to vacuuming. She'd treated that cast as if it were a royal scepter that gave her the right to hand out decrees. Her attitude hadn't changed. No wonder he frowned.

Her frustration had risen every time she'd had to do something one-handed. Working on her computer became such an ordeal that she nearly threw it out the window. Instead, she screamed and cried. Mike had tried to rescue her more than once, but she'd turned her back on his every attempt.

As Carol watched Mike conversing with George and Betty, the cake in her stomach turned to rock. When was the last time they'd talked like that? He seemed so disconnected from her, but here he was, talking with these strangers as if they were his long-lost parents. Maybe that was why Carol liked them.

Betty reminded her of her own mother. If only she'd been able to talk to Mom, she might have avoided some heartache. Mom always offered sage advice. That guiding voice had died with her.

Carol shook free of the lingering grief. She excused herself from the table and weaved through the overcrowded room, intent on beating the crowd to the restroom before the next session.

After washing up, Carol gave herself a cursory glance in the mirror, grimaced, and dug into her purse for a brush. She definitely needed a new cut and color. When she returned to her seat in the meeting room, Mike was still missing. Disappointment sagged her heart. She'd hoped for a few minutes to chat.

The rich dessert somersaulted in her tense tummy. Hildebrandt's words had convicted her. She wasn't sure what to do with the guilt.

****

Ceiling lights brightened in the hotel conference room as the seminar concluded. The audience gave the Hildebrandts a standing ovation. Carol and Mike applauded with the rest of the attendees, and Mike seemed downright enthusiastic. Halfway through the morning, he'd set down the book. He'd worked on the exercises and listened to the messages. Could this all-too-short seminar make a change in their relationship? Could *she* change? Mike said he was willing to work on their marriage. Was she?

"Did you enjoy the conference?" Betty's question bounced her out of her speculations.

Carol decided on a vague answer. She thought she'd bawl if she admitted how much the seminar had affected her. "Oh, yes. I think it was very helpful."

"Well, he sure gave me a lot to think about." Mike rarely displayed his emotions in public, but Carol saw him wipe a tear from his eye. She smiled. Fighting the mastodons, indeed.

As George and Betty left to greet the Hildebrandts, Carol faced her husband and squeezed his hand. "Honey, thanks for attending this with me. I know you wanted to trim the hedges this weekend. I appreciate your sacrifice." Carol couldn't think of the last time she'd said thank you. She could start with that.

Mike dismissed her worry with a shrug. "I can always do it next week." Then he gave her that lopsided grin that always spun her on her toes. He paused for dramatic effect. "Or maybe I can talk you into going skiing with me instead."

"This late in the year?"

"A few runs are still open. I like spring skiing."

"You know I don't ski anymore." Carol regretted her argumentative tone. "I wish I could, but I'm just afraid my carpal tunnel will kick in again."

"I don't think it'll hurt your wrist after all this time. You can check with the doctor if you're that concerned."

Carol considered her options. She could get an appointment next week. She was probably just babying herself. A slight smile curled her mouth before she frowned again. "It's been so long since we've skied. I'm sure I've forgotten how."

"Nonsense." Mike launched into his most persuasive tone. Carol didn't mind. "You could take a refresher lesson if you're uncomfortable, but it's like riding a bicycle."

"Maybe." Carol hated her lack of excitement at the

prospect. She'd been down in the dumps too long.

"Or you could go shopping while I conquer the slopes, then we could find a nice restaurant."

"Hmmm." *Maybe a romantic dinner.*

"Tell you what. I'll spring for a weekend in Aspen, complete with shopping, if you'll ski one run with me. One more condition. Help me clean up the yard on Friday. It's beginning to look like a jungle. I'll finagle an extra day off somehow. We can get an early start on the yard and then head up to the slopes late afternoon."

It didn't take long for Carol to consider the offer, although Mike was such a perfectionist that helping him prune the roses made her nervous. But Aspen…

"Deal." She doubted the glow would last, but she felt valued. A glimmer of hope shone its rays on the future.

Thanks, Lord.

13

"I"

Worth navigated his way down the stairs at the side of the stage. The auditorium hummed with conversation as people stood and stretched at the end of a long day. George waited for him at the bottom step, and Worth slapped him on the back. "Thanks for being here, old friend."

"Wouldn't have missed it." George grinned. "Betty and I always enjoy your seminars."

"And I always appreciate your prayers."

"Our pleasure. Come. Thy chariot awaits."

They shuffled toward the back exit, George acting as bodyguard. "I'm so sorry," he said to a woman as she elbowed her way through the crowd, asking for just a word or two with Worth. "I'm afraid I need to haul this man off to the airport. His daughter is an astronaut, you know, and she launches on Tuesday."

"Oh, that's right. Have a nice flight." Her raspy voice faded behind Worth as George hustled him through the crowd. On the other side of the room, Betty hurried Laura through a knot of admirers.

Finally, they escaped. Worth panted as if he'd just boxed three rounds with a heavyweight champion. Seminars always drained him.

The four of them raced out the door to George and

Betty's car. They climbed into the black Lincoln Continental, and George pulled out of the parking lot before they had time to buckle their seatbelts.

"We really appreciate the lift, but we could have driven ourselves," Laura protested from the back seat. "Three days of overnight parking wouldn't break our piggy bank."

"No more of this, dear," Betty said. "We're happy to do it, and we know how exhausted you and Worth must be. And excited. I just can't imagine having my own daughter launching into space."

"I wouldn't be able to drive straight if I were in your shoes." George's eyebrow quirked.

Laura chuckled. "Incredible, isn't it? And to think we were worried when she went to college."

A glorious sunset disappeared behind the Rocky Mountains, igniting the clouds streaming east. Worth loosened his red tie but couldn't unknot the lump in his throat. "We're very proud of her."

George pulled into the drop-off area and helped them with their carry-ons. Worth glanced at his watch. They were early by a couple of hours. "Thanks again."

"Have a wonderful time, dear. We'll be praying." Betty's face expressed regret. "Wish we were going with you."

They exchanged hugs, and then Worth lifted Laura's flowered carry-on and his battered one out of the trunk. He and Laura *whooshed* through the double doors, rolling their suitcases behind them. He gripped his wife's hand briefly before they mounted the escalator to ticketing.

Their own daughter, an astronaut. Pride, worry, and prayers churned together in his stomach. *Reconciliation*'s flight to the International Space Station would be just another routine mission. He hoped. Doubt nipped him as he remembered the *Challenger* and *Columbia* disasters. Worth reached over to grasp Laura's hand. She looked up to him and frowned. No need to say anything. She was as worried as he was.

****

Worth woke at five o'clock. The time change always fouled up his biorhythm. Resigned, he slid out of bed and padded to the kitchenette, grateful the bedroom had a door so he wouldn't disturb his wife. He prepared a pot of coffee and inhaled the aroma as the brewer spat its way to completion. He sipped a cup while he squeezed in a little prayer and Bible reading. He studied the map to the Kennedy Space Center Visitor Complex, the beach house, and NASA's Banana River viewing site. Seemed pretty straightforward.

At seven, he woke Laura with a kiss. She yawned and came instantly alert. Always the morning person. Worth envied her ability.

"Morning." She sat up then placed her hands on her hips. "And where's my coffee?"

"Coming right up." Worth returned to the kitchenette, poured a cup, added creamer, and carried it to his waiting princess. The serving-her-coffee ritual had become a part of their daily routine since...well, since he turned his life around and returned to his true love.

They dressed for a cool morning outdoors, ate the motel's hot breakfast, and drove to the visitor's center. The tour group assembled for a briefing. Worth scanned the crowd but didn't see Frank's or Dan's parents. He and Laura boarded a bus and joined the other visitors for the tour.

Hours later, the bus belched its occupants onto the parking lot of the center. Worth thanked the driver and guide before leading his wife by the arm. "We should get going."

Laura nodded. "I'm glad NASA does a farewell barbeque two days before launch. It sounds lovely."

Worth programmed his GPS unit before starting the car and leaving the parking lot, but the navigator proved unnecessary. They drove to a secluded beach area, reserved for astronauts and their families, and pulled up to a cottage with multiple decks. Worth breathed in the salty tang of the Atlantic Ocean mixed with the aroma of grilled meat and watched the waves caress the sands.

They walked up to the cottage simply known as the beach house. The first people they saw inside were Frank's parents. "So good to see you again." He grasped Dick's hand and winced at his strong grip. The man's broad shoulders testified to his linebacker days, but his hair had turned silver.

His wife Debra joined them, her blonde hair framing a pixie face. She wrapped Laura in a bear hug. Worth was still amazed at their continuing friendship with the couple whose son had devastated their daughter's life. Laura had persevered. She'd bridged the gap of awkwardness. Regret still tinged his thoughts of the marriage that could have been.

"Where's your son?" Debra frowned. "Where's Chet?"

Worth grimaced. "Not coming."

"Still angry." Laura shook her head. "I'd hoped he'd at least come for Evie's sake. He knew about it, of course, but he never returns our phone calls."

Glass shards pierced Worth's heart at the pain in Laura's voice.

Then Evie appeared in the doorway, and all thoughts fled Worth's mind except love for his daughter.

****

"That was a great dinner." Worth's stomach complained that perhaps he should have stopped gorging himself earlier.

Laura had hardly touched her steak, caught up in conversations with the other members of Evie's crew. Grateful that all the astronauts had decided to attend, he shook hands with Larry and Jasper. Frank donned his armor of bravado, avoiding them as much as possible. They danced politely around rhinos in the room. A broken engagement, the dangerous launch, and six months in outer space.

After dinner, the families strode the beach. Worth locked arms with his wife and daughter as they stepped barefoot onto the warm sand.

"I still can't believe you'll be in space in two days." Worth's grip tightened.

Evie grinned, skipping on the uneven sand and pulling her parents along. "After two years of training, I can hardly believe it myself. It's just awesome. And I can't wait to play with that virus in microgravity."

Laura frowned. "I wish your brother had come."

"I knew he wouldn't. He's jealous. He can't stand the fact I might get ahead of him in scientific recognition. But he can't catch me now," Evie whooped.

Worth's sadness grew like the lengthening

shadows. Daughter and son still at odds, consumed by competition. The repercussions of his *stupid* actions still rippled through his family. Their children had escaped from a broken home by entering hazardous careers. But he clamped his mouth shut and kept smiling. This was not the time to berate Evie for her ambition.

Laura's eyes glistened as they embraced. "We'll be praying. You know that."

"Love you, Mom. Love you, Dad."

Worth squeezed her tight one more time. "We're proud of you, daughter."

They left weeping.

14

"I" Plus Two Days

Dan poked his head in the bustling room on his way to a late dinner. The backs of fifteen men and women blocked his view of their computer monitors but not the display of the world map dominating the front wall. Mission Control was now manned around the clock—a clock standing at T minus ten hours. He yawned as he sipped a cup of black coffee strong enough to wake a hibernating bear.

Tomorrow, once *Reconciliation* launched and it cleared the tower, control would be theirs. Then he'd begin his job of relaying commands.

He strolled to his work station and gripped the shoulder of his bald-headed counterpart sitting in the CAPCOM chair. "How's it going, Dave?"

"Quiet. Thought we'd have the traditional delay or scrub by now, but everything's nominal. See you in the morning."

Dan smiled and walked away. He hoped the man would dispose of his pile of candy wrappers before then. He yawned. Tossing his empty cup in the trash, he nodded at the shift's flight director and closed the door. Food then bed.

He bumped into Sheldon Baxter, his commander for the next Rigel mission. "Hey, buddy. How's the rat race?"

"The rats are winning." Shorty leaned against the wall as if hoping it would hold him up. Judging from the dark circles under his eyes, he'd been keeping the same hours as Dan. "Long day."

"Eaten yet?"

"Nope. Interested in steak?"

Dan checked his watch. "Guess Perry's is still open."

"You'll just have to suffer through a New York, medium rare—"

"Enough. You talked me into it. But we should leave now. I've got CAPCOM duty in the morning."

They left the building and walked to Shorty's Camaro. He revved the engine and peeled out of the parking lot, apparently more than ready for dinner.

The smoky aroma made Dan's stomach grumble even before they stepped into the restaurant. He ordered a Cowboy rib eye, Shorty the pork chop.

Dan picked at his salad. "Can I ask you something?"

Shorty leaned forward. "I'm all ears."

"You and Joan seem especially happy. How do you do it?"

"It ain't easy." Shorty swallowed his last bite. "Joan's a special lady. She knew what she was getting into when she married a space jock. We spend a lot of time together, just the two of us, and with the girls when I'm not gallivanting around the universe." He shrugged. "We just work at it, that's all. Why? Don't tell me you're thinking about marriage."

"Don't know. Hildi and I—"

"Hildi? You've kept that quiet."

"Well, you know how NASA is."

Shorty harrumphed as the server presented their salads. "You're a fool if you let Hildi get away."

"I almost proposed before she left for the Cape. She got mad that I didn't. I think."

"Women." Shorty forked a piece of lettuce. "Why'd you get cold feet?"

Dan studied his sweet tea. "It wouldn't be fair to her. She has a career she loves. I can't ask her to give it up, and I can't see how we could keep a marriage and our jobs."

"Why does *she* have to be the one to give it up?"

Dan stared at him. "Give up the astronaut corps?" *Give up the moon?* He shook his head. "No can do."

"Marriage is all about compromise. You need to learn that."

The steaks arrived. Dan found his appetite had taken a vacation but made a brave show of it. His efforts to rectify his relationship with Hildi were on hold. She was at the Cape awaiting launch, and he was here.

His mind chased a stray rabbit. Frank's affairs had devastated Hildi, but now she displayed her usual self-confidence. Her smile was back. She even smiled at Frank. Was something brewing there?

Dan drained his tea. Hildi and Frank would only be together in space for a few days, and they'd probably be too busy to talk. Of course she wouldn't let Frank sway her.

Or would she?

****

Hildi wrapped herself in an afghan she'd brought from home. She sat in the armchair of her Cape

Canaveral apartment, still wide awake. The hefty textbook, *History of Space Flight*, lay in her lap, guaranteed to put her to sleep. Instead, her mind drifted between prayer and the conflicts with Dan, Frank, and Chet. She glanced at the clock then speed dialed Francine's number.

"Hildi!" Francine's squeal always made her smile and left her partially deaf in one ear.

"How are you? How's work in the lab?"

"Same as always. Shouldn't you be asleep by now? I mean, don't you have a launch or something tomorrow morning?" Francine chuckled.

"Just *you* try sleeping when you're about to ride a rocket and spend some quality time with the guy you almost married."

"So how is he, anyway?"

Hildi huffed out a breath. "I really don't know. We've been so busy with the last phase of training—"

"Didn't you spend eight hours in that simulation with the whole crew? That sounded worse than the New York Marathon."

"Yeah." Hildi smiled at the memory. "It went really well, though it was kinda weird sitting behind Frank and hearing Dan in our headsets."

"And how's the love of your life?"

"Don't be so nosy."

"What do you expect from me? We haven't talked in two days. Hey, I got a right to know." Francine's voice lowered to a conspiratorial whisper. "And I don't suppose he's popped the question yet?"

Hildi's pulse banged an angry beat. "Nope. Romance is still—shall we say—up in the air."

"Is he crazy or just plain stupid?"

"I'm glad you're on my side. I'd hate to run into

you in a dark alley when you've got your claws out."

Francine guffawed. "What's a mama bear to do? You're not having second thoughts, are you?"

"I haven't had a thought for three weeks. No time."

"He'll come around."

Would he? "Sometimes I wonder if I was too hasty in breaking it off with Frank."

"I take it back. *You're* the one who's crazy."

Hildi yawned.

"Glad I'm so entertaining. By the way, how was the barbeque?"

"It was great to see Mom and Dad. Had a long talk with Frank's parents. They vowed to keep in touch. They're great."

"No Chet? Wait, don't tell me. The microbe didn't show for his own astronaut-sister's farewell."

Hildi tamped down an angry retort. "Nope."

"Well…have a good flight." Francine had the sense to drop the sensitive subject. "Don't take any wooden nickels."

Hildi laughed. "I won't. I'll try to send you an e-mail or something. We can do that from orbit, you know."

"Wonders never cease. *Vaya con Dios.* I'll be praying."

Hildi punched the off button and returned the phone to its cradle. Her mind U-turned back to the Frank question. He'd shattered her trust. Could they make the torturous climb back to a healthy friendship? Maybe with her father's help? Her Father's help…

Hildi drifted back to prayer. *Father, I need some peace with Frank. All these superficial niceties just don't cut it.*

Other thoughts tumbled in her mind like clothes in a dryer. She'd cleaned out the refrigerator in the efficiency apartment, but the layer of dust coating the maple coffee table would just have to wait.

Lord, protect us in the coming flight, be with the ground crew, and please, no delays. Delays happened for a variety of reasons—weather, fuel problems, hangnail…Ah, the joys of a bureaucracy that had seen too many tragedies. Caution flavored every decision.

But she couldn't stop grinning at the enormous opportunity NASA had handed her. Working on a virus in space could answer some of her professional questions. She might even make a breakthrough in the field. Journal articles, magazine interviews, Nobel Prize.

Catch me if you can, little brother. Got spacecraft?

Her mind kept jumping to the station and back to Earth, refusing to shut down. Frank, Dan, Chet, Vomit Comet, microgravity, scientific satisfaction.

Besides, she'd have a lot of fun floating around.

Her grin turned into another yawn. Hildi stood, stretching her arms over her head. She folded the afghan over the back of the couch and headed for the bedroom. Four o'clock would come way too early.

****

Frank lay in bed with his hands behind his head, unable to sleep. He knew *Reconciliation*'s controls backward and forward but kept reviewing every move. The team at Kennedy had tried to trip up the crew during the long dress rehearsal, throwing in a few emergencies that were either impossible to occur or impossible to scrape out of. He wished he could have pulled a James T. Kirk and rigged the training program, but Tom wasn't a guy who could take a joke.

He couldn't wait to man the spacecraft's controls and feel *Reconciliation*'s power at his fingertips. Being pilot had its compensations, including—hopefully—a little prestige. Oh, it wouldn't be like *Apollo 11*'s landing on the moon or *Apollo 13*'s nail-biting flight, but plenty of people would be watching. Maybe. He grimaced. It seemed these days the media considered every flight to be routine.

He gave up on sleep and pulled out a suspense novel. His mind rejected his command to shift into reading gear. He'd be with Hildi. Somehow, he'd finagle a time to talk to her in private. He'd had enough of shallow women and shallower relationships.

He stared at the ceiling, random thoughts snubbing his demand to shut down. Hildi and Dan had argued a few weeks ago, but neither had mentioned it. That was just before the crew left for Kennedy. The elephant in the room. During the simulation, Frank had wondered what was going on in Hildi's pretty little mind as Dan relayed instructions to the capsule.

As he thought of tomorrow, he smiled. The preparations were always a pain, but waiting for countdown ratcheted his anticipation with every tick. Nothing like sitting on top of tons of explosives to get the blood flowing. *Please, no delays.*

Frank closed his eyes and willed his body to relax. His body refused.

15

"I" Plus Three Days

Worth and Laura munched energy bars as they drove in the early morning light to the Banana River viewing site, reserved for VIPs and the astronauts' families. A security guard checked their tickets and IDs. "Mr. and Mrs. Hildebrandt? Are you Hildi's parents?"

"Yes." Worth and Laura spoke in unison. They looked at each other and laughed.

The guard smiled then pointed to his right. "Please drive to the fourth row and follow the attendant."

Worth parked the car and opened the door for Laura. She grabbed her camera and handed Worth a pair of binoculars. Humidity weighted the air.

"Want more coffee?" He pointed at the building that housed a cafeteria, gift shop, restroom, and a small museum.

"Nothing right now, thanks."

Worth scanned the crowd, looking for familiar faces. Dick and Debra joined them. "We're finally here. Beautiful day for a launch." Debra's smile competed with the sun. "T minus two hours." She called attention to the huge digital clock as the seconds snapped by.

Worth nodded. "I'm glad we have a couple of

veterans in our midst. We're new to this daughter-astronaut launch thing."

Dick pointed at the countdown. "Don't get too attached to the countdown. We've seen Frank's three shuttle launches, and each of them was delayed."

Lifting his gaze to the Banana River, Worth's breath caught in his throat. Beyond it and the lush Florida greenery, the heavy-lift rocket stood in defiance of the skies.

Laura hugged her arms. "I still can't believe it. I can't believe our little girl is an astronaut. Do you ever get used to this?"

"Not really." Debra frowned. "Sometimes I wish I didn't know all the details of space flight."

All the dangerous details, that is. Worth forced a smile as his mind wandered another lane. How would Evie handle the next few days in space with her ex-fiancé? She said she had moved past the hurt, but Worth knew how anger could rear its dragon head and spew fire at unexpected moments. Unfortunately, he knew it firsthand from Laura's unbridled rage in the early days of their painful road back to a loving relationship.

Worth coughed. Laura pulled him aside. "Think you're catching a cold?" Her eyes mirrored concern.

He shook his head and coughed again. "No. My throat's just a little sore from speaking." Hiding his increasing symptoms of illness had been tough during their tour of Florida's theme parks, the amusement parks an ineffective attempt to get their minds off today's launch. Worth's attention instead became fixed on his persistent hacking and body aches.

She searched his face but finally smiled. Always protective. His compromised immune system welcomed every bug like a long-lost friend.

He offered coffee again, and this time Laura agreed. She turned her gaze to the launch pad.

Returning from the cafeteria with two paper cups, he glanced at Frank's parents, now engaged in a television interview. Worth ducked his head and pulled his ball cap low over his eyes. Maybe the reporters wouldn't recognize him.

He handed Laura her coffee and sipped his own. The brew scalded his tongue and throat. He juggled the cup between his hands, the heat burning his fingers through the protective sleeve. "Every time I see Dick and Debra, I wish things had turned out differently."

As usual, Laura read his mind. "That Evie and Frank had overcome the pain? So do I."

He turned to her and grasped her hand. "I'm still amazed you took me back. Have I told you today I love you?"

"You can always say it again."

****

"Ten, nine, eight, seven, six, ignition sequence start—"

Worth held his breath.

"Three, two, one, zero, liftoff. We have liftoff. The first manned mission of *Reconciliation* and the new Rigel series is on its way."

Fire blazed from the engines of the rocket. It rose in slow motion as if reluctant to leave the safety of Earth. The roar hit Worth like a physical blast. His jaw dropped. Dick was right. Even at this distance, words couldn't describe the spectacle seen live. Billows of steam poured along the ground as tons of propellant launched his daughter skyward.

The rocket cleared the tower. Launch Control now handed the reins to Mission Control in Houston. With Dan as CAPCOM.

Was he their future son-in-law? Or another man who'd break Evie's heart?

****

Hildi gripped her chair in the cramped quarters of the space capsule.

"The clock is running." Larry verified the rocket's status from Launch Control in the same matter-of-fact voice he'd used in the simulator. Nothing seemed to rattle him. Hildi's teeth, however, threatened to rattle out of her gums as *Reconciliation* launched. Pressure increased as gravity protested its loss of another space-bound vehicle. The engines screamed, answered by the whoops of the astronauts.

Hildi laughed. Any roller coaster ride paled in comparison. She shifted her head to the left toward Jasper, a true feat as two g's and a bulky pressure suit plastered her to the couch. She immediately regretted the motion as her stomach complained about the difference between her sight and her inner ear. She returned her gaze to the front row.

Frank turned and grinned. She tried to return the smile but inwardly tensed. He'd seemed overly friendly before they suited up, but at four in the morning, everyone sounded too chipper. At least she'd only have to endure his attention for a few days, until Frank piloted *Reconciliation* back to Earth with a couple of station-weary astronauts.

The shake in the capsule eased and the weight on

her chest decreased, only to be replaced by the jolt of first-stage separation that slammed her against her harness. Then the second stage ignited, sinking her weary bones deeper into the couch.

She'd been in preparation for hours, submitting herself to assistants who eased her into her suit and checked her vital signs. Even with the amount of time she'd spent in the blue suit at the CDC, the final lock-in of her helmet gave her shivers. For the next six months, she would breathe only canned air.

The final stage propelled them toward their intended orbit 250 nautical miles above Earth. They would be weightless and officially in space after a mere nine minutes, with a day and a half before docking. Then her ground-breaking work would begin.

She prayed again for the mission, the other three astronauts, the crew on ISS, and herself as the lone scientist passenger—a payload specialist in astronaut lingo. In this case, the payload was a tiny vial of a mild influenza virus.

"Quite a ride, eh?" Jasper's deep voice echoed in her helmet. He should have been a radio announcer with that rumbling bass of his.

Hildi grinned. "Not sure my pearly whites appreciated it, but yeah, what a ride." Hildi gasped as she glimpsed the blues and greens of Earth rotating beneath them. "And what a view."

Her heart fluttered at CAPCOM Dan's voice "*Reconciliation*, Houston. You're GO at eleven and a half. Main engine cutoff is twelve plus thirty-four."

Twelve minutes and thirty-four seconds into the flight, silence wrapped them as the computer killed the main engine. Hildi longed to float free and taste the microgravity of space. Flights in the Vomit Comet had never been enough with a mere thirty seconds of weightlessness at a time.

"OK, people, time to get to work." Commander Larry took charge and reminded everyone of their duties.

"Let's get to it." Frank sounded like a drill sergeant. Hildi inwardly harrumphed. She'd decided not to let Frank bug her, but she feared her attitude needed adjusting. She especially didn't want to respond with some caustic remark in the middle of a mission. They'd part soon enough. She needed to keep the peace.

Hildi suppressed a sigh as she worked with the others to check systems. She felt like a passenger on *Reconciliation* in spite of her duties, although she had trained as hard as the others and could take over any position. Once they got to the space station, she could concentrate on the work she loved best. She and Maria, a virologist already on board, would run experiments as they observed the effect of microgravity on influenza. Perhaps a vaccine would be easier to develop there.

"Dr. Hildebrandt? Is the payload secure?" CAPCOM's voice from Houston interrupted her musings. Dan's rich baritone goose bumped her emotions in spite of their last argument. Kissing and making up would have to wait. She smiled at the prospect.

Hildi glanced at the locker imbedded in the wall, holding a sandwich-sized metal case that cradled the virus sample. She spoke into her headset. "Yes, Mission Control, payload is secure." NASA had insisted on the protocol codes for the sample as if her work were a top-secret military project. The media had already reported it, so why did NASA bother? Most people were blissfully ignorant that influenza, which seemed a mere annual nuisance, could turn into a deadly pandemic. The truth lay in history books, especially with accounts of the World War I outbreak. Scientists at the CDC were unsung heroes as they risked their lives so the public would remain safe and oblivious.

This would be the first study of influenza on the station. Perhaps her work would help future astronauts—and lunar colonies—deal with the diseases that were determined to follow them into space. Her mind wandered. *The Hildebrandt vaccine for HIV. Dr. Hildebrandt, Nobel Laureate.* She would enjoy surpassing her brother in their field, although the launch into space certainly qualified. *Heh, heh.*

The capsule lurched, jerking her back to reality. That couldn't be good.

"Houston, we're encountering a little trouble with the attitude jets." Unflappable Larry sounded tense. Hildi's insides plummeted.

"Roger, *Reconciliation.* We confirm."

Frank manipulated the controls to correct the sudden yaw and pitch of *Reconciliation.* It quickly settled into calm.

Larry turned to Frank. "That shouldn't have happened."

Frank lifted his hands. "It wasn't me."

Larry tapped a finger on the instrument panel as if that would solve the mystery.

A moment passed as Dan silenced the radio switch and apparently consulted with various people monitoring their instruments. Hildi's stomach continued its free-fall. Dan's CAPCOM voice finally returned. "Larry, we don't know why the jets hiccupped. You sure it wasn't Frank pulling a practical joke?"

Frank shook his head.

"Houston, this is *Reconciliation*. Frank says he didn't touch the controls."

Hildi chewed her lip. Would Houston order them back to Earth after only a few orbits? Missions had been aborted for less. Doggone it; she hadn't come all this way just to admire the view.

"*Reconciliation*, this is Houston. Our boards show no malfunction of the systems. We'll just chalk it up to a pilot twitch. You are still GO."

"Roger."

Frank muttered under his breath.

Hard to believe they were a mere thirteen minutes into the flight. Hildi's nausea stabilized, but her pulse still danced the cha-cha. This particular scenario hadn't been a part of their training. How did the simulator team miss inflicting this situation on them? What other glitches would they discover in this shake-down flight of the Rigel series? Her brain shied away from her worried thoughts and concentrated on the discussion among the astronauts.

Jasper snorted. "Well, that was fun, though I think I prefer bucking broncos. At least I have the illusion of control." He glanced at Frank, suspicion reflected in his eyes.

"Oh, let's not get wrapped around the axle." Frank answered Jasper's concern with maddening nonchalance. "I think that's the one problem we're gonna have. Every mission has one."

CAPCOM interrupted their conversation. "*Reconciliation*, Houston. Looking good."

"Roger." Larry's grin showed through his voice.

Frank continued to test the pilot switches then leaned back and huffed out a breath. Hildi sneaked a glance at him every so often. He caught her eyes, his lips curling into a smile.

What was going on in his mind? Was he trying to re-establish their relationship, maybe even re-propose? Yeah, like *that* would happen. Hildi could ignore his attempt at reconciliation without getting wrapped around the axle, to use his own terminology. She'd forgiven him, and that was the end of it.

Hildi released a long breath. Frank's status as a space jock kept the ladies in awe and attracted them like ants to a picnic. Had Mr. Charm-the-Ladies-and-Make-Them-Cry really changed as he claimed, or had he been searching Florida's beaches for a new conquest?

Thankfully, Dan was from a different strain entirely.

****

After shutdown, Frank removed his helmet and unbuckled his restraints. His stomach performed a rare rollover, though he expected it for the first day or two in space. He shouldn't have eaten the astronauts' traditional steak-and-eggs breakfast. He oriented himself in the weightless environment, happy to regain his space legs.

Hildi hit her head on the roof as soon as she floated free.

"Easy, girl." Frank offered his hand and drew her down. "Move slowly, or you'll get sick for sure."

"Sorry. Should have remembered."

"Happens to all the rookies." He grinned as she hung her head, then he helped remove her helmet.

Frank shrugged out of his pressure suit and set it on an intentional trajectory. It floated across the interior and struck Jasper in the face.

The bulky suit muffled Jasper's protests. "Who turned out the lights?" He finally pulled it off and threw it back.

Frank laughed. He knew he'd pay for it later. He and Jasper had a friendly rivalry in the practical-joke department.

Hildi removed her own suit and threw it like a basketball toward Jasper's open arms. He faked an attempt to dribble. Definitely not possible in weightlessness.

"Enough." Larry switched on his commander voice. "Stow 'em."

Hildi's cheeks turned a pretty pink.

As Larry and Jasper removed their outer gear, Frank stretched out the kinks in his stiff muscles. The blue NASA jumpsuit he wore underneath was infinitely more comfortable. They rolled their pressure suits into compact bundles and stowed them in the designated lockers. Hildi's movements were already becoming as effortless as a space chimp's. Even in the uninspiring crew attire, she looked beautiful.

He'd always been a sucker for the beautiful women who wanted an encounter with a real astronaut. His conscience pricked him. Those roving days were over. If only he could convince Hildi of that.

Frank turned away. His stomach felt heavy, and it wasn't breakfast. His hope of reconciliation with Hildi was probably a lost cause, and he suspected his old childhood buddy was reaping the benefits. Maybe he and Hildi could have a little heart-to-heart before they docked...

Privacy on a spacecraft? That would be the day.

****

Dan listened to the chatter on *Reconciliation*, finally relaxing in his chair after a few nail-biting moments. He loosened his tie and stretched out the tension of the last few minutes. The mission was still GO, the apparent malfunction a no-show on Mission Control's monitors. It could have been disastrous. His job as CAPCOM had one big drawback. No control. No control over the spacecraft, no control over the crew's actions, and no control over The Jerk ferrying his girl to the station.

He jettisoned his feelings like a used rocket stage. Dan grinned. Hildi would be stuck without a test tube for a day and a half until the capsule docked, one part of the mission she would hate. She even insisted on driving every time they were together, though her tiny Smart Car gave him a stiff neck as it forced him into an uncomfortable imitation of the Hunchback of Notre Dame.

Dan closed his eyes. After the last argument with Hildi and their forced separation due to the mission, he wasn't going to take her for granted again. Shorty was right. Once she returned to Earth, he'd make it up to her. Big time.

16

"I" Plus Three Days

Carol stomped her foot. "But you promised!"

Mike shrugged. "I'm sorry, hon, but things just piled up at the office. I really have to go in this weekend."

"We were going to *Aspen*. Since when would you rather work than ski?" *And be with me?*

"Why don't we do it the weekend after next? I'll make reservations for that European-style hotel."

Carol wouldn't let him off the hook that easily. She'd been looking forward to this weekend ever since the seminar. She should have known his change of attitude wouldn't last. Slamming the crusty casserole dish into the sink suds, she charged upstairs, cries ripping out of her throat. Maybe her tears would make him feel guilty. She slammed the bedroom door.

She flung herself on the bed, but her little tantrum ran out after a few minutes. So much for a good, long cry. She washed her face and took a few deep breaths. Mike must be working in the garage, judging from the hammering.

She waffled between apologizing and making her husband suffer, not that he seemed to be suffering. Heaving a sigh, she wondered who she could call to dump on. Her sister was working...

A business card lay on her nightstand. Carol hesitated then punched in the number before she could change her mind. She walked to the closet for her comfort slippers as the phone rang at the other end of the line.

"Betty here."

"Hi, Betty. It's Carol Hardesty. Remember me from the conference?"

"Carol. Of course I remember. How are you, dear?" Betty paused. "You sound upset."

Carol's faucet started dripping again. She brushed angrily at her cheek. "Mike and I had a fight."

"Just a moment."

Carol heard a vacuum cleaner, the noise muffled as someone closed a door.

"There. I have a housekeeping service once a week, and that vacuum of theirs could wake a deaf corpse."

A giggle escaped Carol. "Aren't most corpses deaf?"

"Well, come to think of it, they are." Betty chuckled. "Now, do you want to talk about it?"

Carol took another deep breath. "It started when Mike said he had to work this weekend. He promised to take me to Aspen." She paced to dissipate her temptation to throw something.

"I'm so sorry, dear. I'm sure you were looking forward to it."

"He never keeps his promises."

"Now, I know I'm doing a little meddling here—"

"Meddle away. That's why I called. I don't know what to do. We go to a marriage seminar, he seems to change, and then he's right back to his old habits in two days."

"Dear, one of the first things Worth talks about is to stop using 'always' and 'never' during an argument."

Carol sighed. "I know. Mike just makes so mad. He never—"

"He never?"

"I get your point." Carol forced her teeth to unclench. Much easier to talk that way. "But I'm tired of being ignored. Why won't he pay attention to me? Maybe I should get some of those cosmetics of yours, maybe lose some weight."

"Dear, I'd be happy to come over and do a makeover for you. Just let me know when. But I think your main problem right now is *you*."

"Huh?" Carol didn't like where this conversation was going. She wanted sympathy, not a lecture.

"Dear, you can't change your husband, but you can change *you*. Start by apologizing. Anger festers the longer you ignore it. Marriage is not all daisies and buttercups, you know. You need to work at it."

"I know you're right, but I don't want to do it. It's his fault."

"And you did nothing to—uh—escalate the disagreement?"

Carol huffed out a breath. "I guess I did. But he did, too."

"Never mind that for now. If you were wrong, you need to tell him that."

"It's so hard."

"Of course it is." Betty's chuckle chimed. "It's called pride, and it's a stubborn thing indeed."

"What if...What if he doesn't accept my apology?" Carol sniffed as she sat on the edge of the bed and reached for a tissue.

"Do you really think he would do that?"

"Well, no, but—"

"No buts. Just apologize."

"OK."

"I'll be praying for you, dear. And call me anytime."

"Thanks."

Carol hung up the phone. She checked her image in the bathroom mirror. Grimacing, she used get-the-red-out eye drops—which did more stinging than un-reddening—brushed her hair, and added lipstick. Maybe the trip postponement was just as well. She felt achy, like she was coming down with something. She walked downstairs, feeling as if she were walking to an appointment with a firing squad. She opened the door into the garage.

Mike's truck was gone.

17

"I" Plus Three Days

"Looking good, *Reconciliation*." Dan breathed a sigh of relief. They'd achieved orbit. Rendezvous with the space station would occur tomorrow.

"Good job, people." Steve Walters stood and stretched. The Mission Control crew turned toward him. He grinned.

Vince from ISS control walked in, concern on his face. "Steve, the station was unable to maneuver away from micrometeoroids."

Dan gulped. ISS had always avoided collision before.

"We'll inform *Reconciliation*." Steve gripped his wooden pencil and snapped it in two. He reached for another one from the cup at his elbow. "What's the damage?"

Dan rolled his eyes. Steve was one of the savviest techies he knew, but the man was in the Stone Age when it came to his preference in writing implements.

"Don't know yet. Joe did a fair amount of cussing, but the crew's safely tucked away inside the Soyuz."

The ISS crew was supposed to take refuge in the capsule at the first sign of risk. Dan's shoulders relaxed.

Vince nodded and left, still frowning. Ten minutes

later he returned with a deeper frown. "The station crew determined the skin of the Soyuz was punctured. They've abandoned it and closed the hatch."

Dan swallowed. Another emergency averted, but his guts insisted it wouldn't be the last.

"Thanks, Vince." Steve dismissed him with a wave of his hand. He smirked as he turned to Dan. "Wait 'til you hear what those space chimps on *Reconciliation* are going to wake up to."

Dan chuckled. "The mind boggles. I'm sure you picked something appropriate."

"Indeed. Tell them it's time for bed."

Dan cleared his throat and returned to CAPCOM mode. "*Reconciliation,* this is Houston."

"Larry here. Hey, I hope this won't take long. We've had supper and are ready to bed down."

"Finish up and go to bed. That's an order from the flight director. We want you fresh for docking tomorrow, Frank."

"Acknowledged, Houston. The crew's settling in their sacks except for Jasper. He seems a bit tangled up in the sheets."

"Am not," said a muffled voice. "I'm snug as a bug."

"All right, people. Beddy bye until 8:00 AM, Houston time. We've got something special planned for your alarm clock."

"That's what I'm afraid of." Larry groaned.

****

The strains of "Good Morning, Starshine" blared from the speakers and startled Hildi out of a sound sleep. Groans from Larry and Frank accompanied the wake-up call. Jasper whistled along until Frank glared at him. She shook her head. Leave it to the flight director to pick something as corny as the fields in Iowa.

She slipped out of her mummy bag. Rolling her tongue around her mouth confirmed her suspicion. Her breath could kill three Doberman pinschers. Brushing her teeth was her first priority.

"Rise and shine, people." Dan's voice from Houston sounded entirely too cheery.

"Houston, this is *Reconciliation*. Acknowledging your sick sense of humor." Larry yawned.

Dan chuckled. "Hey, you sleepwalking?"

"Can't do that in space."

Dan changed into his CAPCOM authority voice. "Busy day, folks. Get some breakfast and prepare to catch up to ISS."

Hildi listened to the rest of the mission chatter with one part of her brain as she stowed her bag. This time, Frank and Jasper weren't playing football. They were all a bit groggy from a short night's sleep. Well, all except Jasper.

She'd drawn kitchen duty, so she added water to three bags of powdered eggs, smooshed them around, and put them in the microwave. She opted for oatmeal for herself. Everyone ate a tortilla, the only form of bread allowed in space since it didn't crumble. Crumbs in the instruments could foul them up something fierce. She slathered the tortilla with peanut butter. Coffee and orange juice completed breakfast. Frank cleaned up, a chore that required pitching all the containers into the trash compactor. She was grateful that meals in space didn't require much work. She hated cooking, even when the eggs stayed on the plate.

After they strapped in, Frank initiated a rocket burn to adjust their orbital inclination and join the exact orbit of ISS.

Frank's shoulders tensed. "Attitude control feels a little wonky again."

Hildi's insides flipped when she heard the worry in Frank's voice. More problems, or was he just being his grumpy old self?

"Let me try." Larry exchanged seats with Frank, an interesting ballet without gravity. "I don't feel anything." He floated back to his flight chair.

Frank fiddled with the joystick then huffed out a breath. "It's gone now."

The commander flipped on his talk-to-Houston voice. "Mission Control, this is *Reconciliation*. Request another reading on our attitude jets."

"Acknowledged."

Hildi willed her breathing to slow. She didn't want Houston's flight surgeon to panic. She heard mumbles through the radio as Dan consulted with the specialists in Mission Control. His CAPCOM voice returned. "Larry, our instruments do not indicate a problem. You sure Frank didn't sneeze or something?"

"No!" Frank's outburst fried the air.

"Uh, Houston, that's a negative."

"OK, Larry. *Reconciliation*, you're still GO for docking."

"Roger." Larry swiveled his head. "Frank, what do you think?"

Hildi knew that stubborn stance when she saw it, even with Frank sitting down. "I could swear the control felt sloppy a minute ago."

Jasper chimed in. "Maybe you weren't awake."

"I know what I felt."

Larry glared at both of them. "Cool your jets."

Jasper clamped his mouth shut.

Frank had the decency to mumble, "Sorry."

Larry nodded then cleared his throat. "Prepare for docking."

****

Hildi's heart hummed as she spotted the station, a bright star in the heavens. The long and spindly object, bristling with antennae, soon filled the window. Home for the next six months.

They approached the American docking port at an inch per second. Frank guided the capsule forward, one hand poised over the autopilot switch per protocol. No one trusted the software. The tiny jet bursts hissed, but Hildi couldn't feel any acceleration.

A sudden lurch snapped her body against her flight chair.

Frank grabbed the controls and slowed their approach. Not enough.

The astronauts jerked forward against their restraints. An odd *crunch* rang through the capsule. From outside in the silence of space? Impossible, unless…Hildi's heart galloped around in her chest.

Larry's voice took on an ominous calm. "What happened, Frank?"

Frank stiffened. "Autopilot failed. The jets jammed. How am I supposed to know?"

Larry grasped his shoulder. "Run the tests. We'll figure it out." He keyed his mic. "Houston, we have a problem."

Hildi's nerves knotted. James Lovell had uttered the same words after the explosion on Apollo 13.

"Acknowledged, *Reconciliation*. What's your status?" Dan's nothing-can-ruffle-me voice sounded frayed.

"Uh, Houston, we're still analyzing the situation."

The astronauts checked every instrument on the capsule. Jasper pointed at the viewport. All Hildi could see was the skin of the station. She gulped.

"Uh, Houston, as far as we can figure out, we rammed the port." Larry scratched his head.

"Houston, this is ISS. They sure did." The new voice had a Texas drawl as thick as Rio Grande mud. "This whole thing shuddered like a rattlesnake with a bad cold."

Hildi chuckled as Jasper stage whispered, "That's Cowboy Joe for you."

"The blasted control malfunctioned again." Frank's voice rose.

"Enough." Larry gripped the pilot's shoulder. "You want to try it manually, hotshot?"

Frank shook off Larry's hand. "You bet."

"Houston, *Reconciliation*. Request permission to re-dock manually."

"*Reconciliation*, you are GO for re-docking maneuver. We still show no problems with the controls."

Jasper muttered, "Well, *that's* a relief."

Frank purpled from rage...or fear. "They malfunctioned. It wasn't me."

"Your attitude"—Larry enunciated every word— "does not solve the problem."

Frank huffed out a breath then nodded.

Hildi's insides refused to settle as a debate raged over the next couple of hours.

"Let's back up and see if we damaged anything."

Larry spoke calmly, as if he were used to crash dockings.

"Roger." Frank spoke through clenched teeth.

"Prepare for undocking."

Hildi tightened her death grip on the couch.

"Here goes." Frank pulled back on the joystick. The jets puffed.

The spacecraft stayed put.

Frank tried again.

No effect.

"What's wrong?" Worry creased Larry's forehead.

"We're stuck," Frank said.

Larry keyed his mic. "Mission Control, this is *Reconciliation*. Unable to undock from ISS. Please advise."

Frank's eyes narrowed. "I'm going to spin this sucker to the right. Hang on."

"Wait!" Larry roared.

Hildi's stomach spun one way while the capsule spun the other. *Reconciliation* lurched free. Frank corrected the spacecraft's spin until it matched ISS again.

"You had no authority." Larry spoke through gritted teeth.

"It worked, didn't it?" Frank's defiance thickened the air.

"Next time, you wait for instructions from Mission Control and from me as commander. Understood?" Larry's bellow rang in Hildi's ears.

Frank slowly sagged like a deflating balloon. "Yes, sir."

Hildi released a breath as the tension eased.

Larry gave a curt nod. "OK, Frank. Back us up a bit."

"Yes, sir."

"*Reconciliation,* Houston. What's your situation?"

"Houston, we have successfully undocked. Assessing damage visually."

Hildi stretched her neck to see through the forward ports. Dents and gouges glared at them from the docking ring's surface.

Larry leaned forward and peered at the damage. "Looks like we scraped it up. Doesn't look serious from here, but we should ask the boys on the station."

"Acknowledged, *Reconciliation.* ISS, can you get someone to evaluate?"

"This is ISS. Joe and Maria will go." A slight Russian accent identified the speaker as Leonid, an astrophysicist.

Hildi sighed. This would take a while. At least the new Z-1 space suits were quicker to get into than the old ones and didn't require pre-breathing.

An hour later, Joe and Maria emerged from the station's airlock. Joe waved at them against a backdrop of stars. "Howdy, folks." They tethered themselves and then used handholds to pull themselves toward the damaged collar. "It ain't too bad. I think we can get it fixed in no time."

Joe turned his body to face the capsule. His voice hissed over the radio. "Now, your spacecraft there is a horse of a different color entirely. The mating ring has a dent the size of Texas. They cain't dock with that."

"ISS, Houston. Will it compromise the capsule's integrity during reentry?"

"Might."

Hildi's heart plunged into a tar pit. They'd never dock.

They'd never go home.

****

Don't panic. Hildi willed her breathing to slow as time crept like a snail on tranquilizers.

Frank threw up his hands. "How long is this going to take? We can't wait forever for NASA to make up its mind."

Jasper rested his chin on his hand as he gazed at the station. "I think our best bet is reentry. Take our chances with the damage we sustained."

Hildi shook her head. "So close."

"The first manned mission of the Rigel capsule, and I mess it up." Frank scowled.

Larry gazed at Frank. "You said yourself you did nothing wrong. When we get back, and we *will* get back, the techs will crawl all over this spacecraft to find the malfunction, and they'll find it." He gripped Frank's forearm.

"I wanted to eat hot dogs on the station." Jasper's wistful sigh drew chuckles from Hildi and Larry.

Frank stared off into cold space. "That's not going to happen."

The radio crackled. Hildi tensed, awaiting NASA's orders.

"*Reconciliation,* this is Houston. The team here sees no problem with reentry. You are GO for—"

A raucous buzz startled Hildi. The master alarm.

Frank cursed and pointed to the oxygen gauge. "Larry, we've got a leak."

"Where?"

Frank scanned the instruments. "Nose."

"OK. Frank, see if you can reach it." Larry gripped the arm rests, but his voice showed no disturbance.

"Jasper, help him."

Frank shot out of his chair and pulled himself to the nose of the capsule. He cocked his head. "Hissing. I think it's near the docking clamps." Frank pried off a panel and handed it to Jasper. He reached in to his elbows and grunted. "Can't get to it. How much time do we have?"

Larry peered at the gauges. "Not much. Not enough to get to the Russian port."

"Anybody got any gum?" Jasper's attempt at humor died in the air.

"Suit up."

Hildi scrambled to obey Larry's command. She ignored shaky fingers as she struggled into her EVA suit. She panted. Was it her imagination or was the air getting thinner? She took a slow, calming breath. *Now is not the time to hyperventilate.*

She secured her helmet and checked Jasper's seals. Larry straightened as he pressed the radio controls with gloved hands. "Houston, could use a few suggestions." Larry's voice raised in pitch a notch.

A slight pause. "Copy that, Larry." The radio went silent. Time stretched into infinity.

A Texas drawl shattered the tension. "Houston, this is Joe. They can't dock, they can't go back, and they can't stay out there forever. I respectfully request permission to lasso that thing and pull her in."

Hildi grinned as her mind filled with the image of Cowboy Joe riding a pressure-suited horse.

"ISS, *Reconciliation.*" Larry spoke as if he were thinking aloud. "We could shoot you a line, tie it off, and spacewalk hand over hand. Houston, do you concur?"

"We concur. You are GO for EVA."

EVA. Astronaut speak for Extra Vehicular Activity. In other words, hang your body out into space and hope your tether holds.

"Roger." Larry turned to his crewmates. "Well, any volunteers to throw a rope?"

"I'll do it." Jasper grinned. "Let me show that Texas cowpoke how we do things in Wyoming."

"Houston, you copy?"

"Affirmative."

Larry turned to the others, sadness coloring his expression. "Never lost a command before."

Bile rose in Hildi's throat. She knew what was coming.

Larry's next command rang in her ears. "OK, people. Prepare to abandon ship."

Abandon ship. Words Hildi never expected to hear on a routine flight. She shoved aside the words from a half-forgotten book. "Abandon hope, all ye who enter here."

****

Frank flashed a reassuring smile at Hildi, but she didn't acknowledge it. Probably a bit preoccupied with the change of plans. He'd hoped for a little support from her, sympathy, *something.* He huffed out a breath, fogging his faceplate, wishing he could replay the last few minutes. Larry hadn't said anything, but Frank could hear the blame as clearly as a telepathic link. He hadn't regained control after the computer botched the docking, and he'd made it worse by pulling *Reconciliation* free. He should have known better than to act without orders. Now they had to perform an Extra Vehicular Activity to reach the station. *Extra* for "extra dangerous."

Pulling himself back into his seat, Frank used tiny bursts from the attitude jets to keep *Reconciliation* aligned. The Reaction Control System, or RCS in astronaut-speak, fought his every move. "Having a hard time keeping her stabilized. I think the jets got damaged."

Larry nodded. "Just hold her long enough so Jasper can shoot over the rope and Leonid can get the robotic arm in place."

Frank nodded, putting every ounce of concentration into the task. The system sneered at him.

After Larry vented the capsule, Jasper threw open the hatch. He held a puff pistol, NASA's latest toy. Joe and Maria hovered near the station's docking ring, ready to grab the line as soon as Jasper shot it.

The capsule pitched. The damage must have affected the angle at which the jets fired. The change made it hard to control, but Frank compensated quickly. Jasper rode it out like a bucking bronco.

"How's it going over there, pardners?" Joe could have asked about the weather in the same matter-of-fact voice.

Jasper stuck a hand out of the hatch and waved. "Be there in a sec, cowboy. My horse is a bit balky."

Larry frowned. "Frank, can you keep her steady?"

"Piece of cake." Frank's nonchalant words didn't fool the churning in his gut. NASA wouldn't have allowed such dangerous maneuvers so close to the station unless there was no choice.

Jasper attached a short tether to his suit, secured the other end to the capsule, and eased his body out of the hatch. "Don't worry, Joe. I used to own a gun." After bracing himself, Jasper aimed and pulled the trigger.

Frank's gaze followed the line's trajectory while he kept most of his attention on the joystick. The weighted end hit Joe in the breadbasket.

"You got me." Joe clutched his middle and bent double.

"I also won most of the sharpshooter contests, old-timer." Jasper gripped his end of the line and knotted a thick rope to it.

"Hey, who're you callin' old?"

Frank shook his head. He was getting tired of the Wild West banter while he worked his tail off.

"You OK, hotshot?" Larry's concern was an intrusion into his black thoughts.

"Yeah." Frank forced a smile.

Jasper leaned out. "You ready, Joe?"

"You bet."

Joe and Maria pulled in the rope hand over hand. Then Joe whipped the end around a handle, tied it off, and held up his hands. Frank couldn't remember where he'd seen that gesture. Oh, yeah. Calf roping. *Figures.*

Jasper knotted his end of the line to a handhold. "Yahoo!"

The cowboys were at it again.

"I used to rope heifers, too, folks. Got the fastest time, more often than not." If Joe's chest had puffed out any more, he'd have burst a hole in his suit.

Frank immediately sobered. A hole in the suit equaled death. An astronaut never let his imagination wander in *that* direction. And it wouldn't take much. One snag on a protruding antenna.

Larry keyed his mic. "Houston, this is *Reconciliation.* Line secured."

"Roger."

"This is ISS." Leonid's voice entered the exchange. "Will activate robotic arm and hold *Reconciliation*."

"ISS, this is Houston. Go get her."

Jasper floated back to his seat.

Gazing at his fellow astronauts, the commander spoke with a tight voice. "Houston, this is *Reconciliation*."

"Go ahead, Larry." Dan, the cool cucumber.

"We're going EVA. This is our last transmission. *Reconciliation* out."

Frank stared through the port as Jasper hooked his suit's tether to the hastily tied line. The robotic arm grabbed hold of the capsule. Later, someone in NASA would figure out what to do with the crippled ship. Jasper and Hildi would transfer to the station while Frank controlled the spacecraft up to the last minute. Then he'd EVA with Larry taking the rear. Captain is always the last to leave. Stupid naval tradition. It should be him. Malfunction or not, the accident happened on his watch.

Jasper took a deep breath that rattled the radio in Frank's helmet. He attached his tether to the line and jumped off the capsule's hull toward ISS, using the rope only as a guide. Touching down on the station, Jasper turned and thumbs-upped the others.

Hildi was next. She pulled herself out of the hatch, tethered her suit, and grasped the line. She hesitated.

"C'mon, Hildi. You're holding us up." Frank wished he'd sounded more humorous, but his comment flew at Hildi with jagged edges.

Hildi turned, her grin shining. "No worries, Frank. Just admiring the view. It's not every day you see Florida spinning beneath you." She held the line loosely like Jasper, pushed off, and pounced on the station with all fours. Maria pulled her toward the docking area by the strap of her air pack. Frank started breathing again. Just he and Larry now. They worked together to shut down all systems. He stared at the gauges. "RCS isn't responding."

"Can you shut it down manually?"

"Negative."

"Leave it. Let's get out of here."

Frank propelled himself through the capsule to open space. Larry followed, securing the hatch after he emerged. Frank stood on the hull, watching the lifeline between the spacecraft and the station grow taut.

The line snapped.

Reconciliation shuddered free. Frank and Larry grabbed nearby handholds. The craft broke away from the robotic arm and accelerated with a pronounced yaw. The high-gain antenna snapped off against the arm as the space capsule spun out of reach.

Frank winced at Leonid's cursing. He knew Russian, of course, but had never heard those particular words. The torn rope, still knotted to ISS, waved at them in a sinuous I-dare-you-to-catch-me dance.

They crouched on the capsule. Larry grabbed him, lifted him like a sack of potatoes, and hurled him toward the rope.

Frank captured the line with one hand and scrambled to the docking port, gasping. Where was Larry? He jerked his head back. Larry clung to the spinning spacecraft as it drifted farther away with every breath. "C'mon."

Larry sprang.

He strained toward the line, floating with

exaggerated sluggishness, like those frustrating movie scenes with slow-motion action. Frank tensed, willing Larry to make it.

Larry missed.

He collided head first with the station.

His limp body floated away.

18

"I" Plus Three Days

"Worth, you know I'm right." Laura glowered at him, hands on hips. The morning sun's glare filtered through the bedroom blinds and silhouetted her trim figure. A breakfast tray sat on his nightstand. Worth's lagging appetite refused to perk up at the smell of tea and cinnamon toast.

"I can't cancel a seminar. I know I'll be fine in a couple of days." He tried to rise from bed but lay back with a groan, pulling the comforter under his chin to hide his shivering. "It's only the flu."

"No, it's not. Whatever this is, it's worse than that Hong Kong flu thirty years ago. I should know. That thing laid me low for weeks. That's why, C. Worthington Hildebrandt, you are going to the doctor."

He felt like a microwavable meal left in the oven for three days, but he wasn't about to tell her that. As Laura plumped his pillow, he reached for the glass of ice water on the tray and chugged it.

She sat on the bed, forehead furrowed. "Worth, you know how susceptible you are to these things, even with a flu shot. You need to see the doctor. I won't have my husband dying on me." Laura sniffled as she reached for a tissue.

Worth grasped her hand. "You always were too good for me."

She gained her composure with remarkable speed. "Let me take your temperature." She grabbed the digital thermometer from the nightstand and jammed it in his ear.

"Hey, no fair. You're drilling that thing into my brain." Maybe she wasn't so composed after all.

"All's fair in love and illness. Or don't you remember the words, 'in sickness or in health'?"

"Hmph."

Beep.

Laura checked the readout. "One hundred two point four. You're not going to the doctor's today."

Worth sat a little straighter. "See, I told you it wasn't serious. I'll make an appointment for tomorrow."

"You're not going to the doctor's tomorrow. You're going to urgent care *now*." She pulled open a dresser drawer and threw a pair of briefs and a T-shirt onto the bed. "Get dressed." She crossed her arms and tapped her foot the way she had when their children misbehaved.

Worth didn't have the strength to protest. "Yes, ma'am." He swallowed a cough to hide his ragged breathing. "Maybe they can give me some antibiotics or something."

He fought the gravity that bound him to the bed, and he reached for his clothes like a good little boy.

Laura left the room with a smile of triumph that didn't extend past her lips. She was really worried.

The receptionist at urgent care handed Worth a clipboard with a pen and several pages of forms. While Laura paced like a caged tiger, he sat on one of the

institutional armchairs—blond wood, blue vinyl seat—
and stared at the papers. Other patients, many of them
coughing and sneezing, occupied chairs lining the
room. A minty medicinal smell wafted from a senior
citizen maneuvering through the door. His walker had
yellow tennis balls on its feet.

A chill invaded Worth's body and made his hand
tremble. The typeface on the forms blurred. "Hon, will
you do this? Your handwriting is so much neater."

Laura gave him a long stare before grabbing the
clipboard. The floral scent of her cologne nearly
neutralized Mr. Ben Gay. She sat down, balanced the
clipboard on her knee, and pursed her lips. Fifteen
minutes later, she delivered the forms to the
receptionist and dug in her purse for the medical
insurance card. Worth smiled at her before another fit
of coughing racked him.

"Worth Hildebrandt?" A nurse with horn-rimmed
glasses waited in a doorway for her next victim.

Several pairs of eyes glanced in his direction. Even
here, he couldn't escape his notoriety. He kissed his
wife's forehead before disappearing through the door,
head held high.

The nurse seemed friendly enough, though she
yawned as if she needed another cup of coffee. She
ushered him into a chilly exam room. After
questioning him endlessly while typing on a laptop,
she took his temperature and blood pressure. The cuff
squeezed his biceps so hard that Worth looked to make
sure his arm was still intact. She finished her notes,
said she would inform the doctor, and left. As the
minutes stretched, Worth wrapped his arms around
his chest, longing for bed and a blanket.

A doctor entered, wearing a white coat, short-cropped brown hair, and the latest in beards. He scanned the intake info on the laptop and the medical history Laura had completed, frowned, and turned the clipboard toward Worth. Dr. Beard pointed to one of the yes/no questions. "Is this correct?"

Worth nodded.

The doctor pulled on blue exam gloves without further comment. He poked, prodded, and told him to breathe deeply. Worth took a deep breath and coughed, his chest rattling, as the man pressed a refrigerated stethoscope to his back.

Dr. Beard gave him his diagnosis. "You appear to have double pneumonia. I'm starting you on oxygen."

The nurse returned, clipped a sensor to Worth's forefinger, and turned to the pulse-ox display. Then she inserted a cannula in his nostrils and nodded at the improved numbers on the machine. Worth knew the procedure all too well. He tried to ignore the itching invaders in his nose.

As the oxygen flowed, he relaxed. Tension drained away, now that he didn't have to battle for every breath. The nurse ducked out and returned with Laura.

"So, doctor, what do you want this husband of mine to do? Take two aspirin and call you in the morning?"

Worth recognized Laura's I'm-going-to-joke-because-I'm-really-worried ploy. He shook his head and regretted the movement. His body wasn't the only thing that ached.

The doctor wasn't fooled by Laura's tactic, either. "We're way beyond aspirin, I'm afraid. Your husband has double pneumonia. I've asked the nurse to call an ambulance. He needs to be hospitalized."

"Ambulance? Hospitalized? I'm not *that* sick."

Worth's eyebrows slammed together.

"Yes, hospitalized." The doctor wasn't backing down. "He's doing better on oxygen, but he needs intravenous antibiotics. Of course, the pneumonia may be a secondary infection. With his high fever, age—"

"But I'm only 57."

"—and this other complication, we've got to use aggressive treatment." The doctor jabbed his pen at the clipboard.

Laura pinned the doctor with her eyes. "I hope you understand this needs to be kept quiet. If word ever reaches the press—"

"Don't worry, Mrs. Hildebrandt. All our patient records are confidential." The doctor handed her another set of forms. "If you'll just sign this authorization for transport, we'll get you on your way." Dr. Beard left the room.

Laura rolled her eyes. "I hate forms."

****

Worth felt like an Egyptian mummy as the EMTs strapped him onto a gurney and secured an oxygen bottle.

Laura squeezed his hand. "I'll follow you."

"Sure you know the right hospital?"

"Hmph. Just don't give these guys any grief."

"If he does, we'll just throw him out the back." The EMT's levity made Worth smile, but Laura remained stoic.

They loaded him into the ambulance and shut the door. Worth closed his eyes and tried to pray for wisdom for the doctors, but concentration wouldn't come. All he wanted was his own bed and untroubled sleep. He couldn't form a cohesive sentence. *Help, Lord.*

At the emergency entrance, the men deposited him onto another gurney in an examination room surrounded by white drapes. A nurse plugged him into more machines than he could count. Laura soon joined him, a little out of breath. She'd probably run from the parking lot. She frowned at all the equipment.

A doctor entered the cubicle, blonde hair pulled back in a ponytail. She looked at the information provided by urgent care, squeezed Worth's shoulder, and examined him. He endured another round of poking and prodding while Laura found a chair in a corner. The doctor announced her diagnosis. "He appears to have double pneumonia. How long has he been sick?"

"A couple of days." Laura frowned.

"Has he been traveling? Like to Michigan or Ohio? The bacteria there aren't your run-of-the-mill bugs, and we use different antibiotics for treatment."

"We give marriage seminars all over the country. We were in Chicago two weeks ago, then home in Denver."

Dr. Ponytail's gaze traveled to Worth's face. "So you're *that* Hildebrandt. I've seen you on television, but you looked a lot healthier."

"I felt a lot healthier."

She chuckled, scribbling notes on another form. "I'll order blood work. It could also be a secondary infection to influenza, but it's a bit early in the season. Was he vaccinated?"

Worth's temperature rose. He resented being talked about in the third person.

One side of Laura's mouth quirked upward in a you've-got-to-be-kidding-of-course-he-does expression. "Yes, he got a vaccine, just like he does every year. He's at risk, after all."

Dr. Ponytail made another notation. "Mrs. Hildebrandt, if you'll wait in the reception room, we'll get your husband settled in a room. You can join him there after you fill out the forms from the admitting nurse."

As the doctor stepped out, Laura muttered, "Paperwork."

Worth winked at her as he suppressed another coughing fit. "Don't worry. I'm in good hands. God's hands."

She nodded, her eyes staring at nothing. "I just didn't expect this." She swallowed and attempted a fleeting smile. "I'll see you as soon as they let me. After I finish their stupid forms." She stomped out.

Worth sank into the gurney's thin mattress and shivered again under a cold, scratchy sheet. The nurse inserted a needle for an IV drip and hung the bottle on the pole attached to the gurney. She tucked his personal belongings on a shelf underneath. His vision filled with the ceiling and its acoustic tiles as an orderly wheeled him through the corridors. The tiles with their precise holes formed a colander, straining out his life force.

An elevator, a slight sense of rising, and a voice intoning "Fourth floor." Worth knew the hospital well from numerous visits to sick friends. He racked his tired brain to remember what was on the fourth floor. He caught a glimpse of the sign above the double doors as they pushed him through.

Intensive Care Unit.

19

"I" Plus Three Days

Carol groaned as she woke. Every muscle ached. She snuggled deeper into the comforter, shivering.

"C'mon honey, time to rise and shine." Mike yanked off the comforter.

Carol dove for it. "No way. I'm not moving from this bed. I feel awful."

Mike's brow creased. "Caught a cold?"

"No, I think it's the flu. Knew I'd catch something at that seminar. They kept the rooms so icy."

Mike shook his head. "You can't catch the flu that way. Someone in that crowd probably exposed everyone there."

She huffed a breath that morphed into a cough. "I know that." She kept her tone level. Although she and Mike had apologized to each other after their argument yesterday, she still winced at the memory.

He'd left without a word but pulled into the garage after twenty long minutes. Carol struggled with the urge to cross her arms. "Where have you been?"

"Hardware store. Needed some screws." He cocked his head. "Something wrong?"

"I...need to apologize. I flew off the handle. I'm sorry."

Mike's head dropped. "I'm sorry, too." He held

out a bouquet of daisies, her favorite. "I figured you needed some cheering up. Come here." He opened his arms.

Carol launched herself into them. After a long hug, she sniffed and pulled away. "Let's put it behind us." She had fixed a nice dinner. Chinese takeout.

The vase of daisies sat on the dresser. He acted like nothing had happened, but she couldn't forgive herself that easily.

"Can you get me the thermometer? I think I'm running a temp."

"Sure." Mike walked to the bathroom. Carol heard the medicine cabinet open, then the clink of bottles. "Where do you keep it?"

"Second shelf, right side."

Mike returned with the thermometer already inserted into its sanitary sleeve. Carol placed it under her tongue, grimaced at the plastic, antiseptic taste, and waited. He folded his arms, and she felt her anger rise. He never took her illnesses seriously.

Enough with the "never" stuff.

Pulling out the instrument, Carol squinted at it. "Hmmm. One hundred degrees. That's a little high." She set it on the nightstand.

Mike picked it up and read it as if he didn't trust her to do it properly. "Looks like you're right. But it can't be the flu. You had a flu shot last month."

"Must have gotten some weird strain. The shot's only good for the most popular one. With all of those people at the seminar, who knows what I was exposed to."

"Ending a sentence with a preposition is something up with which I will not put."

Usually his quips brought a smile to her face, but

not today. Carol hoisted herself out of bed to use the bathroom. Her bladder was quite insistent.

Mike yelled through the closed door. "Is there anything I can get you? I need to leave for work."

"I really don't feel like eating. Maybe some ice water."

"Coming right up. You should take some ibuprofen."

"I will." Carol rummaged through the cabinet. "We don't have any here. I think there's a bottle in the downstairs bathroom."

"Water and ibuprofen. Got it."

Carol shouted down the stairwell. "And could you stop at the store and pick up some of that nighttime stuff? We're out."

"OK."

Carol eased back into bed. Mike's retreating steps made her head hurt with every pounding footfall. How could someone so slight sound like a fullback on the stairs? She sat up as Mike returned with the medicine and a tall glass of water, ice tinkling. After gulping down the pills and water, she snuggled deeper under the comforter. "Thanks."

"Call me if you need anything." A worry line creased his forehead.

"I'll be fine. It's only the flu."

****

Carol rinsed her mouth after another bout of vomiting. Odd. She didn't think this was the stomach variety of flu. Shivering, she crawled under the covers.

The creak of the oil-starved garage door announced Mike's arrival from work. As he tromped up the stairs, Carol hid her head under the pillow. She just wanted to be left alone.

"Can't fool me." He lifted the pillow and pecked her on the cheek. The tender gesture warmed her. "How do you feel?"

Her words emerged as a croak. "Terrible. I'm burning up. It's gone into my chest."

Mike took her temperature again. "Hmmm. One hundred three. This isn't good. Have you eaten anything today?"

"Just a few crackers. I'm a little sick to my stomach. I vomited all morning."

"Maybe it's a stomach virus. Water?"

"A little. I'll go to the doctor's tomorrow if I don't feel better." Carol coughed as if her insides wanted out.

Mike took his familiar I-won't-budge stance. "I know a sick wife when I see one. You could be dehydrated. And you're so pale." He pulled off the covers, gently this time. "Put on some clothes. I'm taking you to Emergency."

"No. I'll be fine."

"You're going. Stop arguing."

Carol nodded. She did feel lousy. She downed a couple more ibuprofen as she slipped into jeans and a T-shirt. Even that simple effort made her feel fifty pounds heavier. Trudging downstairs to the garage, her worry gland started kicking her insides. She would never admit it to Mike, but she'd become a little concerned herself. The flu had never flattened her like this. She eased into the passenger seat.

"Drive, James." Her smile was a weary one.

"Yes, ma'am."

Emergency was jammed with a few people

holding blood-soaked sterile pads to their extremities, but most of them were coughing their hearts out. Carol thought she recognized a couple from the marriage seminar, but she wasn't sure. A few of the coughers walked through a door when their names were called and returned a few minutes later, clutching what she assumed were paper prescription orders.

Her turn finally came. She sat on the cubicle's bed and answered questions from a nurse while Mike watched from a nearby chair.

Finally, the doctor entered, giving a cursory glance at the information the nurse had gleaned. "And how are we feeling today?" He looked too young to wear a stethoscope.

"Rotten." Carol almost gave in to tears. She'd tried to sleep that afternoon, but no dice.

"What the nurse wrote is consistent with dehydration and pneumonia. This virus is especially virulent, so I'm admitting you."

Mike's eyebrows rose.

"Don't worry. We'll start her on an IV drip and oxygen right away, and I'll order blood work and an X-ray. We'll fix her up in no time."

"OK." Carol would have agreed to a lung transplant if it would help her breathe.

The doctor turned to Mike, who'd pulled his face into a deep frown. "You can stay with her if you like, or at least 'til we transfer her to a room."

Mike nodded.

The doctor left without another word. On to the next patient, Carol supposed.

"Mike?"

"Hmm?" His head was already buried in a book.

"Could you get the book out of my purse, please?"

Mike grunted and rummaged through her tote bag at the foot of the bed. He emerged with a small paperback. "Here it is."

"Thanks." Carol opened her novel. Escape or distraction seemed a good idea, but the words swam. She couldn't focus. She laid it on her chest.

A nurse came in a moment later with a portable X-ray machine, took images, and left. Another nurse inserted a needle for an IV. Carol watched with a certain fascination.

"You're good," Carol mumbled, closing her eyes. "I barely felt it."

Mike turned away. He didn't like needles.

The second nurse hung a bottle of saline on a hook, inserted plugs or something up her nose, and turned a valve. Carol's breathing eased.

She blinked at Mike and closed her eyes again. How long had they been here? She sagged into the sheets. "All I want is my own bed."

Mike looked up. "You'll be OK." He squeezed her hand. She tried to smile back.

When the doctor returned, Mike was in fidget mode. "Well?"

The doctor ignored his tone as he displayed the X-rays. "It appears your wife has double pneumonia. I suspect it's influenza, but I'm concerned about her dehydration and high fever. I'm admitting her to ICU."

Carol gulped. She was sicker than she thought. Vaguely she heard the doctor talking to Mike as if she were an inanimate object, but she was too worn out to argue.

The orderlies appeared. They wheeled her one way while Mike went another, probably hunting for a latte. He promised to meet her once she got settled in her room. Only after Carol was hooked up to a bazillion monitors did they allow Mike in.

"You look like a Borg from *Star Trek*." He plopped into the chair and slurped from a paper cup.

"Thanks a lot."

She surveyed her surroundings. Her room had a glass wall that looked out to the nurse's station and a few rooms opposite her. Most people were in worse shape than she was, judging from the moans. One patient, with his wife sitting nearby, caught her attention.

"Mike," she whispered. "Isn't that Worth Hildebrandt? Over there?" She tilted her head.

Mike leaned toward the window and squinted. "Hard to tell at this angle. I think I recognize his wife. Wonder why he's here."

"Probably caught the same bug."

A nurse came in and checked Carol's vital signs. "I'm Annie Burton. I'll be your nurse tonight. Is there anything I can get you?"

"No." Her tongue felt thick. "Wait. Maybe something for nausea."

Annie frowned. "I'll have to check with the doctor first. But I can give you Tylenol if you're achy."

"Thanks. I feel like a steamroller's flattened me."

Mike surfaced from his novel. "Do you know if that's Worth Hildebrandt over there?"

The nurse grimaced as if she'd just tasted bitterness. "I'm not allowed to say. We have a strict policy about confidentiality." She cocked her head. "Do you know him?"

"Uh, not really." Carol glanced at her husband. "We attended his marriage seminar three days ago."

"Interesting." Annie tapped her little finger on her

cheek.

"I think I caught the flu at the seminar. Maybe he did, too. So cold in the hotel." Carol allowed Annie to fluff her pillow before lowering the bed to a prone position.

"I told her it didn't work that way." Mike touched her hand again.

"I know that, Mike." Carol sighed. "It's an expression, I guess. I must have caught it there, though. I'm sure of it."

"You're probably right." Annie looked thoughtful again as she adjusted the water pitcher on the bedside table. "Flu is transmitted either by sneezing or by personal contact. That's why we're always telling people to wash their hands. Even with all the announcements from the CDC, the public misunderstands how it's spread."

Mike nodded. "Like that swine flu several years ago. Some people refused to eat pork."

"They haven't nicknamed this strain yet. Maybe they'll call it the tofu flu." Annie chuckled.

Carol smiled. She liked this nurse.

"Speaking of late, it's about bedtime for you. But first, I want you to drink some water."

Carol stared at the clock and tried to calculate. Two hours had disappeared since she and Mike had left for Emergency.

Annie turned to Mike. "You can stay if you like, but she needs rest."

"You have my cell phone number?"

The nurse nodded then stepped out of the room and greeted the patient next door.

"Do you want me to stay?"

Yes. But she couldn't ask him to. He had to work

tomorrow. "No, I just need sleep."

Mike stretched, stood, and pushed the chair against a wall. He leaned over and kissed her. "I'll see you first thing in the morning."

As Mike left, she heard a confusion of voices and Nurse Annie hissing, "You're not allowed in here. This is an ICU unit, not a photo op." The brilliance of a camera flash seared Carol's eyes. Her husband merely said, "Excuse me," and slipped past the photographers. Carol guessed the fuss was over Worth Hildebrandt. He had to be the patient she'd seen. Why else would the media be here?

As Carol tossed in bed, she wondered what was going through Mike's mind. Was he thinking about her health, their relationship, or the next book to read?

20

"I" Plus Three Days

Chet groaned as he turned over in his stateroom's queen-sized bed. His throat felt like someone had lit a bonfire in it with sharp sticks. He used every tissue in the room, and still he dripped. Coughing only made it worse. But the symptoms were all wrong for the flu.

Four years as a vaccinologist working with the deadliest diseases on Level 4, and he catches a common cold.

At least it wasn't the flu he'd unleashed. When he caught a run-of-the-mill cold, he usually recovered in a day or two. Probably caught it from someone on the plane.

The blue sky visible through the fluttering sheer drapes confirmed late morning. The salty sea breeze blowing in through the sliding glass door was too brisk for him, an unusual occurrence. He wanted the outside world to just go away.

Someone knocked on the door. Probably the steward wanting to make up the bed. "Come in." Chet sat up and reached for a used tissue. Even that slight effort made him cough.

The stateroom attendant stuck in his head. "Señor, you look so pale. You are ill?"

"Yeah, Enrique. A cold."

"You want I should ask ship's doctor for medicine?"

"No, I have some, thanks. Maybe some water and another box of tissues."

"Sí. Do you want me to close the sliding door?"

"Yes, please."

Enrique slid the door shut, grabbed the carafe and ice bucket, and left the room. He returned a few moments later, the clink of fresh glasses resonating uncomfortably in Chet's head. "Do you need anything else, Señor? Food? Another blanket?"

Chet held up a hand to avoid any more questions. He wasn't up to it. "Just make my apologies to my dinner mates tonight. If I feel like eating, I'll call you. Oh, and yes, I would like another blanket, please."

"Very good, Señor."

Chet sighed as Enrique returned with the blanket, arranged it on his bed, and shut the door. Chet got up and fumbled in his kit for a couple of aspirin, zinc tablets, and vitamin C. He downed them with a full glass of water. A faint ringing in one ear confirmed his diagnosis. He submerged himself under the covers, grateful the mattress wasn't a slab-o-pedic.

Clutching the blankets under his chin, Chet wondered about the spread of the virus. He should have heard something by now on the Internet. The outbreak of an unexpected strain usually raised ominous warnings in the media reports. The flu he'd inflicted wasn't too nasty, just enough to make his father and those hypocrites suffer. Too bad he couldn't tailor it for his father alone, but that technology was decades in the future. When he felt better, he'd plug his laptop into the ship's Internet system and check the news again.

Chet smirked. Maybe he'd send his father a get-well e-card. He shook his head. He wanted his gift to be anonymous.

He drifted in and out of sleep as the cold ran its course. Nothing he could do except wait it out in slumber land. He dreamed about innocuous things until the recurring nightmare reared its ugly head.

He lay on the backyard lawn, pointing at the cloud shapes. A horsie, a kitty, and a sailboat. Grass tickled his neck as he watched the clouds. Butterflies flew around him.

Groans drifted from an open window of the house. He skipped over and tried to peek in, but his four-year-old frame couldn't reach the sill. He jumped up and down but still couldn't see. Running to the back door, he opened it and let the screen bang closed behind him. He bounced into the house and stopped at the open bedroom door.

"Daddy?"

His father lay on the bed. Someone was underneath him. They must be playing a new game. He laughed and jumped onto the bed, ready to tussle.

The lady in the bed yelled, and Chet saw her. Miss Tanda, his Sunday school teacher.

Daddy turned his head. He was angry. He rolled out of bed. He wasn't wearing any pajamas.

Chet crawled backward. He knew he'd done something bad, but he didn't know what.

Daddy lifted him.

"Daddy, you're hurting me."

"Don't you ever tell Mommy, or I'll whip your hide. Understand?"

Chet nodded as a tear ran down his cheek.

Chet startled awake, the memory still screaming in his mind. The nightmare had plagued him ever since regression therapy. Boy, was *that* a mistake.

Remembering what his father had done only reignited a smoldering fire. And revenge hadn't put it out.

21

"I" Plus Three Days

Hildi's breath came in ragged gasps as she stared at Larry's body tumbling in a macabre dance alongside the drifting capsule.

Body. He couldn't have survived.

Someone bumped her. Frank strained against Jasper's grip on his shoulders.

"You can't go after him!" Jasper twisted the struggling figure until they faced each other.

Blobs of tears pooled in Frank's eyes. "He shoved me. The idiot shoved me." Frank's voice ringing through her helmet's radio held conflicting tones of anger and desperation.

"Listen to me. His faceplate cracked. I saw vapor escape and his suit depressurize." Jasper shook him.

"Let me go!" Frank tried to wrench himself from Jasper's grasp, their movements a slow dance in the bulky pressure suits.

"No, Frank." Jasper's voice jangled Hildi's heartstrings. "You'll never reach him in time. No one can live in a vacuum. You know that. If you go out there, we'll lose both of you." Jasper hung his head. "He's dead, Frank."

Frank shook off Jasper's grasp and shoved him away. Jasper clung to a handhold and swung back. He blocked the pilot's next attempt to launch himself toward the inert body. Hildi feared Frank would start a fight as he raised his gloved hands.

"ISS, this is Houston." Dan's strained voice broke the tension. "Flight surgeon confirms the loss of Larry's vital signs. He's gone."

Hildi felt as if space itself mourned.

"C'mon, people." Joe's defeated voice had lost all trace of Texas fire. "Time to go inside."

Hildi cycled through the airlock and unfastened her helmet in a daze, trying to comprehend. Larry, dead. *Reconciliation* gone. She breathed the slightly stuffy air, grateful for the expanse of the station. Although she knew better, her brain associated more room with more air to breathe. Her heart froze, imagining Larry's last gasps of life.

Maria emerged from a section's doorway. Short, black hair framed her sad face. She hugged Hildi.

Joe cycled through the airlock, followed by Frank and Jasper. He removed his gloves and helmet. With his mousy hair and pale complexion, Joe looked like an accountant, not a sun-weathered cattle rancher. Grief grayed his eyes as he extended a hand. "Hi, Hildi. Welcome to—"

A piercing alarm assaulted Hildi's eardrums.

Joe's jaw clenched. "Leonid, what's going on?"

Hildi's heart hammered in response to Joe's switch in demeanor. She dreaded the answer. This couldn't be happening.

"We have air leak." Leonid hung parallel to the floor, examining the gauges.

"Where?"

"Docking area. Damage from accident, I think."

Joe's curses blued the air as he propelled himself

to the control board. "Houston, this is ISS. We have a problem. Air leak." Joe pronounced it as one word.

"Say again?" Dan's matter-of-fact voice confirmed Hildi's suspicion that he already knew. Maybe they wanted to record the moment for posterity.

Joe took a deep breath and tried again. "We have an air leak in the docking area. Request permission to repair."

"Acknowledged."

Hildi's heart took up permanent residence in her throat. Everyone had suited up and clicked their helmets in place. Normally they would have huddled in the Soyuz, but it was damaged and six people couldn't fit.

An hour creaked by. If NASA took their usual sweet time, it would be hours more before they made a decision.

Leonid said something rude to the gauges. "Leak is getting worse."

Joe keyed the mic. "Houston, we need an answer pretty bad."

"Roger, ISS, you are GO for repair."

"Acknowledged, Houston."

Leonid looked up from his instruments. His fair hair and complexion contrasted with Maria's dark features, but their faces wore identical worry lines. She'd already pulled a patch kit and toolbox.

Joe grabbed the supplies in one fluid motion. He and Jasper floated to the docking area. *Reconciliation's* shrill decompression alarm still rattled Hildi's memory. ISS had meant safety as she fled the crippled capsule, but that assurance had evaporated into the air. The rapidly escaping air.

Everyone waited in silence. Maria and Leonid

checked and rechecked every gauge. Finally, Joe panted into the mic. "Hole was mighty big, 'bout the size of a plug nickel. Patch is holding."

Hildi's shoulders relaxed at the return of Joe's accent.

"Copy that, ISS. We confirm." Dan's standard CAPCOM voice seemed cold and out of place, but Hildi welcomed it, anyway. She could listen to him for hours.

Hildi released the breath she'd been holding as Maria, the first Mayan astronaut, helped her remove the bulky pressure suit. "We usually don't have *this* much excitement here. Welcome, by the way." The scientist's calmness soothed Hildi's fight-or-flight state. The instinct soon descended into numbness.

"Hey, Joe, where do we stow our suits?" Jasper sounded like he was asking a party host for the guest closet, but his lips pressed together in a thin line.

"Put them in the locker there. We'll figure out room arrangements later."

Hildi frowned, her thoughts swirling like leaves in the wind. She'd forgotten something, like an umbrella. But she didn't need an umbrella in space...Her eyes widened. The virus sample.

"What's the matter, Hildi?" Frank pushed off from a wall and grasped her forearm. His eyes reflected pain, grief, and despair.

Hildi's heart lurched with Frank's touch. She bit her lip, determined to keep a professional focus. "I left the flu vial on the capsule."

But Larry was dead, and nothing would bring *him* back. Her irritation at Frank and at forgetting the virus sample shriveled to nothing.

Leonid floated up behind them. "Houston has lost

telemetry with *Reconciliation*."

"No!" Frank balled both fists.

If Houston couldn't reestablish control of the spacecraft, *Reconciliation* could circle the Earth for years before its orbit decayed and it either crashed or burned up. Recovering the spacecraft intact was crucial to proving Frank's insistence of instrument malfunction. Hildi's heart ached.

"They'll get it back." Joe cleared his throat. "But Larry—uh, Larry's body—will float alongside us 'til we update our orbit. Should do that mighty soon. His body's a danger to the station."

Hildi winced at the macabre thought. The astronauts stared at the floor, ceiling, anywhere but at each other. The somberness in the station weighted the air.

Everyone went to their assigned cabins. She brooded, trying to think of nothing. Instead, all she could see was Larry hurling Frank into a life-saving trajectory.

Joe's voice over the intercom jarred her out of her bleak thoughts. "I'd like y'all to mosey over to the main cabin."

Hildi pulled herself into the crowded common area, noting the red-rimmed eyes on everyone. Frank arrived last.

Joe cleared his throat. He clutched an ancient copy of the *Book of Common Prayer* in front of his chest like a shield. "Folks, I think we should pay our respects." He opened the book to an earmarked section. He paused. "That is, if no one objects. I know y'all have different faiths." His gaze touched each one in turn and settled briefly on Maria, but everyone nodded.

"ISS, Houston. We're with you." Steve Walters

took the mic as Dan softly sobbed in the background. Hildi's heart tumbled.

"Uh, I'll be reading from the Burial of the Dead. It's meant for burial at sea, but...I think it's appropriate." Joe acted as ship's captain as he read the words, occasionally wiping his nose on his sleeve. "'I am the resurrection and the life, saith the Lord...We brought nothing into this world, and it is certain we can carry nothing out. The Lord gave, and the Lord hath taken away; blessed be the Name of the Lord.'"

Hildi glanced at the others, all floating in microgravity and oriented the same direction, heads bowed. The service was more than appropriate for a man who'd sacrificed himself as a career astronaut venturing into the sea of space. She jerked her attention back to Joe's words.

"'Lord, let me...let me know my end, and the number of my days...'"

He droned on as the astronauts listened in silence except for a few sniffles. The lump in Hildi's throat grew into a grapefruit.

Joe stopped. "Y'all, let's recite the Lord's Prayer together. 'Our Father, who art in heaven...'"

The radio crackled as the people back in Mission Control joined them a beat or two delayed. Frank and Jasper whispered the words while Leonid floundered. Maria floated in respectful silence. Hildi's voice cracked at every other word.

"Amen." Joe swallowed. "These, uh, are the last words. 'We therefore commit his body to the deep...uh...*depths of space*, looking for the general Resurrection in the last day, and the life of the world to come, through our Lord Jesus Christ; at whose second coming in glorious majesty to judge the world, uh...*space* shall give up its dead; and the corruptible bodies of those who sleep in Him shall be changed, and made like unto His glorious body; according to the mighty working whereby He is able to subdue all things unto Himself. Amen."

The final word echoed in the cabin. Hildi couldn't choke back her tears. No one else managed it, either. Tiny spheres of salty water escaped and drifted in the weightlessness.

Good-bye, Larry. See you in Heaven.

When Joe finished, he took a deep breath and shifted into a serious mode. Very serious. Hildi tensed. *Here it comes.*

Joe resumed his station commander's voice. "I've been doing a little calculatin' on our current inventory. *Reconciliation* was supposed to re-supply us, but 'course that didn't happen. We have fifty days left of food and water." Joe exhaled. "The crucial shortage is oxygen. We lost a lot with the leak. We have fifteen days."

The station *always* had a forty-five-day supply. Hildi's brain tried to comprehend how a routine spaceflight could go so terribly wrong.

When the murmuring faded, Leonid raised his voice. "Russian supply rocket leaves in ten days, da?"

"Doesn't look good. They're having 'technical difficulties' as they put it. Seems to me they ought to launch anyway, or we could be in a world of hurt."

"And if they can't?" Hildi's stomach rolled.

"Don't know."

22

"I" Plus Three Days

Dan released the breath he'd been holding. Joe had repaired the leak without too much trouble. The station commander lost his Texas drawl, a sure sign of stress, but everything seemed under control for the moment. Under control with fifteen days of air left. He thanked God they didn't have a full crew on ISS. Three more astronauts on board would have stretched the oxygen supply even thinner.

A geeky-looking engineer with a white shirt, pocket protector, and thick glasses burst through the door, a member of ISS monitoring team in the next room.

"What is it, Alex?" Annoyance tinged Steve's face.

Dan's stomach nose-dived. *Please, Lord. I don't know how much more I can handle.*

"Steve, ISS had an air leak." The engineer announced his news in a quavering voice.

"We know, Alex. Joe just patched the leak on the station. They'll do a more permanent repair once we know the whole situation."

Alex frowned.

Steve gestured to a chair. "We have other issues we need to address. Sit. We need your expertise."

Apparently mollified, the engineer sat. Dan smiled

at him. Geeky, but the best brain around.

"Ladies and gentlemen." Steve stood and took command. His words now would color the White Team's struggle between sorrow and responsibility. Fifteen men and women, eyes glistening, turned from their consoles.

Steve cleared his throat. "We have six astronauts marooned on ISS, damage to the docking ring, and a capsule that's tumbling out of control. We need to focus, people."

Every head nodded.

"Give me the readouts, by the numbers." Steve sat and pulled a pad of ledger paper toward him, his back rebar straight, a supervisor coordinating a building's construction. Dan prayed the building wouldn't collapse on its foundation. He rubbed clammy palms on his pressed slacks.

"Do we know where *Reconciliation* is now?" Steve jotted notes on a yellow sheet.

The woman at the tracking console swiveled in her chair. Dan noted her red-rimmed eyes and smeared mascara. "Sir, we have an orbit. Well off that of ISS."

"How is that possible?"

Another controller turned to Steve. "The attitude jets are still firing intermittently on their own. We have no maneuvering capability of the spacecraft at this time. Still working to reestablish telemetry."

Dan shifted in his seat. Worst possible scenario. Steve scribbled more notes and looked at the controller. "Opinion. Can we regain telemetry?"

"Yes." The man fidgeted. "I think so."

Alex the Geek blinked. "Flight, we can do it."

Steve leaned forward. So did the ground-control engineer, apparently annoyed at the interruption.

Alex stood and paced. "The S-band high-speed comm link is inoperative. The antenna was probably broken off during translation. We can't engage Remote RCS and maneuver her back to the station. But" —he paused—"we *can* deorbit her. We can initiate the automated reentry sequence by DTMF over the VHF voice comm, using the backup RCS. It should work."

Steve looked skeptical. "What if the primary RCS system is still compromised?"

"It'll work." Alex bounded over to the engineer's desk and started pointing at the dials and numbers, talking in a low voice. Finally, the engineer nodded. "He's right."

"Do it. I want the spacecraft on Earth and in one piece." Steve stabbed a finger on his ledger. "*Reconciliation* is a memorial to our fallen astronaut. It's also a valuable piece of government property. If we can retrieve her intact, we can find out what happened." He glanced at Dan. "*Valiant* is due to launch in three weeks, but of course now it'll be delayed."

Dan's heart sank. There went his next mission and possibly the moon as well. The NASA guys would be hashing and rehashing the problem for months— years—with or without the capsule.

He dreaded the next question he knew Steve had to ask.

"Have we determined the location of the body?"

A woman swiveled in her chair to face him. She swallowed. Dan admired her control; her voice barely broke. "Sir, he's in a parallel orbit with the station, thankfully out of view."

Alex interrupted. "ISS will adjust orbit soon to avoid possible collision."

"I'll notify the family." Steve took a deep breath

and continued his relentless assessment of the situation. Dan marveled at the man's concentration and thanked God he wasn't sitting in the director's chair. "How are the vital signs on our astronauts?"

The flight surgeon turned from her console. "I'm showing elevated levels of pulse and blood pressure, but that's understandable considering the circumstances. Jasper's vitals barely moved. I'd say they're in decent shape."

"Thanks, people. Good job." Steve leaned back in his chair.

Dan stared at the computer screen as the station's video camera showed two objects tumbling away. Silent tears and inner rage battled for supremacy. Larry gone?

Space work was dangerous. Everyone knew that. Each mission could become another disaster, and there had been too many of those. He just never expected it to be Larry.

He'd just spoken to him. Larry had been upbeat, facing the emergency with his usual competence. How could he be dead?

Dan swallowed, trying to shake his emotions into a corner of his mind for later processing. He had to concentrate. He couldn't let grief affect his job as CAPCOM—the voice of calm to a crew in shock.

Everyone in Mission Control had listened while Joe conducted the first memorial service in space. Most stared at their consoles instead of each other.

"An honorable end for any astronaut," Dan murmured.

Those close by nodded.

He ducked his head. He hadn't meant to speak aloud.

"You're right, Dan." The flight director met his gaze with a ghost of a smile. "But I prefer old age myself."

Alex collapsed against his chair. Steve's stare pulled him back to an upright position. "Just how much oxygen *do* they have left in the tanks?"

"I'll get back to you." The man hurried away as if his tail were on fire.

23

"I" Plus Four Days

Chet glanced at the late-afternoon sun reflected on the sea then returned to surfing the Internet in the computer room, looking for news articles about an influenza outbreak. The papers should have reported something by now, unless his tactic of spraying the napkins had failed. He weighed the possibilities. Maybe it was a bit early. If doctors didn't report flu to the CDC, it would take a while, and hopefully they'd never trace the outbreak to the seminar.

He stretched, grateful he'd recovered so quickly from the cold. He wasn't contagious any more, but he used the hand sanitizer dispensers often. However, his steward had looked a bit peaked the other day. This morning a fellow from Indonesia had taken his place.

Chet gave up on his flu hunt and typed "Worthington Hildebrandt" into the search box. Google listed a ton of links. The first one sent him to his father's website. He scanned the information, noting the next seminar had been canceled. Maybe he'd gotten the flu after all. *Good.* Other sites contained denouncements of dear old Dad as an adulterer. *Hear, hear.*

One news article caught his eye from the search results page, "Seminar Leader Hospitalized." Chet frowned. The virus wasn't *that* potent. His neck prickled as he clicked on the link.

The controversial pastor-turned-seminar-leader became ill on Tuesday and was admitted to Littleton Hospital's ICU ward with double pneumonia. His doctor refused comment.

Hmmm. Chet tried another article, this one from one of those sleazy tabloids. Just the usual garbage about his father's ongoing love affairs, this time with a ninety-two-year-old woman. How anyone believed such trash was beyond him.

The paper's headline caught his eye. "Flying Saucer Attacks Space Station." Always alien this, alien that. Wait a minute. Shouldn't his sister be on the station by now?

Chet started a new search for "Hildi Hildebrandt." The first result was an article from the *Los Angeles Times*. "Capsule Crashes: Kills One, Astronauts Stranded." His jaw dropped.

He read the article in full, stomach knotting. Hildi wasn't the one killed, and his stomach relaxed a bit. He didn't know the other astronauts except for Frank. *The sleazeball.*

Chet had zero tolerance for adulterers, wishing they'd all eternally rot. But Hildi had not only forgiven their father like a good little Christian but had forgiven Frank as well for cheating on her during their engagement. Chet never would forgive either of them. And to think he'd actually liked Frank.

He felt himself being watched. He turned his head and admired the slim, smiling woman who met his eyes. She wore a cruise name badge. "Can I help you with anything? I'm roaming the room and answering questions."

Chet deleted his search. He'd probably overstayed

his welcome on the Internet connection. "I'm done if you're waiting for this."

"No, no." Her laugh was a tinkling bell. "Take as much time as you need."

Chet faked a concerned frown as he pointed at the minutes remaining on the Internet card he'd purchased from the cruise line. "Wow. I should daydream less often. Guess I should pay more attention when I'm doling out money by the minute."

"It adds up quickly. Do you need help in increasing your Internet time?"

She was blonde and well dressed. Chet admired her graceful form and sea-gray eyes. Taking a deep breath, he plunged in. "Hi, I'm Chet Hildebrandt." He stuck out his hand.

She shook it. "Sandy Andrews. Pleased to meet you." The woman had a firm grip in spite of her wrist splints. She also had short fingernails.

Chet smiled. "You're a harpist."

Her mouth quirked upward. "How'd you know?"

"Used to hang around concerts backstage." He glanced at the splints. "Carpal tunnel?"

"Yeah. Occupational hazard."

"How'd you wind up in charge of the computer room?"

Her laughter tinkled. "Oh, no. I'm just the relief person. Jeff is the real expert."

Disappointment clipped Chet's hopeful wings. "Jeff?" *Drat, she's married.*

"Jeff Huth."

Chet hoped Jeff was just a coworker. He glanced at her left hand. No wedding ring. "Do you play for symphonies or chamber ensembles?"

"I play for both occasionally. I signed up for this

gig a few months ago. Pays the bills, plus I see the world."

He raised an eyebrow. "I'd love to hear you play."

"Well," she whispered, "I'm playing in Le Pouvre from eight to eleven tonight."

Le Pouvre was the fancy French restaurant on board. He'd tried to schedule a reservation. His hopes skidded to a halt. "They're booked tonight. I checked."

"If you want, you can sit in their lobby and listen. I'm trying to arrange a little recital, but the cruise director hasn't figured out a time. Keep checking with the daily schedule."

"I will. I'd like to—"

"Hey. Hellooo." An overweight woman in an aloha shirt that screamed *vacation* interrupted them. "If you're quite through with this touching conversation, I need help with getting my e-mail." She scowled from a nearby seat as if it was their fault.

Sandy winked at him. "Gotta go," she whispered, then turned on the charm as she addressed the woman. "I'm so sorry. What seems to be the problem?"

Chet quickly packed up his laptop and left, hiding a grin. He walked up several flights to his stateroom, noting his regular steward was still missing. The Indonesian only said, "Very sick, sir."

Striding across his room, Chet opened the sliding glass door to his balcony and stepped outside, enjoying the cool air. The gray, churning sea reflected his worry about Hildi in jeopardy, stuck in space with The Creep. The news piece had mentioned a problem with the air supply, but he never took the reports seriously. Sensationalism was the name of their game.

The breeze glued his pants to his legs. He stepped back into the room and closed the door, convinced the wind had also pulled his hair off his scalp. A quick comb with his fingers yielded only snarls.

He glanced at the clock. Time to dress for one of the formal dinners. He changed into his tux, tamed his hair, fussed a bit with his cufflinks, and was ready. He looked forward to sitting in the mezzanine with a drink and the mellow sounds of a string quartet.

Before he exited, he paused. He pulled his empty suitcase out of the closet, rummaged through its pockets, and found the vial he'd snatched from the CDC. He pulled it out, examined the label, and froze.

This vial didn't belong in Level 3. It wasn't the mild flu virus he thought he'd taken. It wasn't the variant of H1N1 that hit the U.S. in 2010. This was much, much worse.

24

"I" Plus 5 Days

Worth sipped his tea, trying not to cough the hot liquid all over the bed sheets. A nurse's aide was kind enough to fetch his comfort beverage. He'd steeped it a little too long, but the bitter, scalding brew with lemon and sugar eased the ache in his throat, at least for a moment.

Craning his neck, he glanced at the pulse-ox meter. Temperature up, oxygen down. Still going down, as he expected.

Yesterday evening he'd sent Laura home for some much-needed sleep. She'd protested, of course, but even Annie, his night nurse, had thrown her out. He was too weak to insist himself, a fact he tried to hide, but he couldn't fool Laura.

"OK, I'm leaving. I can take a not-so-subtle hint." Her tired smile attested to her drained energy. "I'll be back in the morning." She kissed his forehead like he was a fevered child. Her shoulders slumped as she turned and walked out.

Worth eavesdropped on the conversation at the nurses' station. He doubted they knew he could hear them, but his room's glass doors had been left open to the bustle of the caregivers. He could see their faces as they watched the patients. Worth had learned to read lips, a useful skill he'd picked up before getting a decent hearing aid. Between his clear line of sight and the stage whispers, he had no trouble understanding them.

Annie and another nurse—was it Diane?—spoke with worried tones.

"How are you doing?" Diane sipped her coffee. She looked as tired as Annie had earlier.

"There's not enough coffee in all of Colorado to keep me going." Annie gulped. "I'm in the middle of a double shift, like you and everyone else. Intermediate Care is handling overflow, and still it's not enough. I don't know how long we can hold out."

"Did you talk with Dr. Stephens?"

"Yes. He thought it could be something like Hong Kong flu. The current vaccine doesn't work." Annie huffed a breath. "It'll take months to develop a new one."

Diane drained her mug. "We could have dozens more cases by then and who knows how many across the country."

Worth sensed hesitation in Annie's lowered voice. "I wonder if it's H1N1, the original one from 1918. I did some research on it in nursing school. Nasty. The media will probably speculate about it. Once they do, it'll be the lead story on every news program." She took a deep breath as if she were plunging into the deep end of a pool. "Any word of this, and the population will panic."

"Well, the papers didn't hesitate to spill the beans on Mr. Hildebrandt's health. They've been out to get him for a long time. Boy, once they get their jaws around some scandal, they're like guard dogs." Diane looked pensive. "I wonder how they found out about his HIV."

Worth tensed.

Annie sighed. "I don't know, unless someone blabbed. Some photographers got in here the other day, but I booted them out. Today's paper said 'unnamed sources,' and that could mean anything." She shrugged. "We may never know." Annie stood and stretched. "I need to make my rounds. I'll check on Hildebrandt again."

As Annie approached his room, Worth quickly turned on the television and pretended interest in a nature program about naked mole rats. He wanted to prop his eyes open with toothpicks to look halfway alert, but what he needed was a nap. She did the usual, checking oxygen and pulse levels, swapping out the expended IV bag for another, and noting the information on his chart. She hung it backwards at the foot of the bed. "Is there anything I can get you, Mr. Hildebrandt?"

"Please call me Worth. Got that lung transplant I ordered?"

Annie smiled. "Sorry. It wasn't in the UPS delivery." She glanced at the bedside pitcher that Worth had barely touched. "Your urine output shows you're not drinking enough. I want you to finish this by noon."

"Aye, captain."

Annie grinned. She turned to leave and nearly collided with Dr. Stephens. They stepped out of Worth's room and spoke in hushed tones with their backs to him, but Worth picked out a few words. "CDC," "index case," and "marriage seminar."

Worth closed his eyes. How *had* the media found out he was HIV-positive? He shivered with a chill that had nothing to do with his fever. Only one person would have relished telling the press. The woman who infected him.

Miss Tanda.

****

Carol's gaze followed the orderlies as they wheeled an empty gurney past her room. Odd. Usually they rolled someone in and occasionally someone out, but no one was on this gurney, unless...oh.

She'd visited an ICU ward when a friend was ill and asked the nurse about it. Apparently, someone who died was usually hidden underneath the gurney on a shelf like they'd used for her personal belongings. The thought made Carol squirm.

"Mike. Did you see that?"

He looked up from his book just as it—the body—disappeared through the double doors. "What?"

"An empty gurney. It could have someone, uh, dead underneath it."

"Huh. That's the first one I've seen leave here without someone on it. Might mean nothing." He shrugged and returned to his book.

Carol coughed into her elbow. She thought she'd feel better by now. She turned her lagging attention back to the TV, a bit miffed at her unobservant husband. But he was here. Her attitude softened.

The evening news anchor switched his gaze to the in-house expert. "We're tracking the unseasonal virus. Here's Dr. Cohen. Brad, what's the situation?"

"Well, Quinn, the CDC reports outbreaks in Idaho, Wyoming, Kansas, and Utah, with the most cases in Colorado. They're looking for the index case—the first known case of this virus—and are confident they'll find it soon." Dr. Cohen frowned. "They've reported three deaths, two of them elderly with breathing problems and one in her twenties."

Mike's book dropped to the floor, startling Carol. "Twenties? Since when has the flu killed someone in their twenties?"

Like me. Carol tried to concentrate on the newscast, but the drugs were making her sleepy. "I heard Worth Hildebrandt is getting worse."

"Hmmm?" He tore his eyes from the TV and looked at her.

Huffing out a breath would only make her cough. After five years of marriage, she should know to get his attention before talking. Mike didn't always hear her when he was deep into a novel or a TV program, and she couldn't talk above a whisper. "Worth's really sick, isn't he?"

"That's what I overheard. Sicker than you are. Probably caught the same bug at the seminar." He picked up his novel, a thick thriller.

She bristled at his lack of conversation and tried again. "I can't imagine feeling worse than I do right now." The effort of talking made her cough, echoing the hacking from the other rooms. She ached all over, and breathing was almost more trouble than it was worth. She wanted him to pay attention to her, argue with her, *something*. "I just wanna die."

Mike clenched his fists. "You're not going to die."

Carol regretted her cheap tactic. They locked eyes, worry etched into Mike's face. He returned to his novel. Mike was usually a fast reader, but he hadn't flipped a page for a long time. He'd also been spending a lot of time in her room before and after work, sometimes reading and sometimes—was she sure it wasn't the drugs?—just holding her hand. She reached for a tissue. Lack of sleep during her long stay in ICU must be the reason for her weepiness.

She dozed, vaguely aware of her husband sitting in the chair in the corner. Slumber wouldn't come. The hushed cacophony of the ward at night kept her awake in spite of her weariness.

The chair scraped as Mike dragged it to her bedside. He held her hand to his heart. Then she heard Mike pray. It shocked her so badly that all she could do was feign sleep.

"Please, God, don't take her from me." His voice cracked. "Please. I love her. Please, heal her." Mike poured out his soul to God. Carol feared to interrupt such a holy moment.

Odd. Comforting warmth spread through her down to her toes. No vise squeezed her lungs. She took one deep breath, then another.

Finally, Mike quieted. Carol opened her eyes. He stared into hers, sniffling. "Feeling better?" His smile held strained edges.

"Mike."

He gripped her hand like it was the only thing saving him from a long fall off a cliff. "I love you. I've never stopped loving you." He blew his nose in a honk that was totally Mike.

"Oh, Mike." Carol tried to hug him, but she only succeeded in knocking the sensor off her finger. The machine beeped indignantly.

They chuckled at the annoying sound. Carol sank back in her bed from the awkward embrace and swiped at her eyes.

He kissed her temple, perhaps afraid of

aggravating her nostrils still irritated by the things in her nose. She reached up to caress his jaw, rough with dark stubble and wet with a single tear. They broke apart reluctantly as a nurse barreled into the room, apparently alerted by the machine's beeping. She glanced at the sensor lying on the bed, re-clipped it onto Carol's finger, and left in a huff. Annie stepped into the room and did the usual, efficient things. Carol smiled back, feeling like a naughty schoolgirl.

The nurse, Annie, checked the machine next to the bed and started to write figures on the chart. She frowned and checked the machine again. She studied Carol's face.

Carol gulped. *Oh no.* "What's wrong?"

Annie's puzzled expression morphed into a grin. "Nothing. Your oxygen rate's improved. And you don't look as pale as you did earlier. I'll ask Dr. Stephens to check on you this morning, but I think you're on your way to recovery."

Carol winked at Mike and breathed a silent prayer of thanks. She cleared her throat. "What happens next?"

"If the doctor decides you're well enough, you'll be released to a regular room. You'll probably stay overnight and then be discharged. How does that sound?"

"Heavenly."

"I'll let him know. Breakfast?"

"Yeah. I think so." Carol wasn't hungry, but eating was one of those things the hospital insists you do before they unshackle you. "Something simple."

"Broth and gelatin." Annie grinned again. "It's what we do."

Carol and Mike stared at each other after the nurse

left. She smiled. "Hi."

Mike smiled back. "Hi."

"So what do we do now about *us*?" She couldn't get past the fear dampening her joy. *Would there be an "us"?* After Mike's confession of love, could she not light one candle of hope?

"Climb back on our horses and ride off into the sunset?" Mike's attempt at levity curled one corner of Carol's mouth, but the other corner reserved judgment. He turned serious. "Something tells me we have to find the horses first."

"Could we try marriage counseling?" Carol lifted her eyebrows.

"Yeah, we could. Whatever it takes."

They were still holding hands when breakfast arrived.

****

Carol sighed. It was a relief to breathe without those pesky things in her nose.

The doctor had released her to a regular room. She really was getting better. She still felt weak, but being sick with the flu and lying in bed for several days will do that. One good sign—the hospital food was starting to taste bad.

Mike sat at her bedside as she ate lunch. The tomato soup was acceptable, but the macaroni and cheese…She tried one more bite and gave up. "*Blech.*"

Mike chuckled. "That bad?"

"Yeah. It's a secret plot. Makes you want to leave the hospital fast." Carol smiled. "Actually, most of the food here is a cut above institutional food and more than a few notches above mine."

"One more night, then you're home."

"I can't wait." She sighed. "What I want more than anything is a pepperoni pizza from Romano's."

Mike raised his eyebrows. "That does sound good. We'll celebrate when you get home." He patted her hand. "I need to return to the office, at least for a few hours. I'll be back after work."

"Promise?"

Mike kissed her forehead. "Promise."

After a short nap, Carol thumbed the remote for a television program more exciting than infomercials. The nurse's aide presented dinner around 5:30. Carol was debating whether to trust the substance that looked somewhat like meatloaf when Mike returned. He was hiding something behind his back, but the aroma of garlic betrayed him.

"Romano's?"

"Nothing but the best. Pepperoni and mushrooms." Mike grinned as he pulled out a white pizza box. He set the hospital food tray on a nearby chair, pulled apart two pizza slices, and put them on paper plates. Two colas appeared from his coat pocket. He winked and closed the door. Then he produced three LED tea lights from another pocket and switched them on. They flickered into happy glows.

For the first time in three years, they said grace.

25

"I" Plus Eight Days

"Pyat, chetirye, tree, dva, odeen, start."

Dan startled from his daydream. The Russian countdown wouldn't happen. They couldn't launch the resupply rocket.

They'd hurried their preparations of *Progress M-09M* and shaved a week from the original launch date. The unmanned spacecraft would have docked tomorrow with food, water, and oxygen for the beleaguered station. The weather still wouldn't cooperate, and now they had another problem.

Steve gripped the Russian liaison's shoulder. "I know your people did their best."

The liaison hung his head. "Da. Russia stands ready to help, but *Progress*"—he heaved a sigh—"*Progress* cannot help."

Dan's hopes sank. How in the world could they reach the station in time? He turned to Steve, who snapped another pencil.

A controller who overflowed the seat of his chair turned to the flight director. "Flight, radar confirms ISS has moved out of danger from Larry's body or *Reconciliation*."

"Good job, Ernie." Steve swallowed.

"With the new radar upgrade, we can find a pin if

we have to."

Steve gave a somber nod. "Ladies and gentlemen, let's observe a moment of silence for our fallen colleague."

Dan bowed his head.

The memorial service on Earth had been with full military honors, of course. Larry's death hadn't really registered for Dan until then, the gloomy day reflecting his mood.

Steve ended the silence with a return of his usual mission intensity. "Tracking, where is *Reconciliation* now?"

Bruce turned, a head above the other controllers even when sitting. "Over the South Pacific."

"Control, how long before we reestablish telemetry?"

Sweat shone on the middle-aged man's bald head. "I don't know. It's tricky with the instruments compromised. I'm having to reset the—"

"I know the difficulties involved, Harry." Steve's smile earned a nod from the man. "I know you're doing the best you can under the circumstances. We certainly never anticipated this scenario."

Harry straightened. "Yes, sir. We'll get it back soon."

"Good." Steve stood and stretched. "OK, people, Blue Team is ready to relieve you. Brief your replacements and be back here at oh-six-hundred hours."

Dan talked with the next CAPCOM. As he filed out, he whispered to Steve, "What do you really think are the chances of recovery?"

Steve's eyes reflected weary confidence. "Good. Very good."

Dan's heart lifted a bit. Recovery of *Reconciliation* had become a symbol of Larry's legacy and a personal issue for all at Mission Control. A second issue filled Dan's mind—the opportunity for Frank to clear his name. He wanted his friend to have that chance. No doubt lodged in Dan's mind that an instrument glitch caused the accident.

He stopped at the cafeteria before heading home. He loaded his tray with everything in sight. Stress eating. Shorty Baxter waved at him from a corner table, and Dan walked over. "Hey, Shorty."

"Hey yourself. Just getting off CAPCOM duty?" Dan's fellow astronaut bit into his barbeque sandwich. "Ah, that's better."

Dan slid his tray onto the table and sat. He stared at his plate. "Yeah. It's been brutal." He slathered his baked potato with the works and smashed it over and over.

"How's Hildi holding up?"

"Fine."

"There's something you're not telling me." Shorty pointed his fork at Dan to punctuate his words.

Dan stabbed at his pork chop. Maybe he wasn't hungry after all. "I just don't know anymore."

Shorty polished off his meal in two more bites. "Sheesh, everybody but you can see it. You love her, right?"

"Yeah." Dan stretched the word. Did he? Maybe that explained the backflip of his brain every time he thought of her. "I think so."

"You know so. So what's kept you from popping the question?"

"I keep asking myself that. Right now, it's 250 miles of space."

"Look, Dan." Shorty gulped his sweet tea. "Take it from someone who nearly let the woman of his life get away. Go get her."

If only it were that simple.

****

Dan readied himself for bed. Six hours' sleep for days in a row just didn't cut it for him. He didn't share Shorty's confidence in NASA. The station needed that oxygen, and he saw no way anyone could deliver it in time. The thought of Hildi gasping for breath dropped his heart into a deep elevator shaft.

He'd never patched things up after their quarrel. Now she'd never know he loved her. If the rocket was lost, so was any hope of rescue.

No rescue. The station would soon become a tomb for Hildi and five other astronauts. Death by asphyxiation.

26

"I" Plus Nine Days

Dan ran tired fingers through his hair as Steve led the discussion. A discussion that was going nowhere. The flight director had called an impromptu and critical meeting.

"OK, people, let's go through this again." Steve cupped his chin in his hand. "We can't reduce the air pressure—"

"No." Another geek from ISS control jabbed his pen at a copy of the report.

"I agree." The flight surgeon's pale face was even paler than usual. "Any lower and we risk unconsciousness."

Dan's heart lurched at the image of Hildi's body floating through the corridors.

Steve tapped his pencil on the conference table littered with papers, laptops, and discouragement. "Other ideas."

The surgeon cleared her throat. "We could order them to minimize their movements. Maybe even make them sleep more with pills."

"What about inducing a coma?"

Dan knew they were grasping at smoke, but they had to come up with something or six astronauts, including Hildi, would inherit the station as their private mausoleum. He squeezed his eyes shut.

The flight surgeon shook her head. "They don't have the drugs on board. I already considered that possibility."

"What would sleeping pills get us?"

"Maybe half a day."

Murmurs and bickering filled the room. Dan rubbed his stinging eyes.

"Folks," Steve bellowed. "We need some focus here. The ISS crew has enough oxygen for only fifteen and a half days. It's pocket change compared to the bankroll we need."

"So what about the Russians? Can't they do anything?" The ISS geek blew his nose.

The Russian-American liaison shook his head. "*Nyet*. They cannot launch."

Steve slapped the table. "Six astronauts' lives are on the line."

The Russian raised his voice. "We could not anticipate problem—"

"Well, it happened." Steve held his pencil in a death grip. "I'm sorry, Nikolai. I know your government did its best. We'll find another way."

Nikolai inclined his head.

Rubbing his neck, Steve stood. "Let's take a break. Ten minutes." He motioned to his assistant. "Arrange for sandwiches and coffee. It's going to be a long meeting."

They filed out of the room, the group unusually silent. Dan exited, trying to walk out the stiffness in his legs. He sent up another prayer for the astronauts. *Please, Lord. We need something. Anything*. He clenched his fists. They had to come up with a rescue plan, no matter what it took.

Dan and the others returned to the conference table. Charlie, the director of NASA, had joined them and occupied Dan's usual seat. He took a chair at the other end of the table, wanting to disengage from the growing despair. He hoped for good news but dreaded the announcement Charlie would likely make. He tensed.

Murmurings became a buzz of agitated hornets. Charlie's voice raised above the din as he reconvened the meeting. "The NASA board has decided on a course of action. After talking with Steve, we believe there's no other option. We launch *Valiant* in twelve days."

Dan stared at him. "Twelve days? You're moving it up from a month to twelve days?" The man was talking miracles. Dan's resolve hardened. If it could rescue his friends—and Hildi—he'd jump off a cliff without a parachute.

The others shook their heads.

"We can do it," Charlie insisted. "She's on her way to the launch pad and will be fueled ASAP. Every flight technician is working around the clock."

Nikolai smiled. "Russia would be happy to provide its finest engineers."

Charlie nodded. "Thank you, Nikolai."

Dan drummed his fingers on the table as if the rhythm could help him think. He and Shorty were here at Johnson, but Dave and Jim were in Alabama. The four of them hadn't had enough simulation time together. He wasn't comfortable with the idea of rushing the launch, but they'd make it work. They had to. In spite of the dire circumstances, his heart leaped in anticipation. He'd be in space sooner than he'd hoped.

Geek scowled. "You're forgetting the damage to our docking bay. The patch Joe made is already under stress, and the last thing we need is more oxygen loss. Joe assures me they have the materials on board, but whether it will hold—"

Charlie pounded a fist on the table then turned to Steve. "Tell the station to go EVA and repair the damage. We need that fix before the patch fails." He huffed a breath, glanced around the room, and stood. "We can do this, people. So let's get to it."

As Dan started to leave, Steve gripped his shoulder. "We need to talk." Dan nodded as the rest of the team filed through the door. Charlie also remained.

Steve's eyes bored into his. "Dan, we can't take the full crew of *Valiant*. We'll need extra room for oxygen supplies."

Dan swallowed. Among the four astronauts for the mission, his position was the most expendable. Everyone cross-trained for a mission. Shorty, Jim, and Dave could easily cover the job.

"I understand, sir." Those were the hardest words he'd ever uttered. Left behind like the one kid not chosen on a baseball team. Without experience with the Rigel series under his belt, he'd never qualify for the moon. But it was a small price to pay for Hildi's rescue. "I'll do my best to see the others are ready on time. I assume you'd like me to concentrate on their training?"

"You misunderstand me. You'll keep your assignment as the pilot of *Valiant,* and Shorty will keep his as commander." Steve's stare bore into his like a laser. "The two of you are it. We can't afford any more weight."

The implications slammed into Dan. His jaw

dropped before he regained his composure. How could he and Shorty tell two of their crew members they had to stay behind? And how could two astronauts perform the work of four? Determination filled him. Dave and Jim would understand. A desperate rescue called for desperate measures. "Yes, sir."

27

"I" Plus Nine Days

Hildi gazed longingly at the treadmill. Normally the astronauts exercised for two hours daily. She really wanted the workout, but they needed to conserve oxygen.

Someone behind her cleared his throat. She turned to see Frank hanging onto a handle near the hatchway. He stared at his feet. "We've hardly talked since this mission started."

She hesitated. She didn't want to encourage him, but she could see pain behind his bravado. He had something on his mind besides their relationship.

Frank lifted his head. "I...I...just can't believe Larry is dead." His voice was strained.

Hildi hung her head. How could she be so callous that she'd ignored his grief? "We all mourn him, Frank. We trained with him, ate barbeque with him, joked with him. He was a good person and a good friend. I know you were especially close to him, but you're not alone in this."

"It was my fault."

"No, it wasn't."

"If I'd taken control of docking earlier, we wouldn't be in this mess. And if Larry hadn't saved my life, he'd be here now. I wish it'd been me instead of him."

Hildi's eyes misted.

Frank's pooling tears threatened to float away on a mission of their own. "And if I had been quicker, none of this would have happened in the first place."

"Look at me. Nobody here blames you. Autopilot was supposed to prevent this. *Reconciliation* lurched. Maybe it was the attitude jets you complained about, maybe something else. But it wasn't your fault." Hildi hoped her little pep talk would lessen Frank's escalating guilt, but hopelessness dulled his eyes. Her heart plummeted.

"I should have been able to compensate."

"You don't know whether that was even possible." Hildi laid a hand on his arm. "Stop beating yourself up."

Frank shook off her hand and turned away, but not before Hildi caught his look of resignation. He mumbled, "I don't know why I bothered to talk about it. Larry is dead, and nothing will bring him back."

Hildi snapped her mouth on a tart reply. Frank had closed down. He needed to work through this, but she wasn't the one who could help him. His despair triggered alarm in her brain. Usually he could compartmentalize his feelings. Maybe Jasper could lift his spirits. She smiled as she thought of their phlegmatic teammate.

As Hildi propelled herself toward a shower, she crashed into Jasper, sending him spinning. He whooped and somersaulted. Hildi grinned in spite of her dragging heart.

He regained a steady position. "We're wanted in the control room."

"Frank, did you hear that?"

"I'll be right there."

Jasper and Hildi sped to the meeting. Frank emerged from the passageway a minute later. "What's up?"

Joe took over without preamble. "Mission Control's on the line. They wanted everyone to be here." He keyed the mic. "Go ahead, Houston."

"Acknowledged." Dan's CAPCOM voice lifted the corners of Hildi's mouth. "We've been analyzing your situation. With some adjustments, we believe you can stretch your oxygen by another half day."

"About what we figured."

Murmuring spun around the room. Frank whispered, "Fifteen and a half days? Who are they kidding? Neither *Valiant* nor another Soyuz will be ready in time. We'll be dead before they get here, and NASA knows it." He glared at the mic.

Joe silenced him with a slashing movement. "Say again, Dandy?"

"NASA's moving up the schedule. Shorty and I will launch in twelve days with loads of oxygen. Special delivery. I'll be switching over to preparations."

Hildi released the breath she'd been holding. The gesture only emphasized how dependent the astronauts were on a little thing like air.

She smiled at the thought of Dan joining her in space. She missed him. Absence makes the heart grow fonder? Definitely for her. What about Dan's heart?

Joe's puzzled frown sobered the station. "Just you and Shorty?"

"Yes. We're loading her to the gills."

"She doesn't have gills." Jasper deadpanned his words.

Hildi chuckled. Jasper ducked his head at Joe's scowl. He continued the conversation with Houston after missing a beat. "So what do y'all suggest for this oxygen-stretching?"

Dan paused as if consulting a list. "We already discussed canceling daily exercise. The boys here can tell you how to tweak the filters so carbon dioxide buildup won't be a problem." He sounded a lot more confident than Hildi felt.

Another pause. "One more thing. Unless you're on duty, sleep. You don't have the drugs on board to manage a coma state, but the flight surgeon says you have enough sleeping pills to keep you happy."

Coma was a last resort, but induced sleep wasn't much better. Hildi didn't want the extra ZZZs any more than anyone else. The medication would hinder their efficiency if they faced another emergency. Probably a moot point. One more emergency and they wouldn't have to worry about sleep.

Joe turned to the crew. "Y'all got any questions? I can't think of anything else 'til the cavalry gets here."

"The capsule can't dock with the damage to the ring." Frank's voice was flat.

"You're right, Frank. That patch won't hold 'til the cows come home."

"ISS, this is Houston. We agree that the docking ring needs to be repaired ASAP. The engineers here are already on it. They're confident they can figure out a permanent fix with the stuff you have. You are GO for EVA."

"Well, Houston, you'd better come up with a good one, on account we can't fool around. It'll have to work and work the first time."

"Acknowledged. Houston out."

"I'll go." Frank's face was set in the don't-deny-me look Hildi knew all too well.

"I'll go, too." Jasper smiled.

Joe smiled at them. "Thanks, gentlemen, 'cause I've already volunteered you." Joe turned to a table strewn with clipped-down photos and drawings. "OK, folks, gather 'round. Leonid extended the robotic arm earlier and got some good pictures of the ring." Joe pointed.

Hildi whistled. The damage was worse than she thought.

Leonid nodded. "We have sheet metal and braces."

"Here's another problem." Joe turned to Frank and Jasper. "Y'all will have about four hours for EVA. That's the limit of your suits since you used a bunch of it on your trek here."

Frank's mouth reflected the determination they all felt. Hildi's mind shifted gears to a stubborn resolve.

Joe favored them with a lopsided smile. "You'll be happy to know this is my last speech for a while. Frank, Jasper, and I will start working on the patch as soon as we coordinate with Houston's engineers. Leonid, Maria, and Hildi will relieve us in six hours. If you're not working, you're resting. Understood?"

Everyone nodded as they again examined the photos. Hildi's disturbing thoughts shouted in her ears. Although everyone had medic training, she was the only doctor on board. She'd be the one to monitor every crew member for signs of asphyxiation. Gasping, confusion, unconsciousness…

Death.

28

Hildi frowned at the latest e-mail from Francine. Amazing to get e-mails in space. Usually she made Hildi laugh, but not this time.

She read it again.

Hi, girlfriend.

Had an interesting day. Hunt sent me to Denver with the CDC team to check out the hotel where we think the index case originated. (I told you about the flu, didn't I? It's bad.) Anyway, it's the hotel where your father had his last seminar. I hate to be the bearer of bad news, but I heard your dad's sick and getting worse.

Anyway, I had the fun task of crawling all over that hotel taking samples. We don't know yet what strain it is. Director Hunt is going nuts because it's way early for influenza to hit the public. I'll be spending a lot of overtime on this one.

Speaking of work and microbes, I haven't seen your brother lately, not that I want to. I think he was suspended or something. Couldn't happen to a nicer guy.

Please be safe up there. Praying.
Francine

Hildi fired back quick e-mails to Francine and then to her mother. Hildi stared at the screen, hoping for an immediate response. None came.

She closed her eyes. Her brother would probably

dance a jig if he knew Dad was that sick. Chet would probably wish he'd unleashed the virus himself.

Her brain kicked into overdrive. Chet could have...no. But he had access to Level 4. He might have had opportunity. He certainly knew how to...*Stop it.*

Her runaway imagination wouldn't shut up. Hildi knew why he'd do it. He still hated their father. But enough to infect everyone at the seminar? Even Chet wouldn't go to that extreme to vent his hatred.

Would he?

29

The new CAPCOM sounded like he'd won a cleanser-gargling contest, but Pete was the sweetest guy at the JSC. Hildi leaned closer to the control board, concentrating on his words. He tried to soften the blow of the inevitable news, but she still felt a golf ball in her throat swelling to a cantaloupe.

"So y'all found Larry's...uh...body?" Joe wanted CAPCOM to repeat it. For Hildi, once was enough.

"Yes. We're tracking it."

The announcement finalized what Hildi already knew—Larry was dead. But when CAPCOM made the statement, she heard nails hammered into a coffin lid.

Pete cleared his throat. "The good news is we got telemetry back on *Reconciliation* and controlled her reentry. The recovery crew salvaged her, and she's in the hangar now. We have the black box."

Frank flinched.

Salvage. Not recovery. The Rigels were designed as reusable spacecraft, like the retired shuttles. *Reconciliation* would never launch again.

Hildi mourned the end of *Reconciliation*'s useful life, but Frank's reaction transmitted utter defeat.

Joe frowned. "Y'all got any idea what happened, Houston?"

"NASA isn't ruling anything out. These things take a while. We'll let you know as soon as we know."

Hildi took a deep breath that morphed into a pant.

Her lungs had to work harder with the reduced air pressure in the station. The crew sounded like a pack of hounds just returned from the hunt.

Joe asked the question foremost in Hildi's mind. Besides breathing, that is. "So, Houston, how's that resupply coming along? We could use a little variety in our diet right about now."

CAPCOM hesitated.

Frank growled. "I told you they couldn't do it. They've been holding out—"

"Quiet." Joe's forehead wrinkled. "Say again, Houston?"

Hildi heard faint voices before Steve apparently wrenched the mic out of Pete's hands. "People, we have the best team in the world working on pre-launch protocol. Dan and Shorty are training all out for this mission. We'll launch on time."

The crew sighed in unison. Hildi's relief couldn't have been more complete if someone had spiked the air with relax juice. Her heart tha-thumped with the thought of her knight in shining armor rocketing to the rescue. She missed him.

"One more thing…Hildi, I'm sorry to tell you that your father is in ICU. It doesn't look good."

Hildi's heart hit a gravity pocket. Frank squeezed her arm. His eyes expressed the empathy she'd longed to see during their engagement. He really liked her father.

Hildi remembered Francine's e-mail. "What about my brother?"

The pause was even longer this time. "He took an extended leave of absence. We've been unable to locate him."

30

Chet lounged in the pool area, the meager sun doing little to warm him. He anchored the blanket under his armpits. At least now he didn't have to fight for a chair. Once the ship left the Bahamas, chugging its way across the North Atlantic to the British Isles, the ocean air turned cold. People usually jammed the Jacuzzis now, but the area was bare. Next time, he'd cruise the Hawaiian Islands. Anyplace warmer.

When Captain Papadopoulos and his assistant strolled by, a slight breeze carried their voices to his corner of the deck. The word "flu" captured Chet's attention. He hunkered down in the lounge chair, grateful that his back was toward them, and peeked over his shoulder.

"I'm relieved the doctor's reported it's the flu and not some weird bug in the ventilation system." The captain's short-sleeved white uniform nearly glowed in the daylight, contrasting with his tanned arms. In spite of his age, he still possessed black hair.

"Unfortunately, we'd already done a thorough inspection of the kitchen, much to Ives's protest." The woman walking with the captain was just shy of anorexic, with blonde cropped hair hugging her scalp like a helmet. They smiled at some private joke.

The captain huffed out a breath. "Of course, that doesn't change the fact we have a very contagious disease on our hands. How many passengers do we have in quarantine?"

"About twenty, but the number keeps climbing. A few have been moved to the ship's hospital." The assistant frowned. The captain turned to her with a grim expression. "Dr. Graves told me she'd contacted the CDC. They think it's the same strain that broke out in Denver."

Chet's guts turned to ice.

"Will they quarantine the ship?"

The captain stopped his pacing and faced her. "We still have five days at sea. Maybe it will blow over by then."

"I hope you're right."

"So do I, Eleanor. So do I. The last thing we need is a panic on board."

After they strolled past him, Chet stood, folded his blanket, and stepped to the railing. He stared at leaden sky, somber sea. He'd become a Typhoid Mary who infected others. He'd carried the disease on board, in spite of his use of gloves and face mask, but hadn't displayed any symptoms. His cold had been just that— a cold. Apparently, he was immune to this particular strain. He'd intended to spread the disease to his father and ultimately to the seminar attendees, but he hadn't counted on *this*.

****

That evening, Chet wore a sports shirt and tie for dinner. He arrived in the grand foyer early to hear Sandy play harp, but the string quartet was playing instead. He worried she'd caught the flu. He asked one of the violin players, but none of the musicians knew. He ordered a martini at the bar, listened while he finished his drink, and walked into the dining room. Not as many people as usual, or they were late.

He greeted the newlyweds at his table who were already immersed in conversation. The young bride's hand seemed glued to her husband's. "What do you think of all this sickness that's going around?" she asked. "I'm worried."

Chet shrugged. "Why? It's only a bug. Lots of people get bugs."

"Yes, but not like this. I went down to the clinic just to get something for seasickness, and it looked like half the ship was there. Some of them were admitted to the hospital. I didn't know they had a hospital."

The husband leaned toward him. "Didn't you say you worked in the health field?"

Chet sipped his water. What had he used as a cover story? "Yeah. Medicare billing."

The other tablemates came. The discussion drifted to other subjects such as the evening's menu. Chet's mind wandered. What had he been thinking? He had worked with influenza before. He knew how deadly it could be. And this one was the worst. The people here didn't deserve the punishment he'd meted out to his father.

He studied his plate. He'd been so full of hate, so cocky, that he didn't think of the innocent bystanders—like that Asian busboy at the hotel—who'd pay for his little prank. Little? Yeah, right.

He wondered again about Sandy's absence and said a little prayer for her health before he could stop himself. His mouth tightened. Probably all that religious brainwashing during his youth.

His father would have been so proud.

31

Dan and Shorty relaxed in the Space Center's lounge during a rare break in training. Dan picked up the *Houston Herald* from the coffee table, set down his mug, and stared at the lead story.

"President Urges Calm"

Washington, DC (AP)—*In an address to the nation yesterday, President Benchley pleaded with the public to remain calm during the recent flu outbreak.*

"I am confident the American people will face this challenge as we've faced all challenges: with purposeful resolve and concern for our fellow citizens," the President said in a televised broadcast from the Oval Office.

"Our best scientists are working on a preventive vaccine, and we will mass produce it as soon as it's developed."

Americans have reacted with everything from stoic fatalism to religious rhetoric about the end of the world. Some have barricaded themselves in their homes as they did during the polio scare of the 1950's.

People are mobbing grocery stores across the nation as supplies of face masks and hand sanitizers run short.

Other countries have not reported any outbreaks yet, but the World Health Organization declared a state of medical emergency in anticipation of a pandemic.

An unnamed source at the CDC revealed the current form of influenza could be a return of H1N1 but would not say whether they had identified the strain.

H1N1 was first discovered during World War I and dubbed Spanish flu. It was responsible for millions of deaths.

Dan's jaw dropped. Millions dead? This report could cause a panic. The reporter apparently considered sensationalism more important than public safety. His blood pressure rose. He continued to read.

A milder strain of H1N1 appeared in 2010 but has not been seen since that time.

Development of a new vaccine could take up to a month plus additional time to manufacture and distribute it worldwide.

The public is urged to use face masks while in public, wash hands often, resist touching their faces, and stay at home if they suspect they've caught the flu.

Symptoms include fever, cough, sore throat, runny or stuffy nose, body aches, headache, chills, and fatigue. A significant number of people also develop diarrhea and vomiting. Anyone experiencing these symptoms should see their physician.

Dan handed the paper to Shorty. "Can you believe this?"

Shorty shook his head. "I always thought the media was manic, but this...this is unprofessional. And dangerous. I wonder how long it'll take for people to start a run on banks."

Dan nodded. The herd instinct of humankind always amazed him. People had a habit of panicking at the slightest thing, like cattle stampeding at a wind-blown Stetson. He smiled at the Joe-inspired expression.

Looking at his watch, Shorty tossed the *Herald* on the table. "We'd better get going. We've got a meeting with Steve in ten minutes, and you know what a stickler he is for punctuality."

"Yes, sir." Dan grinned at his commander's frown. Besides not liking his nickname—which didn't fit his six-foot-four frame—Shorty didn't like formalities. He only stuck with protocol because that's the way it was done.

They strode to Steve's office and arrived with a minute to spare. Dan combed his hair and smoothed the wrinkles of his jumpsuit. Charlie walked out with a worried frown. Not a good sign.

They knocked on the director's open door and entered. Bookcases lined the walls, interspersed with diplomas and citations. Various mementos from space shuttle missions gleamed from their places of honor.

Steve sat behind his walnut desk, the surface bare except for a laptop. Another man turned from the window. The cloudy sky behind him framed his bulk with a halo.

The tense atmosphere startled the hornets in Dan's stomach. Neither of the men looked happy. *Great.*

The flight director gestured toward the stranger. "This is Alan Hunt, Director of the CDC."

"Call me Alan." He shook hands with the astronauts.

"Dan, Sheldon, sit down." Steve motioned toward brown leather chairs. Dan sat on the edge of his seat and waited for the bad-news bomb to fall. His mind raced with questions. Why was the CDC director here? Didn't he have better things to do, such as managing a flu outbreak?

Their boss started without preamble. "You know the situation on ISS. We'd hoped they could buy us more time, but our additional measures haven't been as successful as we'd hoped."

Dan steeled himself for the next announcement.

"We estimate the crew will run out of oxygen in four days."

"We won't make it, will we?" Dan's heart plummeted. Launch time was T minus ninety-six hours but, they'd be in orbit for a day and a half before they could dock. Larry was gone. Now six more would die—Frank, Jasper, Hildi...*Hildi*. His throat tightened into a knot.

"You'll launch on Sunday."

Impossible. How could NASA shave another forty-eight hours from the launch schedule? He voiced his confusion. "But the launch crew can't possibly—"

"Let me worry about the launch crew." Steve's pencil splintered. "*Valiant* will be ready. Question is, will you?"

Shorty answered as commander. "Yes, sir."

Steve locked eyes with Dan. "Are you ready for docking manually? We can't risk the auto pilot after the problems Frank had. We also want you ready to abort if the repair to the ring doesn't hold."

All Dan could do was nod. Six lives depended on them. If they failed, their fellow astronauts and possibly the future of the space program would die. Congress would pull the plug permanently. Along with the moon mission. *His* moon mission.

His mind wandered to Frank, his long-estranged friend. If they failed, Dan would never have the chance to patch things up between them. And he'd never have the chance to tell Hildi how he felt. Except at their memorial services.

The rescue attempt would not, could not fail.

Steve flashed a rare smile. "You're good men. I told Charlie you were up to the task." He gazed at Dan and Shorty. "We have something else you'll need to deal with. You've probably figured it out by now."

Shorty finished the director's thought. "We'll be overloaded. We'll barely have enough fuel to get back."

"Correct. And that's with stripping every redundant system we can reach. You'll have one chance to get it right."

Steve stared at each of them in turn. "Whatever the station crew cobbles together to fix the port, it'll be as delicate as a robin's egg. So I ask you again, gentlemen. Can you handle this mission?"

"Yes, sir." Shorty and Dan spoke as one.

Dan had often bragged that he could pilot any spacecraft in his sleep. He'd now have to prove it. *Me and my big mouth.*

"One more thing. Have you been following the news?"

"Some." Dan wasn't sure which outlandish story Steve referred to.

"The flu."

"Oh, that." Dan snorted. "The media blows everything out of proportion."

"In this case, they haven't." Alan spoke as he paced. He treaded the path in the carpet already worn from Steve's signature cowboy boots.

Now Dan was really confused. "What does that have to do with us?"

Alan approached them. "Gentlemen, we have a big favor to ask. The welfare of our country and even our world may depend on it."

Cut the melodramatics and get to the point. Dan immediately regretted his impatience. Everyone was under stress, and this man had to be carrying Mount Rainier on his shoulders.

"The CDC feels the only hope is to take a sample of the virus to the station and see what Dr. Hildebrandt can do. Weightlessness may help in the development of a vaccine, and she's the second most qualified vaccinologist."

"*Second* most qualified?" Shorty caught the phrase that flew past Dan.

"Yes. The best qualified person is Dr. Chet Hildebrandt, Hildi's brother. Unfortunately..."Alan swallowed. "Unfortunately, I gave him an extended leave of absence before this virus hit. Now we can't find him. I've contacted the FBI for their assistance in discovering his whereabouts."

Chet. Dan's blood pressure rose. Dan had never met the man, but Hildi's friend Francine described him as an antisocial microbe.

"So let me get this straight." Shorty stood and confronted Alan eyeball to eyeball. "You want us to carry a sample of this deadly virus to the station?"

"It'll be perfectly safe." Alan stopped his pacing. "It'll be packed in a secure vial. We'll provide biocontainment suits and other equipment for use on the station."

So that's where some of the extra weight would come from. Not life-saving oxygen and water, but stuff to pull the CDC's fat out of the fire.

Steve must have read his mind. "You willing to take on the extra risk?"

Dan glanced at Shorty, who answered for both of them. "Yes, sir."

Steve leaned back in his chair, fiddling with a new pencil. "Good, because otherwise I would have ordered you."

Dan smirked. "Sir, we risk our backsides every

time we perch on those tons of explosives you call a rocket."

Steve's gaze intensified. "This part of your mission is top secret. I've ordered extra security at the center and at the Cape."

Director Hunt nodded. "We can't let the public know about this, or we'll have crackpots creating havoc. Do either of you read the tabloids?"

Dan and Shorty shook their heads.

"Never mind." Hunt chuckled. "Their investigative reporters have vivid imaginations. They should be novelists."

"That's all." Steve stood and dismissed them with a wave of his hand.

Dan and Shorty rose. Dan almost saluted, feeling he'd just been given orders to the front line.

Dan and Shorty trudged through the halls. Dan's thoughts kept returning to their concentrated training, an army march now bumped up to double time. He'd wanted the *Valiant* assignment, but not under these conditions.

Shorty glanced at him. "Worried?"

Dan nodded, not trusting his voice. It seemed a little tight every time he thought of Hildi.

"Me, too. Lunch?"

Dan smiled. Shorty never skipped a meal. Dan wasn't hungry, but food would probably help bolster his lagging stamina. They matched strides to the cafeteria. A couple of MPs with rifles passed them in the hallway.

Shorty whispered, "Dan, why do you think they want to keep this under wraps? It's not exactly a military secret. Is it?" At the food line, Shorty grabbed a plate and filled it with brisket, mashed potatoes, corn, and salad.

Dan took smaller portions of everything, plus a roll and extra barbeque sauce. "I don't know. Maybe even the CDC doesn't know where it came from. It's not the strain they expected, I can tell you that."

"You thinking what I'm thinking—that it's some sort of terrorist plot?"

Dan's mind flew to other attempts and successes in hurting the U.S. The anthrax scare, the Underwear Bomber, 9/11…He looked over his shoulder at the MPs. "I don't know. One thing's for sure, they're not taking any chances. We've never had a sabotage attempt at launch, but anything could happen with enough hatred for fuel."

They found an empty table and sat. Shorty folded his hands instead of attacking his food. "Maybe you'd better say grace. We could use some."

Dan gave thanks audibly for the food and silently for his friend's rare acknowledgement of God. The simple gesture reminded Dan that God was still in control, no matter how dire the circumstances appeared.

"Do you think Hildi can find a cure for this thing?" Shorty stabbed his brisket and stuffed a hefty portion into his mouth.

"Vaccine, Shorty. There's no cure for a virus."

Shorty sighed. "I just wish all these emergencies weren't piled up at once. I feel like a rabbit hopping around on three venti cappuccinos. We'll be lucky to get a few hours' sleep between now and Sunday."

"If they didn't think we could do it, they wouldn't have asked." Dan kept his doubts of *Valiant*'s readiness to himself. He picked at the rest of his food, which lodged in his craw in a hard lump. He threw his napkin on the table.

"Ready to hit it again?" Shorty gave a lopsided grin.

Dan prayed the word *hit* wouldn't describe his docking attempt.

32

Worth looked up as the day nurse—Annie?—poked her head into the room. He used to be really good with names, but the flu befuddled his brain.

"And we pray for Laura. Give her the strength she needs. Amen." George concluded his prayer.

Annie cleared her throat. "Morning," she said. She had a beautiful smile, but sleeplessness rimmed her eyes.

"Morning yourself," Worth rasped.

"Mind if I crash the party?"

"Not at all." Worth gripped his wife's hand. "I presume you've met my wife, Laura?"

Annie nodded. Worth cringed. Of course she knew Laura. "And our friends, George and Betty?"

"Hi." Annie shook their hands.

"We just stopped by for a minute." Betty held out her arms for Laura's embrace and hugged her like a mom would her skinned-knee child. "I know, dear, I know." Laura sniffled as they broke apart.

Betty reached around Laura and squeezed Worth's hand. She took George by the arm. "We'll be back later. We wanted to see Carol Hardesty before we go. She'll be leaving the hospital today, and we promised to pray with her."

A puzzled frown crossed Annie's face. She didn't seem to know how to react to their prayers. She turned to Worth. "Can I get you anything?"

His brain wouldn't provide the words at first. Glancing at Laura's tear-stained face, he determined to keep his voice upbeat. It still came out as a grumble. "A decent night's sleep?"

A harrumph erupted from his wife, who'd returned to his bedside. "Don't mind him. He's usually this cantankerous."

Worth raised a weak arm in a gesture of protest but nearly knocked the IV loose.

"Enough of that, Mr. Hildebrandt." Annie adjusted the IV.

"Worth, please." He croaked the words.

Annie put her hands on her hips. "Well, if you're so cantankerous, are you going to let me take your vitals?"

"Go ahead." Worth was rather proud of his Eeyore voice. "Everyone else does."

As she placed a new IV bag on the hook and scanned the pulse ox, Worth sighed. He knew the medical terminology all too well from ministering to dying friends.

Annie pursed her lips. Worth didn't need her reaction to know his oxygen numbers were declining, even though they'd elevated his head to help him breathe. Well, he guessed it helped him breathe. It certainly didn't help him sleep.

"Are you in pain?"

"Not really. Just tired and achy."

"Use the call button if you need anything." Annie turned to leave.

"Uh, Worth was saying he hadn't seen the other nurse—Cindy?—lately." Laura's voice was the smooth contralto Worth loved.

"She has the flu." Annie's flat tone of voice told

Worth she was far more worried than she would admit.

"Sorry to hear that." Worth dropped his head on his pillow, a bit breathless from so much talking.

"We'll pray for her." Laura smiled.

Annie looked at them as if they'd just sprouted antennas. She shook her head as she left the room.

Laura squeezed his hand. "We should pray for her. And for Hildi and Chet."

Worth bowed his head as Laura prayed. He managed an "amen," his heart swirling with worry and doubt. He was the one needing prayer. He was supposed to be a Christian leader, for crying out loud, someone people turned to for answers, not some sort-of-a-Christian who couldn't rub two sticks of faith together.

****

Carol waved at George and Betty as they left her room. So nice of them to stop by. She turned her attention to the tabloid. Her jaw dropped at the latest sensational article in *National Exposé*. "Aliens Unleash Virus on Earth"

Extraterrestrials are to blame for the recent deadly flu outbreak, according to Bruce Willit of the Network for UFO Sightings (NUFOS).

"They covered Reconciliation *with disease-laden particles," said Willit. "The virus spewed its poison when the spacecraft entered the atmosphere."*

Willit went on to say that the aliens damaged the International Space Station. "The so-called docking accident was an attack by a flying saucer," he said. "NUFOS has been tracking them for weeks."

Unnamed sources have confirmed that the space capsule was on a secret mission to meet with the alien craft.

"The visitors responded to our peaceful overtures with an unprovoked attack. They intend to destroy all the inhabitants of Earth," said Willit.

One astronaut was killed. The other three barely escaped with their lives.

Carol's funny bone kicked in at the audacity of the paper to even publish such fiction. Mike had brought her a copy that morning along with a vase of daisies. She added the paper each week to her grocery cart of frozen dinners and fresh fruit. Mike frowned every time he caught her reading it, but he apparently had a change of heart with her hospitalization.

She'd been cleared for discharge from the hospital, but the nurse explained it usually took a couple of hours to process the paperwork. She itched to get home and slouch on her own couch.

She flipped through the pages, scanning news items entitled "Boy Trapped in Refrigerator Eats Own Foot" and "Science Fiction Actor Arrested as Terrorist." She finally couldn't contain herself. Her giggles grew louder the harder she tried to stop.

Mike walked in at that moment, consternation wrinkling his forehead. "Something wrong?"

Tears streamed down Carol's cheeks. She wiped them hastily with a tissue and held out the paper for Mike's inspection. "Can you believe this?"

Mike smiled, tired lines around his eyes testifying to his long hours at work and at her bedside. Carol grabbed back the paper. "Listen to this. 'This is the first step in an invasion that space aliens have planned for months. Watch the skies.'" Carol snorted as she handed the paper to Mike. "That's what I like about this tabloid. Cheap entertainment."

Mike scanned the article, then his expression grew grim. "That's not too different from what the newspapers are reporting. I brought you a copy." He handed Carol an edition of *The Denver Post*. Their headline, "Space Capsule Blamed for Virus Outbreak," was barely less out of this world. Her funny bone handed her emotions over to her worry gland as she read the story, frowned, and dropped the paper onto her bedside tray. "So now it's a deadly virus that was on board when *Reconciliation* splashed down?"

"It's ridiculous, of course. Someone at NASA spilled the beans that the space capsule had carried a virus sample for research purposes, but the CDC insists it was just an ordinary flu. It couldn't have caused this."

She read the next column and startled. "The astronauts on the station are running out of oxygen. NASA plans to launch a rescue mission on Sunday. Mike, Hildi Hildebrandt is one of the astronauts. That's Worth Hildebrandt's daughter, isn't it?"

Mike shrugged.

"He must be worried to death."

33

"I" Plus Ten Days

As CAPCOM Pete read the news article to the station crew, Frank's body stiffened in a fight-flight-or-freeze response. He should have seen this one coming.

Frank's rant peppered the air as his hands balled into fists. Joe had awakened him and Maria for this? He'd rather be sleeping instead of facing this nightmare. "So the media is blaming *me* for the crash and want an investigation? *And* they think I'm mentally unhinged?"

"Calm down, Frank." Hildi laid a hand on his arm. He yanked his arm away.

"You gotta cut down on the coffee, bud." Jasper's eyebrows rose. "Oh, that's right. We ran out two days ago."

"Yes, Frank. Calm down." Joe's voice held more of a command than a suggestion. Frank willed his fists to uncurl, but his stomach still churned. "Go ahead, Houston."

Pete continued. "NASA's conducting the investigation." He lowered his voice. "Not some politician angling to get more votes."

"Yeah, like *that's* comforting." Frank clamped his mouth shut as Joe shot him a warning look.

"Frank, no one is blaming you." Hildi's voice was

gentle.

Frank glared at her. She didn't understand. No one did. *Larry died because he saved my life. I could have grabbed him. Should have grabbed him.* "The media will skewer me."

"You're not the only one that's been skewered," Pete said.

Frank frowned, trying to figure out what in the world he was talking about.

"The media claims Hildi caused the virus outbreak. Congress is investigating NASA as well because we allowed a disease-laden capsule to de-orbit."

"How in tarnation did they come to those conclusions?" Joe looked ready to wrestle an angry bull.

"How does the media come to *any* conclusion?" Frank's muscles tightened.

Pete huffed a breath. "Apparently they got wind that the influenza vial was on *Reconciliation* when it reentered the atmosphere. They found some expert who said the virus had mutated when it combined with seawater. They added two and two and came up with seventeen."

Angry voices rose, Hildi's the loudest. "It couldn't have. Viruses don't mutate that way. And the sample vial was securely capped. I checked it myself before launch."

"The vial broke. The CDC's still trying to figure that one out."

Jasper grinned. "Maybe it was aliens."

"You've been reading the tabloids." Pete's voice hinted at amusement. "But enough of the news. NASA wants to know how you're coming on the repair work."

"It's been mighty slow goin'." Joe rubbed a stubbly chin.

Frank bit back a response. He willed himself to change gears and don his mask of professionalism before his mood brought the whole crew down. They all needed to act methodically and logically in this crisis without emotions blurring their focus. The thin air already made that a problem. They'd gathered parts from the station's supplies and cannibalized some equipment. Kluging a patch to repair the docking ring was like using stone knives and bearskins to build a radio.

"Could you elaborate, Joe?" Pete's voice was back to matter-of-fact calm.

"Thing is, it's hard to concentrate right now." Joe straightened. "We'll have it before *Valiant* drops in for a visit on Tuesday."

Murmurs crackled in the background at Mission Control, then Steve took the mic. "People, we've done more calculations here on your oxygen supply. It won't last until Tuesday."

Frank took a deep breath. "So that's that." He grabbed a handhold so he could propel himself to his room and mope in private. *My fault.*

Steve's bellow followed the faint sound of a breaking pencil. "No, it's not. *Valiant* will rendezvous on Monday."

Frank whistled. "And Shorty and Dandy signed up for this suicide mission? Now I know they're crazy."

"Who are you calling crazy?"

Frank's jaw dropped at the sound of Dan's voice. "You, buddy. The whole pack of you, NASA included.

Are you nuts?"

"We're astronauts."

A flame of hope lit Frank's mind, but doubts still hunkered in a dark corner.

Steve's intensity blared from the radio. "So I ask you again, people. When will the repairs be completed?"

"Sunday, sir," Joe said.

"Houston out."

34

Chet sat in the Jacuzzi, his mind swirling as fast as the water. What should he do? If he told the authorities he'd unleashed the virus, they'd throw him in the brig. So much for his vacation. If he didn't 'fess up and contact the CDC, his inaction could slow the vaccine's development. The delay could kill thousands. Millions.

His sister was fighting for her life, and he was responsible for that, too. He'd pushed her into a race for the prize of top vaccinologist, and what better way to lord it over him than to sneer at him from space? Some big brother *he* was. Instead of encouraging her choice to follow in his footsteps, he'd discounted her every academic accomplishment and refused to attend her graduation or her sendoff into space. He'd vented his anger on her as a spillover of his rage at their parents. She didn't deserve that.

His mind jumped back to the deadly threat on the station. An accident had caused a critical air leak. The media blamed it on Frank's piloting. He knew better. Frank was a jerk, but he was also one of the best pilots in the business.

Chet frowned. He was overthinking this. Dan would launch Sunday and save the day.

Or would he?

Valiant had to be carrying a sample of the new virus to Hildi. But experiments could put the astronauts at risk again, assuming they didn't die of asphyxiation before the capsule got there.

He could help her with the research if he were there. If he could get a message to her...

"Hi, stranger." The voice startled him. He looked up. Sandy smiled from the edge of the deck, dressed for performance—a red, glittery formal and no splints on her wrists.

"Hi, yourself. Heard you were sick."

"Yeah." Her grimace was endearing. "What a horrible case of the flu. I think the shot I had last month did some good, but I'm not sure."

He shook his head. "I doubt if it helped. Every vaccine is tailored to the individual strain, and seldom does one substitute for the other. The last flu shot was made for H2N4. This one is...different."

She cocked her head. "How come you know so much about viruses?"

Chet hesitated. He didn't want to give himself away, but he'd have to soon anyway. "I'm a vaccinologist with the CDC."

"In Atlanta?"

Chet nodded.

Sandy whistled then glanced at her watch. "I'd like to talk with you more about that, but I need to hurry. I'm due to play in twenty minutes. Tuning forty-seven strings takes time."

"Where are you playing?" Chet spoke to her retreating back. A rather exposed back.

She twisted her head to answer. "Wine Cellars, deck 4." Her stride was brisk, considering the height of her heels.

"I'll be there."

Chet waited until she was out of view then heaved himself out of the Jacuzzi. He'd never been the athletic type, and she obviously was. Hauling that harp around the ship probably gave her those toned arms. He dried off with a white towel and sandaled his way to his stateroom. As he showered off the chlorine, his thoughts swirled again.

He should tell Hildi. She needed to know what she would be dealing with. He had no idea how to do that. Just call the NASA operator and say, "May I talk to the International Space Station, please?" He just hoped the biology lab module on the station could deliver Level 4 isolation.

Chet donned slacks and a polo shirt for the evening. He paused as he combed his hair then shook his head. Enough introspection.

His stateroom assistant was still missing. He spotted the man who had replaced him. "How's Enrique?

"In quarantine. Flu." Concern creased his forehead.

Chet fled through the hallways but couldn't escape his own worry. Everyone near him had caught it. Typhoid Mary couldn't have done a more thorough job. But why had he been spared? He was seldom sick, but exposure to the flu usually laid him low. Unless, like he'd wondered earlier, he was immune. He stopped before he climbed the stairs. If he was immune, Hildi could be, too. If NASA really was shooting a sample to her, she might have a chance to identify the immunity gene from her own blood. He grimaced. It meant giving away his part in the epidemic.

Passengers in dinner attire crowded the elevators. He took the stairs to deck 4, still preoccupied with his dilemma.

Sandy was playing. He sat at one of the round tables—unfortunately the farthest from her—and ordered a glass of chardonnay. He sipped it while she played popular music then switched to a classical piece. Tension left his shoulders. Hard to be uptight while listening to harp music. The instrument fascinated him. So did the harpist.

Sandy bowed to scattered applause. He debated whether to invite her over for a drink, but she left without seeing him. His gaze followed her until she disappeared past the bar. He glanced at his watch and shrugged. Time for dinner anyway.

A waiter escorted him to his assigned table of eight. So far, he'd tolerated his dinner mates. The newlyweds were more engrossed in each other than inane chitchat. A family of three had never returned after the first evening, apparently appeasing their young daughter with the more casual atmosphere of the ship's buffet. The remaining couple he remembered from his eternal wait before he boarded. The dumpy woman who had dug into a voluminous tote bag for her paperwork was missing.

He nodded at everyone per protocol and turned to the woman's husband. "Where's your wife?"

The bearded man sighed. "Sick. She's in the ship's hospital." He stared out the window.

Chet's tension tightened its grip. "What's wrong with her?" He already knew the answer.

"Flu. Pneumonia."

Chet drew in a sharp breath. Another case. The numbers must be more than he originally estimated. He glanced at empty seats throughout the dining room. He should do something. Send an anonymous tip to the CDC. Figure out a way to contact Hildi. But self-preservation shouted louder in his brain than his conscience.

He picked items from the menu without his usual interest and ordered a bottle of Bordeaux to share. It was his turn. The food came as his appetite failed. The creative dishes lacked their usual flair, at least to his indifferent taste buds.

Before the servers presented the dessert menu, Chet excused himself and headed for his stateroom. He sank to the bed as his stomach churned like the propellers driving the ship through rough waters.

He'd killed his father as surely as blasting him with an Uzi. A bad virus infection and HIV equaled death. He'd lashed out in hatred that was twenty years old. Did the man deserve to die for his hypocrisy? Had Chet played God?

He could blame it on his stupid eyeglasses, but truthfully, he'd been too angry at his boss to notice he'd chosen the wrong vial. After five years as a Level 4 vaccinologist, he knew better than to let his emotions rule him, especially around the lab.

He opened a drawer and pulled out his origami materials to escape his growing self-blame. He folded the paper mechanically. Maybe it would soothe his aching mind. The dove he made by rote startled him. Where did that come from? Throwing the creation on the bed, he opened the sliding glass door. The dove fluttered to the floor as he stepped onto the balcony. The whooshing wind ruffled his hair. Threatening a violent storm, thunderclouds gathered on the horizon.

There was nowhere but down from here. Hunt would eventually make the connection and realize Chet was responsible. He could disappear into London, forever looking over his shoulder for the FBI.

The thought of running rankled him. This wasn't a funny spy game anymore, and he definitely wasn't laughing.

Hide and be caught, followed by a lengthy jail sentence, or confess his crime and face a lengthy jail sentence. Big choice.

He leaned over the railing. If he jumped, would he land in the water or splat on someone else's veranda? It certainly would solve the prison problem.

For the second time since his teenage years, he prayed. "God, help me." But why should he expect an answer? The engines of the massive ship rumbled, the waves slapped against the bow, but heaven was silent.

Hide or confess. Maybe talk to Hildi somehow. There had to be a way. Maybe...apologize to his parents? The thought dropped cannonballs into his strained stomach, but he knew it was right. He wanted to do anything but that, but his lousy conscience wouldn't leave him alone.

Well, he would at least make the effort. He could call. Maybe an e-mail instead...

Coward.

Chet stepped back into his room and closed the door. He wished he could shut off his guilt as easily. He picked up his cell phone before his resolve could vanish. It actually worked in the middle of the Atlantic.

The news had said his dad was in ICU at Littleton Hospital, so he'd start there. The roaming charges would cost a fortune for a connection, but that was the least of his worries. The automated voice of the phone company's information line finally gave him the hospital's number. He endured another long delay before the hospital receptionist dialed his father's room. He nearly dropped the handset when he heard the characteristic buzz of a call going through.

"Hello?"

He recognized Mom's voice. Panic set in. His tongue folded into an origami he'd never tried.

"Hello?" Pause.

Chet opened his mouth but couldn't force a sound out.

"Is anyone there?"

"Mom?"

Silence. Maybe he shouldn't have called.

A gasp. "Chet, I can't believe it's you."

I can't believe it either. "I—well, I just wanted to call. It's been a while." He couldn't have picked a lamer thing to say. He sank back on the bed before he could dash out of the room.

"Hon, it's so good to hear your voice. We've missed you so much." His mom sniffled.

"How's Dad?" Chet was really scoring points on subtlety.

"Not good." A muffled sob escaped her.

He hung his head. Hearing her words made the truth real. "Do you think he could—he would—speak to me?" He forced the words out of his mouth, fearing what the answer would be.

"Yes, of course. Hold on—"

"Mom, I'm...I'm sorry. For everything. For blowing up at you years ago, for turning my back on you, for everything."

"I forgave you a long time ago. And I love you, honey. That has never changed." Her words choked through tears. "Are you coming? To see Dad in case he...?"

"I don't think so. I'm on a cruise."

"Oh, how lovely—"

"Sorry to interrupt, but I'd really like to talk to Dad."

"Of course. Here you are."

Chet heard whispers in the background then a weak voice answered. "Son?"

"Yeah, it's me." Chet cursed his mother for giving him the lump in his throat. She always brought out the emotion in him.

"Are you all right?" His dad sounded wrung out.

"Well, yeah, I guess. But you aren't."

"Truer words were never spoken." His father's wheeze rattled through the handset.

The words punched Chet in the gut. It was one thing to read an Internet report about his father's health, and quite another to hear Dad gasping on the other end. But he seemed so calm about it, like he was reading a weather forecast.

"You have HIV."

"Yes, that—uh—complicates things."

Chet bolted to his feet and paced like a caged tiger. He glanced at his dove origami that now perched on the floor, and his resolve rose. *Just do it.*

"Dad?"

"Yes?"

"Will you forgive me?" Chet's stomach tensed for the expected rejection. Mom was one thing, but Dad had suffered the full force of Chet's anger. How could he expect his father to erase twenty years of hatred with such simple words?

"I forgave you a long time ago, son."

Chet's gut eased its grip on his Beef Wellington dinner. He blurted the next words before his nerve vaporized. "I don't mean just for how I've treated you and Mom. For what I did."

The faint voice on the other end sighed. "I deserved it. Deserved your contempt."

Chet couldn't think of any way to say it except as bald truth. "I mean, will you forgive me for making you sick? What if this flu kills you? Would you forgive me for killing you?"

"What are you talking about?"

He swallowed past the golf ball lodged in his throat. "That flu you have? I infected you. I sprayed it on the luncheon napkins during the Denver seminar."

His father gasped.

Chet exhaled. There. He'd said it. He hoped it would make him feel better, but guilt still screamed in his brain. "Dad?"

"I'm here, Chet."

"I...I...I don't know what to do."

His father paused, apparently struggling for breath. "Ask...God's forgiveness."

"He and I aren't exactly on speaking terms."

"Neither were we."

"OK." The word left Chet's mouth with half a dozen questions chasing it.

"And, Chet?"

"Uh-huh." He squirmed, certain of what he'd hear next.

"Contact...the authorities," Dad rasped.

Chet closed his eyes. "Yeah, I figured you'd say that. But there's something I need to do first. I need to contact Hildi."

His father listened to all his hopes for a vaccine, hopes that rested in Hildi knowing information Chet had. He'd forgotten how, even as a little boy, his father had been a good listener. After keeping rage and fear lately in equal proportions, he needed that.

"Promise me you'll do it, son."

Chet swallowed. He took his promises seriously. "I will."

"I'm proud of you."

Proud? Chet knew he'd blubber if he tried to respond.

"We'll pray."

Chet had run out of things to say. He'd never been in a position of saying good-bye to someone who was dying.

"Good-bye, then. I...love you, Dad."

"Love you, too, son."

Chet switched off his phone. His intestines twisted into tighter knots. The dove origami mocked his lame effort at reconciliation. He should have made a raven, the harbinger of death. He glanced at his briefcase, still containing the vial, and buried his head in his hands.

What have I done?

35

"I" Plus Eleven Days

"Light this candle." Dan didn't care whose eardrums he ruptured as he bellowed into the mic. He would have pulled his hair out by now if he could have reached inside his helmet. NASA had delayed the launch for three hours due to adverse weather conditions, and it didn't look like things would improve at the Cape.

"We can't, Dan." Nate's calm, reasonable voice crackled over the radio from Launch Control at the Cape. "C'mon, you know we can't launch in a thunderstorm. The winds are just too high."

"Skip the excuses. We have a crew to rescue." Shorty had no patience left, either.

Dan shifted in his seat, trying to find a more comfortable position. He and Shorty lay on their backs to minimize the strain of 2Gs during launch, which didn't do a thing for them while sitting on Launch Pad 59-A, waiting. And waiting.

Every moment on the ground reduced the only chance for survival for the stranded astronauts on the station. In the last conversation he'd heard in Mission Control, they were panting like they'd just run a marathon. Dan's mind hovered over the image of Hildi gasping for breath. His breath quickened in empathic response.

Nate talked with someone in the background, maybe the weather guy. Then his voice boomed over the radio. "People, I know this is frustrating, but we have your lives to consider as well."

Nate's reasonable tone did little to soothe Dan. He ground his teeth. "Our friends won't be worth a smashed hen's egg if we don't get there in time, to use Joe's expression."

"Copy that, *Valiant*." More mumbling in the background. Nate returned. "The meteorologist says the winds will calm in about ten minutes. We should be able to resume countdown then. Should be. But we're not risking your lives unnecessarily."

"Well, in case you haven't noticed—" Dan stuffed his exasperation back inside his brain.

Shorty finished the sentence in a softer voice than Dan could manage. "—we're sitting on top of tons of explosives. Not exactly the safest place to be."

"Roger."

Dan and Shorty waited. They checked all systems, but the systems were no different than they'd been the last time. Time ticked by at a snail's pace. Dan drummed gloved fingers on the armrest.

CAPCOM came back in five minutes. "You've got your window, fellas. You are GO for launch."

Dan and Shorty grinned then Shorty responded, "Roger that."

"Restart clock."

The clock had stopped at T minus five minutes. Now it resumed its downward digital trek. Dan heaved a sigh then hurried to finish his part of final preparations before NASA changed its mind. Shorty read from a checklist while Dan confirmed every instrument setting.

Mission Control in Houston was listening in, of course. How many pencils had Steve broken during the delay? Dan smiled at the thought. As soon as *Valiant* cleared the tower, Houston would take over. He would welcome Pete's voice.

After ten minutes into the flight, when they officially reached space, Dan would jettison the Launch Abort System. It sat on top of the capsule, ready to rocket *Valiant* away from disaster if the unthinkable happened. Shorty poised his finger over the control button as protocol dictated.

"Ten, nine, eight, seven, six, ignition sequence start—"

Dan steeled himself.

"Three, two, one, zero, lift-off. We have lift-off."

They whooped as the rocket shuddered. They cleared the tower. Launch Control handed the reins to Houston.

Crack.

Half the instruments blacked out. Altitude and speed displays darkened. Dan flipped all the reset controls while fighting the increasing Gs of launch. "Reset ineffective."

"Switch to backup." Shorty's sharp command held a razor's edge.

"Backup ineffective." Dan's eyes widened as he sought his crewmate's. Shorty nodded.

They knew what had happened.

Lightning.

36

With Joe and Leonid's help, Frank and Jasper suited up for EVA. Hildi and Maria were sleeping. Everyone panted due to the buildup of carbon dioxide. The CO_2 scrubbers labored overtime to compensate, but it was a losing battle.

Frank hoped for a speedy repair—work that never should have been necessary in the first place. For the nth time, he wished he could reverse the last few days.

He inserted both legs into the pressure suit, an interesting operation in weightlessness. Then came the body of the suit. Joe held it by the collar as Frank pulled his head through and hunted for the sleeves.

"Dad-gum arms." Joe gritted his teeth. "Stop flailing around."

Frank tried to grin.

Joe wheezed. "Heard from Mission Control."

Frank's fuzzy brain worked out the meaning of the words. "Hope it's good news. We could use some."

"Dan and Shorty have launched." Joe frowned. "Houston's keeping mighty quiet about it, though. Don't like it."

Jasper nodded. Frank just shook his head. He smelled another complication.

Joe zipped the suit, and Frank locked his helmet in place. Frank opened the air valve and gulped a lungful of oxygen-laden air. Relief flooded through him as his head cleared. Guilt prickled him as he pictured the others gasping, but he and Jasper needed full concentration for this job.

He pulled on his gloves, a nightmare for his hands. It took so much force to make them bend around the tools that his hands fatigued before his body.

After a final check, they entered the airlock, reduced the pressure to zero, and floated out. They tethered their suits. Earth sparkled like an exotic jewel, but Frank had no time to admire the view.

Moving in sync as if they'd practiced this maneuver hundreds of times, they pulled toolboxes and the heavy repair piece from the airlock and closed it behind them. The cobbled-together patch moved easily in zero gravity, but stopping it was another story. Weightlessness didn't suspend Newton's laws—an object in motion tended to remain in motion.

"Nice and easy, Frank." Jasper's reminder was unnecessary as they inched the bulky metal square toward the docking area.

Finally, they reached the port. They guided the piece into place. A perfect fit.

Jasper gave a thumbs-up to Joe, who was videotaping the job from a window. Frank wondered where the odd gesture came from. Roman gladiator fights?

"Roger." Joe's usual banter must be lying on the deck, too oxygen-deprived to reach the mic.

As Frank worked with Jasper to bolt the patch in place, he fought to keep his tether out of the way. The thing was a nuisance but kept him from floating into space. He glanced at the station's antennas, daring him to test the resiliency of his thin EVA suit on their protrusions.

Frank returned to his obsession. *My fault.* Every dent and scrape on the docking ring stared at him in silent accusation.

He cringed at the thought of facing the media and the formal NASA inquiry. The best he could hope for was the Gus Grissom treatment. Gus should have had a hero's welcome but instead was blamed for blowing the hatch early after splashdown, causing the Mercury capsule to sink. NASA later cleared him, but he ran the gauntlet of an outraged public. At least he regained a little dignity until the Apollo 1 fire ended his life.

Frank had destroyed the mission and killed Larry. The crisis he'd caused threatened all their lives with asphyxiation. Assuming they survived, his career and reputation were over. He would be court-martialed, stripped of rank, possibly imprisoned. His roiling emotions conjured up all sorts of ramifications. The scenarios that assaulted him would not, could not happen.

The blackness of space squeezed him in a steel fist. An idea germinated. He *could* redeem himself.

They secured the last of the metal to the docking ring. Frank stared at the toolbox's contents and grabbed an instrument. Jasper gave him an awkward high five and floated toward the airlock. Frank hung behind.

With Jasper's back turned, Frank detached his tether. He felt calm, focused. He held the sharp knife against his suit and pushed off. One slash...

Vise-like fingers closed around his boot.

"What do you think you're doing?" Jasper's stern voice crackled as he clung to Frank's ankle with both hands.

"What does it look like I'm doing?" Frank's words

lashed out. "With me gone, you'll have one less body using up air."

"Are you *insane*?"

Frank kicked at Jasper's grip. Jasper held on, his tether taut. Their bodies swung in a dangerous version of the children's game of whip. Jasper's momentum flung him toward the station's welcoming antennas.

Frank gulped. One more inch and Jasper would be a dead man.

Jasper reeled himself in. He jammed a boot under one of the handholds. Grunting, he hauled Frank into the airlock and pried the knife from his hand. "Of all the selfish, idiotic stunts..."

Frank's body went limp. "At least I could have died a hero."

"Hero? *Hero*?" Jasper slammed him against an airlock wall. "You fool! You nearly killed us both. And for what? So you could make some grand gesture? So we could have another corpse orbiting Earth?" The man was spitting nails.

Shock silenced Frank's protests. He had never seen Jasper so angry.

Jasper's eyes blazed. "We all risk our necks out here. How dare you give up now." He took a deep breath and softened his expression. "We need you, Frank."

Jasper sealed the outside hatch. Frank deflated in defeat. "Let me go."

His fellow astronaut launched into a pep talk. Frank swallowed hard as the specter of causing Jasper's death loomed over him. Finally, he listened.

"Dan and Shorty are busting their backsides to rescue us, so don't be getting all hopeless. And as for your 'ruined career' mantra, forget it. We'll back you to the edge of space if we have to."

Frank saw no condemnation in Jasper's eyes—only the determination of a bobcat snarling at enemies.

Jasper patted Frank's shoulder. "C'mon, hotshot. Let's go in."

Frank sniffled, wishing he had a tissue to blow his nose. Impossible in a pressure suit. He smiled, but a lead brick still weighed down his thoughts.

He followed Jasper through the connecting airlock. The other astronauts stared in silence as Joe helped remove his suit. Then everyone dropped their gaze and avoided his eyes.

Mortification slunk into his brain. They'd heard everything. They'd seen his futile attempt to kill himself. Mission Control, too, and probably anyone who owned a television set. Frank kicked off the suit's legs, floated to the commode, and closed the curtain, the only private place on the station. No one disturbed him.

Dinner was a somber affair, even with the successful EVA and the anticipated arrival of *Valiant*. Tension tainted the room. Frank picked at his food. Finally, he mumbled an apology and turned in. He popped a sleeping pill, wanting dreamless oblivion. Instead, Hildi followed him. *Just what I need. Another lecture.*

"Frank, all of us have the utmost respect for you." She floated near his sleeping bag, more angel than astronaut. "The docking accident wasn't your fault. Larry's death was a tragedy, but you can't wallow in self-blame. It's time to forgive yourself."

"How?" His tone was flat, lifeless.

"Ask God."

Her words echoed her father's and every sermon

he'd ever heard. His anger boiled. "God." Frank flung the word in her face like a curse. "You realize we're all going to die, don't you? Where will God be then?"

"Waiting to welcome you home." Hildi left the comment hanging and pulled herself out of the room.

Frank stewed in his own juices. First Jasper's lecture, then Hildi's meddling. Could his comrades—to use Leonid's expression—really be that loyal to him? Maybe, not that he deserved it. He'd seen fierce compassion in Jasper's eyes and calm assurance in Hildi's. He breathed the thin air, as thin as his hope for redemption. But he did have hope. His relentless self-blame had lessened just a little. Inexplicable.

Unless God had something to do with it.

He forced his rusty-hinged door of prayer to grind open. Finally, he whispered, "God, help me to forgive myself, because I'm no use to anyone here if I keep moping around. Forgive me for being so self-centered. And such an idiot. That's all I have to say."

Sleep trickled in.

37

Worth sagged in his bed as the doctor told him the grim truth.

Dr. Stephens tried to sugarcoat it, of course. Worth finally asked him to stop sweetening the bitter news.

The doctor took a deep breath. "Your pneumonia is worsening in spite of several antibiotics. As a result, your oxygen levels have steadily decreased. Your latest cardio readout shows an irregular heartbeat. Your compromised immune system is unable to fight off the virus." He paused as if hesitant to say the words.

Worth mustered the energy to speak. "I'm dying," he wheezed.

Dr. Stephens nodded. "That's my prognosis." He shuffled his feet then met Worth's eyes. "I'm sorry, Worth. There's nothing more I can do except make you comfortable." The doctor made a notation on the chart at the foot of the bed and left.

Worth wasn't surprised. At the moment, he didn't feel too bad. But his condition was starting to mess with his prayer life. His brain felt muddled, and every breath was an effort.

The do-not-resuscitate order was in place. He and Laura had written their living wills a long time ago. Didn't think he'd need it this early, though.

Laura held his hand. She knew him well enough to give him—both of them—time to regroup. They'd expected this news, but hearing it from the doctor solidified its reality.

Worth took a shallow breath so he wouldn't cough. "Guess we need to plan my funeral."

Laura's grip tightened. A tear crept down her cheek.

His mind cleared just a little, enough to reflect on his regrets and on the way God had redeemed them. God had restored his wife to him. And now God had restored his son. The miracle of their reunion awed Worth. Guess he shouldn't have been so surprised with the miracle of forgiveness God had worked in his own life. He knew what to do to seal that forgiveness. He cleared his throat. "Give my tie to Chet. Tell him what it means."

She nodded, accepting his last wish.

How would she cope with his death? She'd grieve, of course, but she'd bounce back, like she did in every crisis. Even with his infidelity. He'd broken sacred vows and shattered her trust, yet somehow, she'd overcome all that. She'd stuck by his side despite the media circus after Worth confessed his sin and resigned from the pastorate.

Worth stroked her hand. "It's been a good life." In spite of all their heartaches, it *had* been a good life.

There was a little money in savings and some in a retirement plan. And of course the death benefit. She'd be okay.

Before he could tell her again how much he loved her, George walked in, required mask in place.

Worth reached out, but the IV inserted in the back of his hand kept him on a short leash. He grumbled. "Can't give you a proper greeting."

"That's OK."

Laura hugged their friend. "Thanks for coming."

"Betty's outside. The nurses have gotten a little fussy about the rules." George turned to Worth. "So what's the good word?"

"Uh, I'm dying."

Laura stood, mumbled something about needing a break, and fled. George gripped Worth's shoulder, his eyebrows drawn down. He claimed the chair Laura vacated. "So, Laura said you wanted to talk to me." George brandished his Bible. "You know the Scriptures better than I do, but I'm sure I could find a passage to read to you."

The IV site throbbed. Worth rubbed the tape covering it. "No. Want to talk."

George waited.

Worth harrumphed. George was using the same method Worth used in counseling. He sighed. It was effective.

"Well, I...uh...feel guilty." He gasped. "Having to cancel the seminars."

"Guilty?"

Worth gathered his sluggish thoughts. "I've done these seminars to atone for my sins." He fought for another breath. "I failed God. He gave me everything." Worth coughed until his lungs felt like they were falling out. "A loving wife, a successful ministry" — cough — "good health, even a good income. I threw it away."

"So you think you can do better than Jesus did on the cross?" George paused a moment. "Do you believe Jesus's sacrifice was sufficient for everything you've done, past, present, and future?"

Worth wheezed, hating himself. He was supposed to be a paragon of faith. *Yeah, right.* "Yes, but—"

"No buts. Sounds to me like you have a tiny grain

of doubt in your mind."

"More like the Sahara Desert."

"God never condemns us for that. You changed lives through your marriage seminars. Through your preaching. Even through your public confession." George gripped his shoulder again. "You'll never know how many until you talk to our Lord face to face."

Worth turned his head away. "Sooner than I expected."

"None of us knows when we'll die. Our job is to do what God has set before us. You have to leave it at that."

Worth turned back to his friend. "I failed."

The pulse ox machine beeped an alarm. Cindy the nurse stomped in, hands on hips. "You stop talking right now, Worth. Your oxygen levels are dropping."

Cindy seemed a bit pale but otherwise recovered from the flu. Her mother-hen attitude amused Worth. She turned and strode out.

"Stubborn, aren't you?" George's mouth quirked. "God never gives up on us. And He has a habit of using broken vessels. You taught me that."

His friend continued his reassurance of God's relentless love. Worth listened. He started to drink in the grace in small sips, and his parched soul responded.

Maybe his life had counted after all.

****

Annie poked her head into the room. "May I come in?"

"Sure." George's exhortation had drained Worth,

but he felt at peace. A weight had lifted off his spirit. If only it had removed the elephant on his chest.

Annie took a tentative step. Had she heard the conversation? He spoke in a stern voice. "Just don't poke me with another needle."

She chuckled. "No poking this time, I promise." She frowned as she recorded his vitals and checked his IV drip. "Hmm. Your oxygen level is down. Have you been talking too much again?"

"Just a nice conversation with a friend." Worth's Bible lay on his lap. He'd read and re-read the passages George had pointed to.

"What are you reading? The Bible?" Annie grimaced.

"Trying to read a passage in Isaiah."

"When I was a little girl, I could recite all the books of the Bible," she murmured. Her voice softened. "Be easy on yourself. It's the drugs."

Worth raised a hand then dropped it. Just too heavy. "Not only the drugs."

Annie shifted the conversation. "Do you need anything?"

"Got that new pair of lungs?"

Annie shook her head.

"Maybe some pain medication. It hurts to breathe."

"I'll speak to the doctor." She headed to the door, hesitated, and walked back. "May I ask you something?"

"Of course."

"Well, I've been watching you, your wife, and your friends. Your attitude seems...well...different than most patients. You're not fighting death." Annie said it in a rush, her words tumbling like water from a broken dam. "You almost seem to welcome it."

Worth blinked. "I'm not afraid, if that's what you mean. I know I'll be in Heaven the moment I leave here."

"What if someone doesn't believe in Heaven, or God?" A giant neon question mark punctuated her comment.

"Someone like you?"

Annie nodded.

"What do you believe?"

Annie shrugged. "You die and go into a kind of limbo. I don't see how Heaven can be a real place. You can't see it, and no one's come back from the dead to talk about it, except maybe through séances, and I don't believe in them either. How do you know Heaven exists?"

"Jesus talks about it. Look." Frowning, he thumbed through his Bible, laid it open, and turned it toward Annie. She bent down to read the tiny print.

He pointed at one of the paragraphs. "See, it says here—"

Diane interrupted them. "Annie, I need you. Now." She wheeled a new patient past Worth's room.

"Sorry. Gotta go." She brushed the page of the Bible.

"Here, take this." He closed the Bible and held it out, arm trembling. "Read...Gospel of John." He grunted. "New Testament."

Annie backed away. "I can't take your Bible."

"Yes, you can. Please."

Annie grasped it and mumbled her thanks.

Worth sank into his pillows, but his spirit rose. Annie would soon learn the truth about Heaven, Jesus, and a little thing called faith.

38

"Abort! Abort!"

Shorty's finger remained poised over the abort button. He locked eyes with Dan. "We have twenty seconds to comply."

"No way." If NASA wanted a standoff, Dan itched to give them one. He'd fly through a meteorite storm if he had to.

"I'm ordering you to abort, people." Steve's voice boomed in Dan's headset. "Now."

Dan gulped. Fifteen seconds. *Valiant* rattled as she soared heavenward.

Ten seconds. They left the thunderclouds behind.

Five seconds. Blue sky deepened into the black of space.

The Launch Abort System had only a narrow window in which to hurl them from the main rocket. The window slammed shut. They were committed. They were gambling their lives that the instruments would stop their stubborn malfunction.

Steve growled into the mic. "People, that was a stupid decision. Your instruments are dead, and that's just the beginning. We have no idea what else that lightning might have done. *Valiant*," Steve continued in a calmer voice, "please report the instruments you show as nonfunctional."

"Affirmative, Houston." Shorty acknowledged the

request as if his wife asked him to pick up milk and bread at the supermarket.

Dan smelled his own sweat as he glanced at the dark gauges. Maybe the flight director was right. The sole purpose of the Launch Abort System was to avoid another catastrophe like the *Challenger* explosion. The LAS would have rocketed them away from danger. After that, they would have jettisoned it, deployed the parachutes, and landed safely on either dirt or ocean. They would have been safe. The astronauts on the station would have been dead.

NASA could still order them to return to Earth after one orbit if the instruments didn't come back. And the gauges hadn't. Shorty reported the grim news to Mission Control. "Houston, I still show all instruments as nonfunctional. Everything was nominal before the strike, though, and there's no reason to think they won't reset. Sir."

Dan steeled himself for a volcanic eruption. "I'm not going to lose two stubborn astronauts because they *think* their instruments are OK." He wasn't disappointed as Steve's voice sizzled in the headphones.

Dan tried not to crack the eggs he was stomping on. "Do we really have a choice?"

Steve's heavy sigh was *Valiant*'s only answer.

Dan knew they were taking a huge risk that *Valiant* hadn't sustained serious damage, but the hero in him wouldn't keep its mouth shut. "We have to keep going. We—"

"Hold it, Houston." Shorty's voice jolted Dan's attention back to the instrument panel. "Looks like they're coming back."

"We confirm that, *Valiant*. Give us a minute to

assess the situation."

"Yes, sir. Awaiting orders."

Dan's stomach squeezed into a hard lump, even as gravity lessened its hold and stars appeared against the black of space. Now Mission Control would give them the go-ahead or calculate a trajectory for splashdown. He whispered, "Shorty, you know we have to do this."

Shorty expelled a long breath. "Yeah. I just don't want to become the first court-martialed astronaut."

"You'll have company." Dan pursed his lips in stubborn resolve.

All the instruments flickered into existence except one. Shorty stared at the disobedient light. "Don't know how they can clear us without that one." He tapped the altitude display as if it were a stuck gas gauge on a sputtering Model T.

"I can fly this baby blindfolded if I have to." Dan hoped he wouldn't have to. His bravado was as thin as the veneer on cheap furniture.

Shorty snorted. "You're good, but not that good. We're so overweight with this payload, it's a wonder we're not making loops in space."

"How do you know we aren't?" Dan delivered his comment so deadpan that it took a moment for Shorty to groan.

"Very funny. You've been hanging around Jasper too long."

The display light popped on just as CAPCOM Pete spoke. "*Valiant,* this is Houston. You are GO for rendezvous."

Dan breathed again. "Guess we don't have to turn renegade after all."

Shorty signaled two thumbs up. "Roger, Houston."

"Godspeed, gentlemen."
We're going to need it.

39

Hildi knocked the cobwebs out of her head as she struggled into her jumpsuit. Drug-induced slumber always left her groggy. She couldn't have heard right. "What did you say?"

Leonid grinned. "Your brother is on the phone."

Hildi scratched her head. This wasn't a social call. She huffed as she glided to the radio, wondering how much extra oxygen this conversation would cost.

"Chet?"

"Hildi?"

"What's up?" Her question came out as a challenge, but she was at her limits of endurance. Lack of sleep and air, Frank's suicide attempt, Dan's nearly aborted launch. Then there was the virus...

"Just listen. I'm calling from a cruise ship in the Atlantic, and I don't know how long this ship-to-shore...uh...ship-to-shore-to-space connection will last. NASA rigged it."

"OK." Where in the world was this leading?

"The virus NASA's sending you is a Canadian strain. H4N6."

Hildi's stomach knotted. "The one derived from reassortment?"

"Yes. The swine and avian flus."

The one every epidemiologist dreaded would reappear. They'd been lucky last time when the strain was confined to one farm. She glanced at the blue-

231

green Earth below her, imagining the disease spreading across the continents like the stain of death.

"Listen. I did some work on it."

"What?" Hildi wrote furiously as Chet told her what he knew about the virus.

"One more thing. I'm apparently immune. If you are, too, you might be able to isolate the gene responsible and work on the vaccine from that angle."

Hildi nodded. It might help. She still puzzled over his sudden desire to talk to her after avoiding her for months.

"Anything else you can tell me?"

"It's extremely contagious, of course. You'll need to maintain Level 4 protocol."

Now how could she do that? Even with the new lab module installed last month, it wouldn't be easy. "I'll do what I can. Dan will be docking soon with the virus sample and additional equipment."

Hildi waited for Chet's response. Did the lull in the conversation mean he was done? Her heart sagged that she couldn't think of anything to talk about with her own brother other than diseases.

"I took it. I took the sample," he whispered.

Hildi's emotions flashed between a rolling boil and sharp, icy crystals. "You *stole* it? What were you thinking?"

"I wasn't."

"You know that taking anything out of the lab is a federal crime."

"I know." Chet gave a defeated sigh. "It's worse than that. I released it. I released the virus."

"What?" Hildi's eyes widened. She panted, not just from lack of oxygen.

"I sprayed it on the napkins at one of Dad's

seminar luncheons."

"You idiot." Her blood pressure rose. Francine had been right. *Microbe* didn't begin to describe her brother.

"I thought I'd taken a harmless strain, just something to make him—and the other Christian hypocrites—miserable. But I picked up the wrong virus. I killed him, Hildi. Dad has HIV. He'll die from it." His voice had that choked sound from held-in tears.

Hildi's anger deflated. Dad had done well with treatments, but she'd known he lived on borrowed time. She swallowed the sob that tightened her throat.

"Will you...forgive me?"

Hildi frowned, trying to understand her brother's words. Forgive? The word was foreign to Chet's vocabulary.

"I'd better go. Bye."

"I do forgive you," Hildi whispered but heard only dead air. Chet was never one for long farewells.

Joe turned to her. "Swine and avian flu together? How could that happen?"

Jasper's mouth quirked. "Maybe they should call it the flying pig flu."

"That's not funny."

Jasper ducked his head. "Sorry, Joe."

Hildi surrendered the mic to Leonid, who gripped her shoulder before he updated Mission Control on their deteriorating condition. Then he handed the mic to Jasper. "Personal call. Your wife."

Hildi frowned. Why was NASA suddenly arranging calls from family members? Her stomach plunged into a pit. Because NASA didn't expect them to survive.

She looked at the notes in her hand. Chet's

information would give her a jumpstart, but creating a vaccine wouldn't be easy. Assuming they survived until the cavalry rode to the rescue. Shorty and Dan. Dan...Enough introspection. Enough dreaming of a relationship that might never be, rescue or no rescue.

Time had turned into an enemy. *We could use a couple of miracles, Lord.*

Hildi rubbed her eyes. Her fun excursion into space had become a nightmarish drive on a dark, abandoned road. They'd just hurtled past the barrier marked "bridge out."

Jasper finished his call. "Love you." He signed off and pulled himself toward his room, sadness trailing him.

"So, you think you can hogtie this virus?" Joe's Texas drawl was in full force despite an occasional wheeze. As if he wasn't worried. He should be.

Hildi hovered next to a yawning Maria just emerging from slumber. "I don't know. The powers that be think microgravity will help. We have plenty of that." She sighed. "Doing this in weightlessness in an unfamiliar lab makes me squirm."

Frank sped into the room. "Chet was responsible for all this? What kind of madman would poison his own family and then let death loose on the world?"

"He said he didn't know it was lethal."

"How can you believe that?" Frank's face strained at the anger seams.

"C'mon, you know my brother. He's as bitter as they get, but he's honest."

Before Frank could respond, another radio call interrupted them.

"ISS, this is Mission Control." Hildi didn't recognize the CAPCOM's voice. Leonid handed the mic to Joe.

"Mission Control, this is ISS. Go ahead. I hope this isn't the Astronaut Benefit Fund. I already gave at the office." Joe's mouth curled into a semblance of a smile.

"We're patching a call through to Dr. Hildebrandt."

Hildi groaned. "Probably the CDC again." She had a good enough idea on measures to secure the lab, which weren't much. Hunt couldn't give any better solution. She and Maria would do quite fine, thank you. Or as well as they could.

"It's not the CDC," CAPCOM said. "It's your mother."

Hildi gulped. Another farewell call for another dying astronaut? She grabbed the microphone. "Mom?"

"Evie?"

Mom's sobs solidified Hildi's stomach into a solid block of ice.

"Mom, are you OK? How's Dad? Mom?"

Mom's sniffles told Hildi the truth. "You know how much he loved you."

Loved. Past tense. Hildi hung her head. Space suddenly seemed a very lonely place.

"Mom, I'm so sorry." Hildi swiped at her tears, alternating between hot and cold. If it hadn't been for her brother...

Frank wiped tears of his own. He and her father had been close.

Her mother continued. "Chet called and talked to us before...your father left to meet Jesus. He asked for forgiveness."

Hildi's muddled brain tried to comprehend. *There's that foreign word again.*

Mom waited for a response, then cleared her throat. "Listen, I'm planning a private memorial service."

Good luck with keeping it private. Everyone in the world would want to be there, either out of concern or curiosity. Her voice hitched in her throat. "I'm glad Chet called."

"Yes, your father died at peace. Uh, when will you be back?"

Same old mom, changing the subject mid-sentence. "I don't know."

"Hmmm. Well, don't be late for dinner."

"I'll try." She didn't trust her own voice beyond that promise. Her throat constricted. Must be the thin oxygen.

"My five minutes are up. Love you."

"Love you, Mom." Hildi signed off and turned to her crewmates. They'd heard the conversation but pretended to go about their business. Privacy was a precious commodity. They waited.

"My father died. He caught the virus." Her own words of reality sliced through her. Dad. Dead. She wanted to curl into a ball.

"I'm sorry." Joe touched her arm. The gentle gesture from the hard-riding, flea-bitten cowpoke restarted the tears pooling in her eyes.

Hildi took a shuddering breath, willing her mind to switch gears. "I need to get to the lab."

She'd discover the key to the vaccine. Not for glory but as a tribute to her father. The equipment needed to be calibrated. She needed to implement safety protocol so everything would be ready to go when Dan and Shorty got here. She stopped in mid-thought.

If they didn't get here with the oxygen in time, it wouldn't matter.

****

Frank listened to Hildi's radioed conversation with growing grief. He'd really liked her father, even though Worth rankled his own lagging faith. Frank had put on the act, speaking Christianese, saying grace at meals, and attending Worth's gigantic church with Hildi. Worth hadn't been fooled. Neither had Hildi's mom, for that matter. Yet they loved him as a son.

Frank floated back to his room and zipped himself into his sleeping cocoon. The lack of pressure points from a gravity-bound mattress should have sent him to slumberland, even without the drugs the crew was taking. Instead, his brain ran at full tilt.

Valiant would dock in twelve hours, but Frank doubted it would be soon enough. He'd rather step out of the airlock without a pressure suit for a quick death than die gasping or be brain damaged from oxygen deprivation. It was amazing they were still alive. That *he* was still alive. He prayed—for Dan and Shorty, for his crewmates, for Mission Control. He couldn't say he felt better afterwards.

"And, God, help them get here in time."

40

Carol wiped her damp cheeks as Mike bounded up the stairs after work. Still in her pajamas, she stared again at the pregnancy test in her hand. She tried to sniff all the emotions back into her head.

"Hi." Her husband gave her a quick kiss. "Did you get some rest?"

She took a deep breath for the announcement she wanted to make under happier circumstances. She blurted, "I'm pregnant."

"Honey, that's wonderful." He whooped as he picked her up and spun her around. "Do we want a girl or a boy? I..." He set her down and frowned. "What's wrong?" Then he gasped. "Oh."

"Yes, 'oh.'" Carol's emotions took another nosedive. "I caught the flu during the early stages of pregnancy. Remember? The baby could be deformed or mentally...or I could miscarry." She reached for another tissue that joined the collection of damp ones on the nightstand. "Right now, I vote for the latter."

Mike stiffened. "You don't mean that."

"Yes, I do." She stomped toward him and stopped, just inches from his face. "I'd rather have a dead baby than a child who could never"—Carol choked on her words—"run and laugh and skin her knee..."

"Honey." Mike hugged her.

That was the last thing Carol wanted as her tears turned hot. She pushed him away. "Don't 'honey' me.

This isn't something we can fix with a kiss and a hug." She turned her back on him and threw the plastic wand in the trash, where it belonged.

Mike put his hands on her shoulders. "You're jumping to conclusions. We don't know what will happen." He turned her around and held her for a long time.

Carol ran out of tears. She hiccupped as she tried to pick up the shards of her shattered dreams. "I wanted a little girl. A perfect little girl."

The doorbell rang.

"Oh, no." Carol's eyes widened. She winced as her puffy lids stung. "George and Betty can't see me like this. Tell them I'm still sick."

He pecked her cheek. "It'll be all right. Just get dressed."

Carol fumbled with her PJ buttons and tugged on a pair of slacks and a blouse. Her hair was hopeless, her face worse, but she did her best to cover her pain with makeup. She took a few deep breaths, the cure-all for rampant emotions according to the experts. How would they know? They'd probably never had even a bad hair day.

As she trudged down the stairs to the living room, Carol donned a bright smile. "I'm so glad you came." She dropped next to Betty on the couch, wishing she could scoot to a distant corner of the room without being rude.

Betty scanned her face then squeezed her hand. "Do you want to tell me what's wrong?"

Carol dissolved into tears, unable to speak without gulping. She exchanged glances with Mike.

"Carol's pregnant." His voice lacked the joy he should have felt—they should have felt—with such an announcement.

George and Betty beamed. George shook Mike's hand. "Congratulations."

"We're so happy for you." Betty hesitated. "It's good news, isn't it?"

Carol shook her head. She dreaded having to face this response over and over. Maybe they shouldn't tell anyone. Pretend nothing happened.

Mike sat beside her and put an arm around her shoulder as George lowered himself into the easy chair. He and Betty wore puzzled frowns.

Betty gave her hand another squeeze. "You think the flu might affect the baby."

Carol nodded.

"Oh, you poor dears. No wonder you're so upset." Betty reached for a tissue and wiped away her own tears.

Carol started another pile of used tissues as George and Betty waited patiently. She wanted to discuss this privately with Mike, not now. When she could talk without the embarrassing hiccups, Betty squeezed her hand. "Go on, dear."

"I...I already talked to the doctor."

Mike raised an eyebrow.

Carol mumbled, "I didn't have time to tell you." She plowed on, just wanting to get it over. "The doctor said there's a chance the baby could have physical or mental handicaps. All because of some stupid flu." She placed both hands over her still-flat stomach. "He mentioned abortion," she whispered.

Mike shook his head. "We won't do that, of course."

Fresh tears threatened to squeeze past her eyelids. "I wanted a healthy child."

Betty gripped Carol's arm, and the strength to admit the real issue flowed through her.

"I'm scared. Scared for our baby and scared we won't be able to handle a special-needs child." She wondered at her automatic use of "our" and "we."

Mike tipped her head and met her gaze. "Whatever happens, we'll face it together."

"Don't forget God." George's eyes speared theirs. "None of us knows what will happen, but God will give you the power to face it." He smiled. "And He has the habit of giving us the strength when we need it, not nine months in advance."

"It'll be so hard to wait." Carol wrapped her arms around Mike's waist. "And there are no guarantees."

"There never are, dear." Betty patted her shoulder. "Even without the fear of influenza affecting the baby. Our firstborn son was perfect in every way, but the umbilical cord choked him, and he was stillborn. Our youngest daughter was full of life and a sense of adventure, but she was killed in a car crash at sixteen." Pain dimmed Betty's face.

Carol's mouth dropped open. "I didn't know." She frowned at their friends' serene expressions.

"God got us through those tragedies, and He'll get you through this and whatever else you two face as a couple."

Silence descended on the four of them. Then George cleared his throat. "Let me pray." They joined hands. Carol feared her grip would break bones. George bowed his head. "Father, we commit this child to You. Thank You that You love him—or her—more than we can ever understand. Give Mike and Carol the faith and courage to face these difficult days ahead. Amen."

Carol and Mike reached for the tissue box at the same time. She chuckled.

"Uh, I don't know about you, but I'm not in the mood to eat out, and I know Carol doesn't feel like cooking." Mike turned to their guests. "Would you mind if we got something delivered?"

Her man had read her thoughts. But wasn't that what husband and wife were supposed to do? She leaned over and whispered, "Thanks."

Betty smiled. "That sounds just wonderful. I'd be happy to set the table if you'll tell me where you hide the plates."

Carol took another deep breath, grateful for Mike's suggestion. "I'd like pizza."

"Sold. One pepperoni and mushroom, coming up. Is that all right?" He raised an eyebrow at their guests.

George grinned. "Could you order a ham and pineapple, too?"

****

Carol grabbed another slice of pizza with more appetite than she expected. Betty had arranged the dishes and flatware, transferred the delivered food to a serving plate, and even added a candle as a centerpiece. The flame reminded Carol of the newfound resolve she and Mike had for their marriage. A spark of determination ignited, urging her to face this crisis with God and her husband to steady her hesitant steps.

They laughed at George's deadpan jokes. Carol drained the last of her soda as the day's upheaval and her lingering illness caught up with her.

Betty washed the dishes as George dried, waving

away Carol's protests. Betty glanced at her. "You look tired, dear. I think we should be going." The couple stood to leave.

Carol wished they could stay longer, but she was about to keel over from exhaustion. "Thank you for coming. Will we see you again?" *Soon?*

"There's the little matter of bridge and bowling, if I recall." George winked.

"Why don't you come over for dinner at our place sometime? We'd love to have you." Betty leaned toward them. "George makes the meanest hamburgers this side of the Rockies."

"Deal." Mike smiled.

Betty gave Carol a long hug before they left.

Aching for a good night's sleep, Carol climbed the stairs. Slumber might not come tonight with her crashing waves of worry, but she clung to the hope of calmer seas.

41

Captain Papadopoulos sat behind his desk and glared at Chet. "I'm tempted to either throw you overboard or keelhaul you."

Chet winced. Dragging someone under the keel of a ship was an ancient torture. Barnacles scraped skin and much more, and often proved fatal. But he deserved no less.

The officer in charge of ship's security stood at the door, at attention and without comment.

Chet had expected this treatment ever since he'd turned himself in. At least the captain had arranged his patch-in to NASA and his sister. There was nothing more Chet could say or do in defense. He dropped his head.

Papadopoulos stood and paced in front of a sliding glass door leading to his private balcony. In more carefree times, the ocean's surges would have invigorated Chet. Now they only reflected his churning thoughts. The captain turned to face him. "This is going to be a real mess. We're holding position until the FBI can board, arrest you, and take you off my ship. I only hope we can continue our cruise without too much of a delay." He huffed a breath. "You'll be transported to Southampton, but I don't know how the authorities will sort this out. You're an American citizen. I'm guessing you'll be incarcerated in a London prison before you're extradited." Disgust etched his face. "You don't need to know the details. However, thanks to you, we won't be docking anytime soon. The World Health Organization has quarantined this ship."

Chet sighed. Quarantine wouldn't slow the relentless march of the disease. Internet news now reported cases in France and Spain. The world teetered on the brink of a pandemic. Once again, he wished he could go back in time.

Someone knocked on the cabin door. The officer opened it and waved a couple of security guards inside. The captain nodded to them. "Escort this man to the brig." He scowled again. "Bread and water is too good for you, but never let it be said that a captain of Atlantic Imperial Cruise Lines starved one of his guests."

Chet accepted the sentence without comment. They marched him through the bowels of the ship. Sandy blocked their path. "Eric, is it true? Are we under quarantine? I haven't heard any…"

The guard ignored her and motioned for the others to hurry their procession.

Sandy startled as she glanced at Chet, as if she'd just noticed him. "You told me you worked for the CDC. Do you know anything about this quarantine?"

"Yeah. I caused it."

She paused then met his eyes. "I don't believe you."

Chet set his mouth in a grim line. "Believe it. It was my fault. Now I've threatened millions of people." He didn't want to talk to her for fear it might implicate her in his inadvertent—no, evil—crime.

"I don't believe you meant to do it."

Chet stared at her as the guards pushed him

through the hallways to his temporary home in the brig.

****

Chet moped. He hadn't slept last night and felt crusty. He'd tried to read something from the Gideon Bible in the cell, but his childhood verse memorization was in shambles. He half-remembered passages about God's forgiveness but couldn't dredge up the references.

He'd begged some origami paper from his stateroom, a request which the captain granted. Idly he folded another crane to join the others on the floor. Japanese tradition claimed that after folding one thousand cranes, you'd get your wish. Nine hundred and eighty-seven to go. Only he didn't know what to wish for.

Someone had delivered a gourmet meal last night, not the bread and water the captain had threatened. He'd had no appetite yesterday. Now he was ravenous.

A knock on the wall next to the brig's bars signaled the delivery of breakfast. The guard turned the key. The person carrying his tray was the last one he expected to see.

"I talked the guards into letting me bring it." Sandy's lilting voice greeted him without condemnation. She placed the tray on the table. "Eat up."

"What are you doing here?" Challenge barbed his words.

She stepped back, hurt showing on her face. "I just wanted to see how you were doing. You need a friend."

Chet took a deep breath. "Sorry. Guess I'm a bit jumpy this morning. A jail cell will do that to you. Thanks for coming." He pulled up a chair and removed the metal cover from a plate of scrambled eggs, bacon, sticky bun, and honeydew melon, with coffee as a chaser. The aroma of the Costa Rica brew mingled with the scent of caramel. He ate with gusto, grateful for her unexpected kindness.

"How is it?" She smiled as if she wasn't talking to a condemned man.

"Fine." He swallowed and wiped his mouth with the cloth napkin, stopping in mid-wipe as he remembered the napkins he'd sprayed. "I told the captain I was responsible for the outbreak. I stole the virus sample from the CDC and exposed everyone at a Christian marriage seminar my father taught." He shook his head. "I thought I'd taken something as mild as a bad cold, not a lethal strain. I just wanted to make him sick...Instead, I killed him. Maybe others who attended are dead, too—"

Sandy held up a hand. "You shouldn't be talking about this. Not until you have a lawyer."

Chet sighed. "They say confession is good for the soul." *But it's not helping.* "I came aboard to escape, and now people here are dying of it."

Sandy cocked her head. "Why did you do it?"

Chet's eggs stuck in his throat. He set down his fork. "Because I hated my father. He pretended to be a great preacher and Christian. In his personal life, he was a different man. I hated him for it. I hated all hypocrites." Chet wondered why he was referring to his hate in past tense. Had his anger cooled that quickly?

Sandy's eyes widened. "Your father was Worth Hildebrandt?"

"Yes." His shoulders slumped. "Look, I'm under arrest. I'll be tried as a bioterrorist and locked up forever. Maybe even executed. The authorities are probably arguing right now who gets to crucify me. You don't want to hang around me."

"I don't think you meant to hurt anyone."

Was the woman dense? "But I did. My father's dead, dozens of people here are sick, and I don't know what the final death toll will be." His stomach lurched as he imagined corpses zipped into body bags and transferred to freezers for dead people. He winced.

"I still want to be your friend."

Chet pushed his meal away. "Why?"

"I'd like to think I'm a good judge of character."

Chet laughed. "Yeah, right. Just look at me." He leaned forward. "This flu is going to get worse. It'll kill thousands, possibly millions. It will take months to develop a vaccine to prevent people from getting it. Unless Evie—my sister stuck on the space station—can pull it out of her space helmet more quickly. She's as good a vaccinologist as I am, maybe better."

She quirked an eyebrow. "Your sister's Hildi Hildebrandt? You've got quite a family."

"Yeah. And I'll be the first convict."

She locked eyes with him. "I'll pray. I'll pray that the virus won't spread, and that God and the authorities will have mercy."

"Pray?" He rolled the word around his tongue. He gazed into her blue eyes and got nothing but affirmation. He hung his head. "I'm sorry. I should have guessed you were a Christian. I didn't mean to say *you* were a hypocrite."

Sandy laughed.

"Look, I appreciate the gesture, but—"

"But what?"

"You shouldn't associate with me." Chet pulled his eyebrows into a scowl.

"What I do is my own business." She crossed her arms as if spoiling for a fight.

Chet didn't have any fight left. He felt strangely touched by her sympathy. "Thank you." He had a sudden thought as she turned to leave. "Uh, do you think you could help me with something?"

"I'll try."

Chet cleared his throat as he reached for the Bible. "I've been trying to find these verses, and I can't. It's been a long time."

With a glance at the guard, who held up ten fingers, Sandy set down the tray. She sat beside him on the edge of his bunk. "So what are you trying to find?"

"Something about God's forgiveness."

42

"I" Plus Twelve Days

Mission Control's wake-up call startled Dan from sleep. He groaned. "Ode to Joy" definitely didn't reflect his mood.

He glanced at Shorty, already untangled from his sleeping bag. "Mornin'." Dan mumbled a greeting and rubbed his eyes.

NASA had insisted on a few hours of sleep as *Valiant* closed the distance to the station. Dan would get out and push if it would help get them there faster. He chewed his lip.

"*Valiant*, this is Houston. You awake up there?" Pete could have a second career as one of those annoyingly chipper DJs.

Shorty keyed the mic. "*Valiant* here. Nice music."

Dan ran a hand through his hair, not that it would help. Weightlessness made your hair stand on end, a weird sensation.

Pete resumed the usual procedure confirmations. "*Valiant*, NASA has confirmed your instruments are still nominal. You are GO for mission. And for breakfast."

"Roger that."

Dan breathed a sigh of relief at Houston's go-ahead. He glanced at the glowing indicator lights.

NASA could still order *Valiant* to de-orbit if Dan or Shorty sneezed the wrong way. Although Dan had talked tough after the lightning strike, he really didn't want to disobey direct orders. It irritated his sense of duty. It would also end his career. But failure now meant death for the station crew. For Hildi. His stomach clenched.

Shorty hummed NASA's wake-up song. Too bad he was off key. He squished bags holding yellow goo that passed for scrambled eggs. Yum.

"Breakfast is served." Shorty handed Dan a packet of eggs and a second packet that looked vaguely like orange juice. Dan grabbed a flour tortilla and gratefully accepted a bottle of coffee.

"Breakfast of champions. Nothing like astronaut food to wake up the old stomach." Shorty seemed bent on spreading his morning cheer.

Dan shook his head. "At least the station will have decent food." Maybe tomorrow he'd have dinner with Hildi. He smiled at the prospect.

"Yep. The Russians make great borscht."

Dan groaned. At least the Russians usually brought a tin or two of caviar.

They downed their meals in a hurry, expecting an interruption at any minute. They'd just tossed their trash when CAPCOM's voice crackled through the speakers.

"*Valiant,* this is Houston. You are GO for initial burn."

"Acknowledged." Shorty grinned and turned to Dan. "Strap in."

Dan grabbed the back of his flight chair, pulled himself into the seat, and buckled his restraints. He beat Shorty by mere seconds. They went through the checklist with efficient ease.

"Initiate burn on my mark." Shorty switched to his commander voice.

Here we go. Dan gripped the joystick as Shorty started the countdown. "Five, four, three, two, one, mark."

"Firing main engines." The ship's nose pointed upward as they sped toward a matching orbit with the station. Dan prayed that the fix Frank and Jasper had made in repairing the dock would hold. He watched the screens. Time crawled. Dan's muscles tensed with every minute of the slow maneuver. After several hours, a bright spot showed on radar. "Coming up on the station."

Shorty activated his mic. "Houston, this is *Valiant.* We have ISS on our instruments."

Dan pointed. "There she is."

"Houston, we have visual contact."

"*Valiant,* this is Houston. You are GO for manual docking."

Dan made gentle corrections as *Valiant* approached ISS. As sunrise lit the station, he grinned. "We now have matching orbit."

"How does she look?" Pete's voice held a tinge of concern.

Mission Control was talking about damage, not the glint of red and gold on ISS. Shorty keyed his mic. "There are a few scratches, but the repair work looks secure. Ready to rock and roll."

"Very well, *Valiant.*"

Dan slid the joystick forward, then a tiny bit to the left. The controls felt sluggish with the overloaded spacecraft. The sounds of soft puffs from the attitude jets penetrated the hull. When the instruments indicated he was aligned, Dan cut all engines. *Valiant* slipped into the station's docking ring without a bump. Perfect. If he'd been golfing, it would have been a hole in one.

Shorty nodded. "Secure docking clamps."

"Docking clamps secure."

"Station, please confirm docking." CAPCOM Pete spoke with a please-pass-the-potatoes inflection.

Silence.

"ISS, this is Houston. Please confirm docking."

Silence.

Dan's stomach squeezed his half-digested breakfast.

"*Valiant,* this is Houston. ISS does not respond. Repeat, ISS does not respond."

Dan muttered under his breath, "Like they're telling us something we don't know."

"Acknowledged." Shorty's voice tightened.

"This is Houston. Flight surgeon reports the crew's vital signs are weakening."

Dan batted away visions of a floating, dead crew. A floating, dead Hildi.

Mutterings crackled in the headset, and then Steve bellowed, "Get aboard and get those people some oxygen."

Dan and Shorty grabbed eight green emergency tanks, each about ten inches long and with attached breathing masks. They each donned one and carried the rest. After opening the capsule's hatch, they pulled themselves through the airlock and into the station.

"Houston, we're inside," Shorty said.

"Roger."

They split up and sped through empty corridors with their little green tanks of life. Dan stopped at

Maria's side, her body—body?—floating in her quarters. He positioned a mask over her face and opened the valve. He watched her for a couple of breaths before he took one of his own. "Found Maria," he panted. "She's OK."

"Found Jasper," Shorty said. "He's good."

Dan sped into another room, securing a mask to the occupant. "Got Leonid."

"Joe's OK."

Dan found Frank in the next room. He stirred when Dan opened the tank valve. "Frank's OK."

Where's Hildi?

The next room was empty. Dan propelled himself through the modules. Finally, he found her floating in the lab, her body seemingly lifeless, her hair streaming from her head like a red halo. Was it the lighting, or was her skin blue? Heart pounding, he placed a mask over her face and opened the valve.

No response.

"C'mon, c'mon."

No response.

"Dan, she's flatlined." Pete's voice quavered.

"Shorty, grab the AED and get to the lab. It's Hildi." The defibrillator was useless unless Dan could get a pulse. Any pulse.

Dan anchored himself, slammed her against a table, and ripped off her mask. Taking a deep breath, he pulled down his own mask and performed CPR, his thoughts keeping rhythm with his chest compressions. *She can't be dead, she can't be dead, she can't be dead.* He panted with exertion.

"Dan, flight surgeon says we've got ventricular fibrillation." Pete's pronouncement gave Dan a slim hope.

"Shorty!"

Shorty appeared a second later.

Dan ripped open Hildi's shirt. Two buttons floated away. He slapped monitors and electrodes on her inert body.

Dan gulped down the bile of his own fear. "Clear." He pressed the button. Hildi's body convulsed.

He stared at the EKG reading. Shorty shook his head. "No effect."

"Clear."

Another convulsion. No change. A fist of dizziness gripped Dan.

Shorty grabbed Dan's mask and forced it over his nose. "Breathe."

Dan breathed. His head cleared. He gripped the paddles again. *Please, Lord.* "Clear."

Hildi's body convulsed. No change. They were losing her. His throat tightened.

Wait…

"She's stabilizing." Dan's scream probably deafened Shorty and most of Mission Control. Judging from the cheers, they didn't mind ruptured eardrums.

He adjusted the mask over Hildi's nose and watched her breath mist the clear plastic. Her eyes opened. They focused on him. "Are you a dream?" she whispered.

"No."

Hildi smiled.

To heck with NASA propriety. Dan cradled her face in his hands and tried to kiss her forehead. The masks ruined the tender moment as they banged together.

Dan grinned. "I think you need more mouth to mouth."

43

"I" Plus Twelve Days

Carol's stomach smiled with contentment. "That was delicious." She pushed her chair away from the patio table and wiped her mouth with her napkin.

Mike leaned back. "You were right, George. Best hamburgers ever."

Betty laughed. "Well, it's hard to go wrong with George's flair with the fire, and what more do you need than burgers, corn on the cob, and watermelon?"

Summer had come early to Denver this year, bringing with it Carol's favorite foods. She basked in the sun's warmth. Winter had lasted far too long.

Laura set her half-eaten burger on the plate. "I can't eat another bite."

George turned off the grill and closed the lid. Carol turned to him.

"You gave a beautiful eulogy yesterday."

Sighing, George sat. "Hard to fit all of Worth's life into a few words."

A weak smile brightened Laura's expression. "I'm sure he would have loved it."

Conversation halted. Carol remembered the joyful, public memorial. A few of the news people had looked puzzled, but at least they'd respected Laura's wishes for no flash photography.

Betty grasped Carol's hand. "What did the doctor say Thursday at your checkup?"

Mike laced his fingers behind his head. "Just a healthy baby boy."

"Girl." Carol locked eyes with her husband.

"Boy."

"Girl." Carol stiffened as a pang of fear rose then quieted. She patted her still-flat belly. "Well, the doc couldn't tell what sex yet. Too early. But he thought I was doing fine."

"Dear, that's such good news. God is faithful. So when's your next appointment?"

"In a month." Carol frowned. "He wants to do a CVS to test for birth defects, but we've decided to have this baby whatever the results." Carol gazed at her husband, who smiled his agreement.

Mike put his arm around Carol's shoulders. "It's hard to think about what this child might go through, the struggles we all might face. All because of a stupid flu. But we couldn't take the life of our own child."

Carol's eyes started to leak."

"Let's have none of that." Betty lifted Carol's chin. "I think your decision to have your baby regardless of the test results shows a lot of faith and courage."

Not trusting her voice, Carol nodded.

Betty patted Carol's arm before standing. "We have dessert," Betty said. "Brownies a la mode. Coffee, anyone? Regular or decaf?"

"Make mine decaf." Carol patted her belly again. Got to take care of the little one, even if decaf never had the kick of the real thing. Kick. She couldn't wait to feel the life within her.

The clatter of dishes disrupted her musings as George cleared the table. Mike squeezed Carol's shoulder. "We'll face this together with God's help."

We. Carol liked the sound of that.

She dug into her brownie and ice cream for two.

44

With the ISS crew out of danger, Dan and Shorty donned their pressure suits and EVA'd to swap out the liquid oxygen tanks. The exchange took several hours. Dan's hands cramped before they were done.

When they returned, the station astronauts applauded. They all looked a little bleary-eyed, still shaking off the effects of near asphyxiation. Dan gulped as he realized just how close they'd come to death.

He hugged everyone after removing his suit. Frank shrugged him off. His old stubborn friend. Hildi's hug was warm and lasted a little longer.

Joe snapped on the radio. "Houston, this is ISS. Hope you guys haven't fallen asleep down there. Things here are as exciting as watching hay bales rot."

"Affirmative." CAPCOM Pete yawned into the mic. "If you're ready for some challenges, we'll invent a few."

"Nope. We're doin' just fine on our own."

"Flight surgeon has cleared you for work as long as you take it easy." Pete's voice crackled over the radio. "Dan and Shorty, great job. Steve wanted to tell you himself, but he's getting some sleep. Joe, you and the rest of the station missed it, but Dan and Shorty made an amazing rescue at the risk of their own lives. And Dan made a perfect docking."

Frank's eyes narrowed.

"Nothing like being late to your own party." Jasper grinned. His smile was contagious, and soon everyone laughed.

"ISS out." Joe switched off the radio.

Jasper sighed. "I sure could use some coffee."

"We brought some." Shorty smiled. "And a shipload of other stuff."

The astronauts formed a bucket brigade to transfer supplies from the *Valiant* to ISS.

"Tortillas. We were nearly out." Maria grinned as she stowed them.

"Ah, comrades. My government sent borscht." Leonid's eyes glowed. "Now you will taste famous Russian soup. And plenty of hot sauce for your enchiladas." He winked at Joe.

"You tenderfoots will appreciate the extra spice," Joe muttered. "Everything's bland after a few months in space."

Even beet soup with hot sauce sounded good to Dan's growling belly.

Frank still scowled. Judging from the few barbs he'd unleashed, Dan guessed Frank was mad at him for his textbook docking. Why? Frank's attitude went beyond mere jealousy. Lifting an equipment package labeled "thermocycler," Dan guided it through *Valiant*'s hatch to Jasper.

"Makes you think you're a weightlifter, huh?" Jasper flexed his biceps.

Dan grinned. "Be gentle, though. We don't want this delicate equipment to hit the walls."

"Doesn't bounce well, huh?" Jasper pushed the package toward Shorty, who handed it off to Hildi. She and Maria secured it in the lab with straps until they were ready to unpack it. Leonid stowed the food supplies.

Joe peered inside *Valiant*. "Is that it?"

"Except for the virus sample. I'll get it." Dan reached into *Valiant* for the case cushioning the sample vial. "One influenza virus, coming up." He glided to the lab module and delivered the case to Hildi. Their fingers touched. She smiled.

Hildi snapped on gloves, opened the case, and extracted the vial. Dan squinted over her shoulder. The liquid inside appeared harmless. Deadly viruses didn't emit blood-red sparks.

Frank bolted into the lab, his face contorted. "We just got another report from NASA. How does it feel to be a hero?" He spat the words at Dan. "Surviving a lightning strike, making a perfect docking, and rescuing us poor astronauts, while the press blames me for the accident. I still say my controls were faulty."

Dan floated back a few feet. He had to do something to calm Frank. "What do you mean, *hero*? We delivered the oxygen. That was our job. If you'd had the mission, it would have been your job."

"*You* haven't been vilified by the press. And *you* didn't have your fiancée stolen from under your nose."

Dan's jaw dropped. Frank blamed him for the breakup? It didn't make sense. "I didn't steal her."

"Frank." Hildi stepped between them, clutching the vial in her hand. "I knew him only as your best buddy while you and I were engaged. Dan and I didn't even date until six months later. And it was my decision to break our engagement. Dan had nothing to do with it."

Frank clenched his fists, his breathing ragged. He wasn't going to listen to reason.

Dan glanced at Hildi, hoping she could talk some

sense into him. She took the hint. "Please, Frank. We'll always be friends, but I've moved on. Dan's the man in my life now."

Man in my life. Dan's heart sank. Not fiancé. He swore he'd fix that soon.

Frank exploded. Curse words pierced Dan like shrapnel.

"Stop it." Hildi tried to separate them as Dan held Frank at arm's length. Frank spun away, colliding with Hildi.

The vial flew from her hand with the speed of a fastball. It struck the corner of a box. The cap flew off.

Hildi pushed the men out of the lab.

Dan froze, staring at the floating globules of deadly virus. Dread knotted his guts.

Now they were all exposed.

45

Chet woke disoriented from a fitful sleep. Then he saw the bars of the brig. *Right.* What had disturbed him? The rumble of the engines had changed. The ship had slowed, and the sea's whoosh had softened to a whisper.

He rolled from his cot, stretched, and tried to smooth the wrinkles out of the clothes he'd slept in. He couldn't see anything from the cell. He did the usual morning stuff, stood at the bars, and waited. No one bothered to offer breakfast.

A security guard came to his cell, escorting the chaplain. The man of the cloth had a wrinkled smile and kind eyes. "You wanted to see me?"

"Yes. They'll be hauling me away soon."

The guard opened the door, and the chaplain entered, grasping Chet's shoulder before taking a seat on the one chair in the brig. Chet lowered himself onto the bunk.

"Five minutes." The guard walked away, scowling.

The chaplain lifted a worn Bible. "Do you want me to read you some Scripture?"

"I'd like that, Reverend."

"Please. It's Jack."

"Jack." Chet took a deep breath. Time to take the plunge into the deep end of the spiritual pool. "I doubt if anyone in this world will forgive me for what I've done. Will God?"

"I think you know the answer to that." Jack opened his Bible and searched through the middle of the book. Chet grabbed the Gideon's Bible beside him and flipped the pages.

"Psalm 103:12. 'As far as the east is from the west, so far has He removed our transgressions from us.'"

Chet's shoulders slumped. *Not for me.* "I'm having a hard time believing that. My father drilled that verse into me as far back as I can remember. It never stuck." He sighed. "And I sure don't feel it. My prayers for forgiveness haven't gone any farther than the ceiling."

"Feelings are, at best, unreliable." The chaplain smiled. "There's an old saying, 'God said it, I believe it, that settles it.'" He frowned. "There's also something called repentance."

"I know, I know. I've heard it all before." Bitterness coated Chet's tongue. "Turning from sin and going another direction. I guess my father—a pastor by the way, who committed adultery—did that. I'd always assumed the hog would return to the mud." But his father had never had another affair after he repented, at least not that Chet knew—and he'd been watching. Guilt chewed Chet's insides like a hungry tapeworm.

Jack raised an eyebrow. "A pastor, huh?"

"Worth Hildebrandt."

"I thought your name was familiar. Now there's a prime example of God's forgiveness."

Chet shifted on his bunk.

Jack pointed again at the passage. "You'd do well if you read this psalm over and over." He grasped Chet's shoulder. "The apostle Paul was a murderer, and he spoke a lot about God's forgiveness."

"I guess. He couldn't undo what he did, though."

Jack nodded. "Neither can you. But you can admit what you've done."

"Guess that means I can't plead 'not guilty by reason of insanity.'" Chet's mouth quirked while his guts twisted into tighter knots. "I must have been crazy to unleash the virus and kill my own father."

Confusion creased Jack's forehead. "You killed him? How did you come to that conclusion?"

Chet lifted his head and locked eyes with the compassionate man. "I killed him, as sure as pulling a trigger. I didn't know he was HIV positive, but that's a flimsy excuse. His wrecked immune system couldn't survive an assault like that." He paused. "A lot more people are dying because of my actions." How many more? He only hoped Hildi could develop a vaccine in time, before everyone on the planet succumbed. For once, he wished for her success instead of wanting her to fail. Her obsession to surpass him professionally had rankled him. Now he didn't care if she got the accolades. The stakes were too high and his guilt too deep.

He snapped his attention back to Jack. "Sorry. Woolgathering. What did you say?"

"God forgives those who confess."

"I've tried that."

"Sometimes, it helps to pray with someone. Are you willing to do that?"

Chet was desperate enough to try anything. "Yeah."

Jack reached for his hands. Chet grasped them like a drowning man.

The guard returned, took one look at them, and held up a finger. "I'll give you one more minute." He stood there, jingling the keys in his hands.

Chet shifted again then decided he didn't care what the guard thought. He bowed his head as Jack prayed. "Lord, You know this man's heart, and You know what he's done. Help him confess and receive Your forgiveness."

When Jack stopped and the silence deepened, Chet cleared his throat. "God, I...I admit I did a terrible thing. I don't deserve Your forgiveness, but I ask for it."

"Amen." Jack stood and motioned to the guard, who at least had the decency to look embarrassed for eavesdropping. He opened the door.

Jack gripped Chet's shoulder. "I'll be praying for you."

Chet nodded his thanks, fighting the lemon lodged in his throat.

As Jack's steps faded to a hollow echo, Chet settled on his bunk and turned to Psalm 103.

****

Time crawled. Chet shut the Bible and pulled out his origami papers. Not many left. Would they allow origami in prison?

He chose a red paper and folded it. He grunted. A cross. Where had that come from? He'd just folded his fifth cross when he heard heavy footsteps in the hallway.

The captain ushered three strangers in dark suits who stared at him with undisguised disgust. Curious employees ringed the men but didn't get too close.

The security guard turned the key in the lock. The door clanged open. One of the suits stepped forward and flashed a badge. "Special Agent Collins, FBI. You're under arrest for domestic terrorism." He turned to the other men. "Cuff him."

Chet made no protest as they read him his rights and handcuffed him behind his back, pinching his wrists with a bit more enthusiasm than necessary. "Am I allowed to make a phone call?" Having a lawyer right now would probably be a very good idea.

Collins growled. "After we get off this boat."

The captain stiffened. "Please remove the prisoner from this *ship* as quickly as possible. We don't want to alarm the passengers."

"Maybe they should be alarmed with nutcases like this running around." The guard scowled, twirling his keys.

"I'm not a nutcase." No, he'd committed his crime with full control of his faculties.

"Save it for the judge." The guard raised one eyebrow as he gazed at the origami crosses. "Getting jailhouse religion? Bit early." He shrugged. "The losers always do. It never sticks."

Chet hung his head but said nothing. *Loser.* He trudged out of the room. He craned his neck to peer through the doors leading to the kitchens but only caught a brief glimpse. He wished he'd had the chance to take the tour.

The agents herded him like a steer to the slaughterhouse. Crewmen gazed at him with accusing eyes, murmuring among themselves.

"Did you see the ship alongside us?"

"Maybe it's to keep us from violating quarantine."

"Maybe it's for this guy. I heard he's a terrorist."

"The sooner he gets off, the better. The guests are already spooked."

The entourage took a service elevator to the third deck, the usual level for launches. Chet had a stray thought about his personal belongings. He'd never see them again except in a courtroom as damning evidence. He'd chucked the empty vial into the ocean, but that wouldn't slow their investigation. They'd condemn him to life in prison or execution. Right now, he voted for the latter.

A woman waited near the elevator. She wore wrist splints. "I'll visit you as soon as I can."

Chet stared at her. "Don't."

Sandy crossed her arms. "What I do, mister, is my own business." Her face softened. "I'll be praying for you. God's not finished with you yet."

Chet shook his head as the agents marched him past her.

Alongside the ship, a launch bobbed in the water. Looked military. Chet lifted his gaze to the waiting vessel and startled. A naval destroyer?

Well, at least he'd be traveling in style.

****

The next morning, Chet felt like a squeezed-out dishrag. The FBI had grilled him for hours. Now he wished he'd kept his mouth shut.

The destroyer's engines changed in pitch as it apparently slowed for docking. Agents escorted him to the ship's disembarkation ramp. In the distance, hoisting cranes skewered the sky as far as he could see. Southampton looked more like an industrial area than a destination for luxury cruise ships. He envisioned nearby London as a bustling metropolis with double-decker buses and international restaurants, not that he'd get a chance to sample any exotic foods now. At least Navy food was passable. His stomach rumbled.

Chet suspected the virus had already reached Great Britain. Everyone on the pier wore face masks.

An unmarked black sedan and four police motorcycles waited. His transportation. He descended the ramp and emerged into cool early morning, moody fog clinging to the ground. The stench of diesel fuel tainted the fresh salty air. Chet smiled when he recalled Sandy's promise to visit, and his stride became a little lighter. Until the cameras flashed.

The press swooped down like seagulls on fish guts. Their barrage of questions bounced off the agents who ran interference for him. Chet refused the FBI's offer to shield his face as they marched him to the waiting car.

Collins turned to address the crowds. "Dr. Chester Hildebrandt is under arrest for domestic terrorism." The man droned on, stealing all the credit for the capture of a dangerous criminal.

Two agents waited at the car. Pain skittered up Chet's arms as they bent in an awkward position, and one of the agents pushed him into the back seat.

"Oh. Sorry." The man sounded sincere.

Chet nodded. "No problem."

The car smoothed into gear. Chet peered once more into the miserable fog before someone slammed the car door.

46

Hildi's heart thumped into overdrive. She grabbed a plastic bag from a locker, collected the vial, and herded globules of floating liquid into it. The stuff misted the air like a violent sneeze.

Rage and panic fought for control. "Of all the lamebrained, idiotic stunts..." Professionals, ha. She strangled the bag in her hand.

It would only take a few droplets to infect the crew. Level Four protocol wouldn't help now. But first things first. She had to capture enough of the sample for analysis.

Maria had quickly drawn a clear curtain to seal the room with Hildi inside. Her effort might slow the spread of the disease, but exposure was inevitable. The crew breathed the same recirculating air in a closed ventilation system.

Hildi held the bag in front of the clear protective curtain for Maria's inspection. She frowned at it. "What's that?"

"What's left of the flu sample. The vial broke." She didn't say how. It didn't matter. She fought to keep her voice level while a panicked part of her screamed, *We're all gonna die.*

****

Frank unclenched his fists as reality slammed into him. He should lick up the virus droplets and at least take the worst of the contagion, not that it would help now. He wondered how it would taste.

He stared at the vial stuffed into the bag. There was nothing he could do except maybe volunteer as a lab assistant. Or guinea pig.

Frank hung his head. He forced out the next words, lame as they were. "I'm sorry."

Joe snorted like a longhorn ready to charge. "Sorry? *Sorry?* You think you can pour spilled whiskey back into a broken bottle?"

Frank grimaced. His simmering pot of anger had boiled over. His old Air Force buddy had been a convenient target, and he doubted he could ever repair the damage to their friendship.

Joe counted to ten aloud. Real slow. His reddened face cooled as he huffed out a breath. "I'm mighty tempted to throw you out the airlock without a pressure suit." He turned to Hildi. "Anything you can do?"

Hildi sighed. "Not much to keep us from contracting it. Chet said he's apparently immune. If I'm immune, too, I can try to isolate the factor in our blood. I think I've got enough of a virus sample." She squinted at the droplets in the bag.

Frank stared at nothing. He'd endangered the crew. Maybe he deserved the airlock. "You can use me as a lab rat if you want. Inject me with the stuff and see what happens." He didn't care if he got sicker than a dog if it would help.

"Mighty kind of you." Joe's words had a tinge of remaining anger, but a slight smile crossed his lips.

Hildi shook her head. "Doesn't work that way. I

suspect all of us will get it sooner or later. NASA sent up some antibiotics to prevent secondary infection like pneumonia, just in case. We'll need them."

What would weightlessness do to their chances of survival? Probably make them worse. Frank shut his eyes.

Joe floated back to the main cabin, muttering he needed to report the accident to NASA. Maria left. Frank stared at the floor. What could he possibly say? "I was out of control." He turned to Dan. "And way out of line. Professionals don't pick fights—"

"Yeah, you should have thought of that." Dan snarled.

"It was an *accident*." Hildi reached for Dan's shoulder.

Dan slapped her hand away. "You stay out of this."

Hildi blanched.

Frank reached for a handhold, gripping it till his knuckles turned white. He forced his contorted face into something closer to normal.

Dan swallowed. "I'm sorry, Hildi. You didn't deserve that."

She nodded.

Frank took a deep breath. "I let this media business get to me. I've been stewing about the docking. And I've been eaten up with jealousy as I've seen the two of you together."

Dan and Hildi exchanged glances.

He met their gazes. "Fact is, I think you could really make a go of it. I hope you do." Frank's throat refused passage for any other words.

Dan nodded. "Thanks for being honest. Let's talk after we've calmed down. Deal?"

"Deal."
It was a start.

47

"I" Plus Fifteen Days

Dan floated to the lab entrance, his insides tightening at the sight of Hildi's drawn face. "Dinner."

She huffed but didn't answer. She turned to Maria. "Still nothing?"

"Nothing." Maria withdrew her hands from the heavy gloves of the clear plastic box and frowned. She pointed to the microscope inside. "No correlation between your blood and any immunity factor."

He floated closer, but they continued to ignore him. The enclosed box kept the sample from floating around, but they could still work with it by using the built-in gloves. Hildi stretched, her back and neck cracking. "Three days of work, and we're no closer to a vaccine."

"Ahem." He raised his voice. "Suppertime."

They finally looked up from their work. Dan's heart missed a beat when he saw defeat in Hildi's eyes. He donned his sternest expression. "You two have locked yourselves in the lab for twenty-two hours. Way past time for food and sleep."

Hildi's stomach growled.

He grinned. "See what I mean?" He coughed into his sleeve, trying to hide the first symptom of the flu. Hildi quirked an eyebrow but said nothing. He'd hoped he wouldn't catch it so soon. None of them could afford to be sick.

"I'll eat later." Hildi turned back to her work.

"You've got to eat. You too, Maria. Can't work on an empty stomach and two hours of sleep."

Maria smiled. "Yes, Mommy." She planted her hands on her hips. "And just who's been monitoring our sleeping and eating habits?"

"I have." Joe jetted up to the lab. "You're eating with us, dag nab it. That's an order."

Maria stuck out her tongue. "You can't order me. I'm a civilian."

"Don't matter. You're under my command. Or didn't you read the fine print on your contract?" He grimaced. "Next time, my crew will all be military, or I'll leave the corps."

Dan fought to keep a straight face. Hildi was a civilian, too, but kept her mouth shut. Her pretty mouth. No one took the old cowpoke's threats seriously. "We'll be along in a minute."

Joe twisted to face Dan. "Keep an eye on these strays and bring 'em back to the herd." He shot toward the dining area.

Hildi headed toward the kitchen, Maria and Dan trailing. Dan's own stomach rumbled at the smell of roast beef, his favorite. They'd finally run out of borscht, which actually was pretty good, and Leonid had promised to open a tin of caviar.

Maria spoke over her shoulder. "Dan, I sure hope Hildi's prayers help with the vaccine. We need all the divine help we can get."

Dan cocked his head. He'd never brought up the subject of religion with Maria. In fact, he'd hardly talked with her at all since she and Hildi had barricaded themselves in the lab. "What do you believe, Maria?"

She faced him, floating in the microgravity. "I was raised Catholic, and my parents still attend church, but I don't follow any belief system. I participate in some of the Mayan dances and festivals that have been part of the Mayan religion for centuries, but they're cultural as far as I'm concerned." She leaned forward with a mischievous grin and whispered, "We've never repudiated human sacrifice, you know."

Dan recoiled in mock horror. "I hope you aren't going to renew that practice here."

"No." She shook her head. "I never understood why the Mayan religion required killing innocent victims, including turkeys."

Dan paused a moment. "The Christian faith also required human sacrifice. But only one."

Maria frowned.

The three of them reached the dining table. The others were already "seated," their legs wrapped around the chairs. Joe and Jasper banged the table and chanted, "Food, food, food." Shorty was tearing into his meal. Frank stared at the wall, his food untouched.

Leonid glanced up from the microwave. "Roast beef for the men, chicken for the ladies." He distributed hot packets.

Dan opened his, forking the meat carefully so the gravy wouldn't escape. Mashed potatoes followed, an excellent choice on the station. The paste stayed on the fork. Chocolate pudding for dessert. They cleared the table for the odd game of catch-the-water, one of the ways to relax after a twelve-hour workday and a game only possible in weightlessness. As orange-sized spheres of water floated above the table, the astronauts took turns batting them back and forth with straws, occasionally sucking them up. Sometimes the spheres got past their defenses, and the giant drop splatted someone's face.

"Third time in a row," Jasper sputtered as he wiped his eyes with a sleeve. "Anybody got a towel?" Dan grinned at Jasper's forlorn expression.

They floated off to bed. Dan dragged himself into his bag, bone tired and aching all over.

48

"I" Plus Twenty-five Days

Hildi rubbed stinging eyes as she bagged another failure, destined to be jettisoned along with the rest of the trash. Days wasted that the world couldn't afford.

Scientists were working around the clock to find the genetic denominator for immunity. They'd had no luck, and neither had she.

Alan at the CDC had reported the virus was continuing its march across the United States. He feared it would spread to undeveloped countries where medication for secondary infection didn't exist. He hadn't used the word *pandemic,* but the unspoken assumption thickened the air. It preyed on Hildi's mind.

She thought she'd discovered a new approach but now had to mark it as unsuccessful. Weightlessness didn't seem to help.

Frank floated to the clear screen of the lab. "Anything I can do?" He still hadn't displayed any flu symptoms. She'd withdrawn a sample of his blood along with everyone else's and compared it to her own, but the key element eluded her.

She was out of options and ideas. "I'm going back to square one and hope I missed something."

"That bad, huh?"

Hildi banged her hand on the counter, anchoring herself so she wouldn't fly across the room. The self-inflicted pain wrenched her thoughts back from the brink of frustration. "I've tried everything in the book and written a few new chapters myself." Sudden inspiration buoyed her hopes. "Maybe the microscope slides were contaminated," she thought out loud, weighing the possibilities on her mind's scale. "Maybe..." She slapped her forehead hard enough to lose her grip on the table. "Duh."

"What?"

"I've been using the remains of what I gathered from the—uh—accident."

"You can say fight." Frank's face radiated guilt. No time to deal with his hangdog attitude now. She gulped. Would any of them have time?

Hildi slipped her hands into the bulky gloves of the glove box. So many hours wasted because she hadn't thought of the obvious problem. "The sample must have been contaminated by something on this station. Even with the environment we maintain, something got into the virus."

Frank quirked an eyebrow. "You're looking for dust on a bug?"

"Yes. I'm going to see if I can salvage enough of the original sample from the vial."

She grasped the plastic bag containing the vial and removed it from the box. Her latex gloves offered thin protection but at least would keep further contamination at bay. She'd taken all her samples from the droplets clinging to the wall of the bag because the vial was empty. She held it to the light. Still empty. Her hopes disintegrated like ashes. She extracted the vial from the bag and dropped it into the centrifuge. The machine whirred. "Pray. This is our last hope. If I can get a decent enough sample from the vial—"

"You can work with it?"

"Yeah."

Frank glanced around the room. "Where's Maria?"

"Sleeping. Doctor's—my—orders. She's running a fever but thankfully nothing else." *Yet.*

Coughs and moans bounced off the station walls. Dan also slept, the sickest among them, now suffering with pneumonia in spite of drugs. She checked on him a little more often than necessary, tensing with his every labored breath. Everyone else dragged themselves through the corridors, performing their duties with sluggishness but doing them anyway. Stubborn astronaut can-do.

Hildi turned off the machine, pulled out the vial, and stared at the bottom. "It worked."

Frank leaned in. "I don't see anything."

"Trust me, it's there. I've worked with smaller samples." She held her breath as she returned the vial to the box, reinserted her hands, and manipulated a micropipette. After extracting a droplet of liquid, Hildi transferred it to an Eppendorf. The tiny tube would be home to the virus for several days as she added chemicals to break down the DNA. "Got it." Hildi secured the Eppendorf and removed her hands then somersaulted with a good imitation of Jasper's enthusiasm. The movement relieved a few kinks in her back.

"Hey, you sure you're ready for that kind of acrobatics?" Frank's sudden grin was contagious—about as contagious as the virus. Fatigue rimmed his eyes.

Maria floated over, rubbing her face. "I heard your

whoop. You made progress?"

"Got a fresh sample. The one we were working might have been contaminated." Her weary bones complained they weren't happy with the task of starting from scratch.

Frank glanced at them and made his apologies. "My turn in the sack." He pulled himself out of the lab.

"Want me to set up the thermocycler?" Maria floated toward the glove box, already focused on the task.

"I'll do it, but thanks."

Maria glared at Hildi, hands on hips. "Get some food and some sleep."

"I can't."

"You're no use if you're asleep on your feet. I am ordering you out." Maria's lilting voice had none of her usual humor as she shook her finger. "Do not try to pull rank."

Maria was right. Hildi hated to admit it, but she was about to keel over.

Hildi heated an enchilada in the microwave, applied liberal amounts of hot sauce, and grabbed a fork.

Joe floated over. He looked like he'd been up all night. "Got the vaccine?"

"Not yet." Hildi smiled in spite of fatigue. "But I have an uncontaminated sample now."

"Well, it's progress." He left.

Hildi toyed with her food, chiding herself. Chet would never have made such a stupid mistake, although he'd made plenty of them lately. Where was he now?

49

Chet squinted as the late morning sun mocked him through a high barred window. He sighed, folding another origami crane. It must be his hundredth since he arrived at Wormwood Scrubs Prison eons ago. At least the governor—the prison administrator—had allowed him his hobby. Origami distracted him from pine-scented disinfectant competing with stale cigarette smoke and sweat. Time crawled like a caterpillar on barbiturates when you awaited extradition, conviction, and sentencing.

Chet had already decided to plead guilty when he faced a judge back in the States. Why make the lengthy trial even longer? The US took none too kindly to individuals unleashing deadly viruses on her population. Chet didn't care much for terrorists either, but now he was one of them.

Footsteps in the corridor interrupted his dark thoughts.

"You have a visitor." The guard yawned as he opened the cell's door.

The Church of England prison chaplain strode in, wearing the usual clerical collar. Chet smiled. The priest had been his only comfort in this stink hole.

"Adjusting to life in the Scrubs?" Father Kirk shook Chet's hand as the guard locked them in.

Chet grimaced. "Not exactly how I wanted to

spend my summer vacation." He glanced at the sterile room—bed, sink, toilet, table. Level 4 had more personality. He gestured to the one chair in the room. "Would you like to sit? I don't have any tea..."

The chaplain chuckled as he lowered himself to the chair. "I assure you, I'm fine, thank you." Middle aged, he kept fit but bore the ravaged face of a life of drugs and imprisonment. Chet had marveled at the man's story of his transformation.

Father Kirk glanced at the Bible lying open on the table. "Read any good books lately?"

Chet plopped onto the thin-mattressed bunk and rolled his eyes. "Yeah. Psalms and Romans mostly."

The clergyman nodded. "Any thoughts?"

"David's raw emotions. I can relate to that, at least."

"Read the Gospel of John. We can talk later after you've absorbed the truths there." Father Kirk glanced at the origami scattered on the bed. "I didn't know you did origami."

"Keeps me from going stir-crazy. These are cranes, a traditional form. Did you know that if you fold one thousand cranes, you get your wish?"

A slight smile curled the chaplain's lips. "And what do you wish for?"

To get out of here. Chet huffed a breath. "A speedy execution—uh, extradition—and trial. I hate waiting around for the lawyers to get their act together."

Father Kirk nodded. "The legal wheels grind slowly. Your government will hasten the process, no doubt, but these things take time. England has cause to try you as well but will honor their extradition agreement with the United States."

"The whole world wants to try me." Chet shook

his head.

"But you gave your sister information to help develop the vaccine."

He shrugged. "I thought maybe it would play well with the judges. Lessen my guilt. Something. But it won't make any difference, will it?" His words tasted bitter.

"I think it will."

Chet cupped his chin in his hand. "I've done a lot of thinking lately."

"I know you have." The chaplain smiled.

"I'd like to do something constructive with my time. I'll never be released from prison, but maybe I could help the inmates somehow. One problem—90 percent of them scare me to death."

"I see your point." Father Kirk gazed at the ceiling. Was he praying or trying to keep a look of distaste from his face? Chet wouldn't blame him for the latter.

The chaplain met Chet's gaze. "You know, this prison holds over nine hundred inmates."

"Yeah." Where was the guy going with this?

"They all need spiritual help." A smile quirked Father Kirk's mouth. "Some more than others."

"I guess you have your work cut out for you."

"I do." Father Kirk scraped his chair across the concrete floor and leaned closer. "I could use an assistant."

"Me?" Chet shook his head. "I'm a vaccinologist, not a pastor. I wouldn't know where to start."

The clergyman smiled. "I've had my eye on you ever since you showed up here. Most of these guys either scream their innocence or boast about their crimes. You don't. I believe your remorse is genuine."

Yeah, but it hasn't done me any favors. Chet huffed

out a breath. "Remorse isn't enough for the authorities. They'll never allow me to work with you. They don't trust me, and I don't blame them."

"I can vouch for you. We'll leave it in the governor's hands and God's." The clergyman shifted in his seat. "Governor Edwards is a big supporter of inmate education. He may even let you attend seminary classes online."

"I certainly have plenty of time to kill." Chet glanced at the heap of origami cranes overflowing his bunk.

"Who knows where God might lead? You might end up wearing one of these." Father Kirk fingered his clerical collar.

Chet stared at him. How could he possibly follow in his father's footsteps, at least his better ones? Forgiveness still battled with residual anger. But the Hound of Heaven had pursued Chet like a beagle after an exhausted fox. He'd run out of denials and excuses for doing what he suspected God wanted him to do. His stomach wrenched at the thought.

Chet's mind whirled. So much had happened in just a few days. The arrest. The surreal drive through the streets of London. The incarceration. The discovery of a speck of faith inside him about the size of a virus. And now this guy expected him to affect others with this faith? He closed his eyes. "I'd like to try. But I don't know how long I'll be here."

The chaplain smiled. "Well, as I said, the legal wheels turn slowly."

"OK." Chet frowned at his own response, the words feeling strange. He didn't know if he had it in him. Maybe God would put it in him.

"Excellent. I'll speak to the governor." Father Kirk

paused as the usual sounds of buzzers and men's raised voices crescendoed several decibels. He glanced at the paper cranes again and cocked his head. "How long have you been doing origami?"

"Years. I teach at workshops sometimes."

"Can you teach the inmates?"

Chet snorted. "Teach *them*? They'd laugh their heads off. Then kill me."

"Some of them knit."

Chet's jaw dropped. "You've got to be kidding. I can't imagine murderers knitting tea cozies."

Father Kirk chuckled. "These men will jump at anything to keep their hands and their minds busy."

"I suppose so." Chet scratched his head, hoping he hadn't picked up lice in this place. Why should he even consider teaching his fellow prisoners? Did he have a death wish? "Do you really think the governor would let me?"

"It wouldn't hurt to ask."

Whiffs of institutional food drifted into the room. Chet wrinkled his nose. The guard sauntered back to the cell and unlocked the door, boredom drooping his eyes.

Father Kirk stood and shook Chet's hand again. As the chaplain stepped out of the cell, Chet blurted, "But what can I possibly say to these guys?"

"Tell them"—Father Kirk paused for a moment—"tell them, as a fellow beggar, where they can find bread."

Chet's blood started a slow boil. The minister's remark was the same inane phrase his father had used countless times. He had no desire to become a Bible-thumping preacher like his father to a bunch of foul-mouthed, hardened criminals.

Never.
The door clanged shut.

50

"I" Plus Thirty Days

Hildi grinned as she announced a breakthrough. Cheers rebounded off the walls. She and Maria were all smiles, but they wanted sleep more than the accolades. The bags under their eyes needed saddlebags of their own.

Hildi acknowledged the praise and turned to the station commander. "We found a single nucleotide polymorphism that accounted for influenza resistance."

"Could you put that in English?" Joe scratched his head.

She laughed. "We found the gene."

Joe grinned. "Ladies, I'd tip my hat if I was wearing one."

Hildi and Maria curtsied, or at least tried to, and burst into giggles.

"I'll get Mission Control." Joe whooped as he sped to the control room. The others followed.

"Houston, this is ISS."

"This is Houston."

Joe handed the mic to Hildi. "You tell 'em."

"This is Hildi. We found the key to the vaccine."

Applause in Mission Control drowned out any response from CAPCOM.

"Roger." A smile flavored CAPCOM Pete's response. "A few million people around the world will be glad to hear that. Congrats."

"It wasn't just me. Maria and I worked together. And my brother gave us invaluable information. Without his help, even with the advantages of weightlessness, we never could have developed it."

"Acknowledged, ISS."

Hildi keyed the mic. "Houston, I need to relay my findings to CDC Director Alan Hunt as quickly as possible."

CAPCOM paused, apparently consulting the communications officer. "Roger. We're setting it up now." Mission Control made the connection within a few minutes.

Hildi slowed her racing words. "Director, we used a thermocycler to conduct polymerase chain reaction. MX1 showed an SNP at marker 75. The people with immunity had thymine at that location whereas the others had a cytosine."

"Thymine, huh?" Hunt's words tumbled together as if he couldn't wait to relay the news to the staff. "We didn't get to that level in our PCR work. Maybe your microgravity made a difference after all. Good job, Hildi."

"Sir, without Chet's preliminary work on this, we never could have discovered the crucial nucleotide so quickly. He deserves the credit."

****

Frank strangled the snarky words on his tongue. Was Hildi actually sticking up for her brother? Her arrogant, belittling brother?

Director Hunt clipped his words. "I don't share your confidence that your brother was such a big help. I'll review the research with the rest of the staff once we receive your e-mail with all the details. Again, thanks for your work. We'll discuss this later after we get through the crisis."

Houston ended the connection with the CDC. Hildi handed the mic to Joe, who continued the conversation with Mission Control.

Pete relayed the assignments for the return home. "The CDC wants Hildi home ASAP. NASA agrees. We'll calculate a return trajectory and use the next available window. Besides Hildi, crew will be Dan, Jasper, and Frank."

Frank's mouth dropped open. Why would NASA want him back on the next flight? A quicker court martial?

"Acknowledged." Joe scratched his head. "Uh, Houston, you mind explaining your reasoning on this one?"

"It's priority one that Hildi be on the flight. Dan and Jasper are the sickest, so they're also going. We also want Frank on board."

"So Shorty, Leonid, Maria, and I will stay." Joe's sigh could probably be heard in Mission Control without the use of radio. He'd been due to rotate back to Earth.

"That's right. The flight surgeon says the four of you are past the danger point, but if any of you get sicker, I want Maria to be there. She has the most medical training except for Hildi."

"So when are you folks planning another trip up here?"

"Russia will have a Soyuz ready in about three

weeks."

Frank caught Joe's lopsided smile. "If y'all hold off another week, I can break my own record." Joe covered his mic and turned to the others. "Wouldn't that be something?"

Joe's happy expression puzzled Frank. The old cowboy was a stubborn and prideful codger, always wanting to beat his own accomplishments. Personally, Frank wouldn't have wanted to stay nine months and deal with the long recovery period after losing all that muscle tone in space. Six months in physical therapy? No thanks. On the other hand, if Frank stayed on the station, the media might ease up on him. *No.* Better to face the music now than let dread of the unknown chew up his insides.

After a muted conversation in Houston, Steve took over the mic. "Joe, I know you're disappointed—in spite of the prospect of staying up there two hundred and seventy days—but that's my decision."

"Yes, sir."

Frank huffed a breath, struggling to keep his voice level. He didn't deserve the driver's seat. "Why do you want me as pilot?"

"Because I want one healthy pilot on board." The snap of a breaking pencil betrayed Steve's strain.

Hildi's eyes widened at his angry outburst. Frank only nodded. The man probably hadn't slept in weeks.

"Dan's too sick to do anything. Jasper's healthy enough to be commander on the return, but you're more experienced as pilot. I need you at the helm. That's an order."

"Yes, sir."

"You'll have to deal with a shortage of fuel since we overloaded *Valiant* for the trip up."

"Do not pass go, do not collect two hundred dollars," Jasper quipped.

Frank smiled, but the thought of flying without wiggle room for emergencies set his teeth on edge.

"Leonid, I'm sorry." Steve's tone turned apologetic. "You were due to rotate back, too. Your liaison here suggested you stay and continue to represent Russia in the spirit of international cooperation."

"So, Houston, when do you want these folks to leave? I'm not complaining about our extra guests, mind, but we're kinda cramped." Joe drawled into the mic.

"Eight hours." CAPCOM Pete returned to his duties. "We want reentry ASAP. The CDC wants Hildi's expertise and her completed work yesterday."

Frank's stomach tightened. He had a bad feeling about this. Then he glanced at Dan.

His friend shivered with fever. He needed a hospital, and any delay would only worsen his condition. Frank would rather risk anything but that. "We can do it."

Everyone gave a thumbs-up. Joe nodded. "The posse here's rarin' to go."

"Acknowledged, ISS. Keep us informed. Houston out."

Frank's guilt and gratitude chased each other around the track of his mind. Was God giving him a chance to redeem himself? He turned to the others. "I still don't understand. Joe and Shorty have plenty of experience—"

"But not as much as you." Dan coughed, trying to catch his breath.

"Some experience."

Dan's eyes drooped with fatigue and fever, but he gripped Frank's shoulder. "Stop blaming yourself. If I'd been the pilot when the accident happened, it would have happened on my watch."

This time, Frank didn't shrug off Dan. He welcomed the reassurance.

Joe leaned toward him. "Bottom line, the flight director gave you an assignment. End of discussion."

Dan wheezed. "You have your orders, soldier."

Frank stared at him. They used to call each other "soldier" when they were kids. Hope surged like a tide finally coming back to shore. Could God repair their friendship? A disturbing thought intruded. Did he really want the friendship repaired? Yes.

Frank scooted to his corner of the station and packed his personal belongings. Remembering his desperate prayers after Jasper pulled him from the brink of suicide, he added another one to the pile. "Lord, I've really made a mess of things with Dan. Help me make it right. And please, take control of my anger. I can't do it by myself. Amen."

He waited for some sign. He didn't feel any different, but what was he expecting? A voice from the stars? He'd have to take it on faith that God would help. *Guess I'm a little out of practice when it comes to trust.*

The tight schedule shoved further thought aside. They removed the lab's curtain, the last psychological barrier in the war against the virus. Frank felt exposed, as if he'd forgotten his underwear. Hildi had insisted on frequent use of hand sanitizer, but Jasper claimed it made his fingers too wrinkled to work.

Frank rolled his sleep cocoon into a compact cylinder and tried to stuff it into his over-packed bag.

Pack. His thoughts swirled. He always packed one thing after another into his bag until it verged on splitting at the seams. Maybe anger was the same way. But how did he unpack? God didn't whisper the answer, but Frank knew what he needed to do.

He propelled himself into Dan's room. Dan had finished stowing his belongings and clung to a handhold, jerking with every cough.

"Dan?"

"What's up?" Dan's croak made Frank cringe.

No one told him it would be so hard. Frank's throat tightened, but he launched the words anyway. "Uh, I just wanted to apologize again. I've been such a doofus."

"Yes, you have." Dan's smile couldn't hide the effort it took him to speak.

Frank swallowed. "Will you forgive me?"

"Yes. Will you forgive *me*?"

"Forgive you? For what?"

"We used to be friends." Dan squeezed his eyes shut. "I knew you were fooling around, and I said nothing. I should have said something."

Frank's blood pressure bounced between anger and sorrow. He wished his friend had confronted him. But would it have made a difference? *No.* He knew himself better now.

He paused, weighing his words. Could he forgive? Frank searched for his jealousy and found it lurking around a corner. *Get lost.* "I forgive you."

Frank extended his hand. It wasn't good enough for Dan. He grabbed Frank into a bear hug. Tears puddled in Frank's eyes. Although he wiped them on his sleeve, droplets escaped, hanging in the air like jewels.

****

Frank didn't relish becoming a human sandwich. Objects had no weight in space, but they certainly had inertia. Grunting, he slowed the movement of some equipment destined for the capsule before it rammed him against the hatch. "Hey, I can't stop a locomotive, and that last piece was coming like a freight train."

"Sorry." Dan's halfhearted smile faded into a grimace. "Don't know my own strength."

"Ha. You have as much strength as a teacup poodle."

Hildi floated over and touched Dan's forehead. "Still warm. Have you taken any acetaminophen lately?"

"Yes, Mommy. Ten minutes ago." Dan's smile barely cracked his weary face.

"You're too sick to keep up the bucket brigade. Go lie down. I'm putting you on oxygen."

Dan gave up without protest. He must be sicker than he looked. At least his buddy had some sense.

Hildi kissed Dan's temple.

Frank stuffed his anger back into his bag of thoughts. *Stop acting like a teenager.* Two of his best friends were batting eyes at each other, and he couldn't even conjure up a bit of happiness for them. He had no one to blame but himself for Hildi breaking off their engagement after he'd shattered it with his flings. Dan would never do that to her. But Frank's jealousy still stank like rotten meat.

Hildi nudged the next box of supplies to Frank, who guided it to Shorty. Dan clung to a handhold in the grip of a coughing fit, his face concealed behind an oxygen mask.

"You OK?" Frank frowned. Dan was *not* okay, but he seldom complained.

Dan held up his hand until he could talk again. "Yeah. This flu is no picnic."

Moans and coughs surrounded them. Frank shook his head. Why was he spared while the others suffered?

His mind snapped back to the piloting job ahead of him. Dan claimed that the lightning strike hadn't caused any permanent damage. Frank still worried.

With the gear stowed, only good-byes remained. The recycled air of the station would soon be history, replaced by the not-quite-so-stale air of *Valiant*. Frank couldn't wait for the first smell of home.

Dan, Hildi, and Jasper hugged everyone and entered the capsule. Frank lagged behind. He turned to face the remaining astronauts and forced out another long-overdue apology. "I'm sorry. I lost control of my temper and broke the vial. I put all of your lives at risk."

They shifted their weightless stance but said nothing. Frank's hope for redemption faded. He turned to go.

Joe broke the uncomfortable silence. "It's gone and forgotten. Don't let anyone back on Earth pester you about it."

Frank nodded, not trusting his trussed tongue. They group-hugged.

"Y'all get off my station." Joe's gruff voice didn't fool Frank, who saw the tears welling up. "You're holding up progress."

With one last grasp of Joe's hand, Frank sped into *Valiant* and took the pilot's seat to Jasper's right, Hildi and Dan behind them. The hatch *whooshed* shut. They check-listed every system on the spacecraft. All nominal.

"Houston, this is *Valiant*. Ready to undock." Jasper craned his neck to the crew behind him. "You backseat drivers got any objections?" Frank caught Dan's tired grin and Hildi's thumbs up.

Dan closed his eyes and croaked, "May the Lord keep us in the palm of His hand."

Frank agreed with every word.

"This is Houston. You are GO for undocking procedure. Godspeed."

CAPCOM Pete's order sent exhilaration down Frank's spine. *Time to rock and roll.* He took a deep breath.

Jasper slipped into command mode. "Release docking clamps."

Frank pulled on a handle. "Clamps released."

"Fire attitude jets."

Frank eased the capsule away from ISS. *Valiant* had a different feel than *Reconciliation*. He shrugged. Each of the simulators back in Houston had its own quirks. This was no different. With the stress and lack of sleep during the last few days, his sensitivity had kicked into overdrive.

"Wow, look at that." Hildi pointed out the window. "I think I can see the Great Wall of China."

"You can see forever." Jasper sang a few lines of the song, his voice raspy. Dan tried to join in but then sank into another coughing fit.

"You're gonna make it." Frank reached behind him and grasped Dan's shoulder. He had to make it.

"Yeah."

Frank's gaze lingered on his friend. He'd never

seen any astronaut so sick during a mission. He glanced at Hildi for reassurance, but the sight below them had captured her attention.

Dan's hacking increased. Hildi offered him a couple of pills. He was snoring within a half hour.

"What'd you give him?" Frank raised an eyebrow.

"Just Tylenol." She grinned. "Tylenol PM. He needed to sleep, and he wasn't about to do so voluntarily."

Jasper nodded his approval. "Good move. Maybe he'll feel better in a few hours."

"Maybe."

Frank piloted *Valiant* into a parking orbit a few miles from the station's docking collar. They would await the command for reentry while catching a few ZZZ's. The wait would allow NASA to calculate a new trajectory that would avoid the typhoon brewing near the original splashdown site.

"Don't worry," CAPCOM said. "The ships are already cruising into position. Super Carrier *George W. Bush* will head recovery." He paused. "They have an excellent team of doctors on board."

"Acknowledged." Jasper glanced at Dan. "Tell them to get ready for four weary astronauts." His voice turned serious. "Can you give us an update on our fuel situation for reentry maneuvers?"

"Extra consumption will be minimal," CAPCOM claimed. "Get some sleep."

Frank shook his head. Houston's vague response indicated *Valiant* would need every drop. Nothing he could do about it except whisper an extra prayer. He willed his steeled muscles to relax and wiggled into a more comfortable position for a catnap. Dandy Dan snorted in his sleep.

"Night-night, *Valiant*."

Jasper answered. "Roger. Wake us in a few hours, will you? Wouldn't want to miss splashdown."

"Don't worry about that."

"Acknowledged. *Valiant* out."

Frank shut his eyes, just for a moment…

****

A trumpet's blare of reveille jolted Frank awake. He glared at the radio.

Jasper and Hildi groaned. Frank held up his hand. "All in favor of telling Mission Control they're calling in sick today, say *aye*."

"Aye."

Hildi touched Dan's arm. "How do you feel?"

Dan shook his head as if to clear the fog from his brain. He smoothed the wrinkles out of his jumpsuit. "Still like death warmed over, but at least I slept." He stared at Hildi and narrowed his eyes. "Wait a minute. What did you do to me?"

Hildi's mischievous smile answered him. Frank knew that smile. Apparently, so did Dan. "Not fair."

She shrugged. "You needed some shuteye."

Dan's pallor remained unchanged in spite of the extra rest. Frank wished Hildi had created an instant cure instead of a vaccine to prevent others from catching the flu. He gulped air in response to his friend's labored breathing.

Jasper radioed Mission Control that they were all fully awake now, thank you very much.

CAPCOM Pete chuckled. "*Valiant*, the flight surgeon asks for Hildi's visual assessment of the crew."

Hildi checked everyone's temperature, including her own. She spoke into her mic. "Houston, Frank still has no sign of the virus. Jasper and I have mild cases." She paused. "Dan has double pneumonia. He should be hospitalized as soon as we land."

Dan glared at her. "I feel better, honestly."

Jasper craned his neck. "And pigs pilot space shuttles."

What would the short time under g load do to Dan's lungs? Frank's momentary discomfort would be nothing compared to Dan's.

"Earth to Frank, Earth to Frank." Jasper grinned as Frank tore his focus back to reentry procedure. They checked off the final systems. Jasper switched to command voice. "De-orbit on my mark."

Frank gripped the joystick, eager to fire the main engine that would slow the capsule and tip them into reentry. Going home. Always the best—and saddest—part of any mission.

"Thank you, ISS," Hildi whispered.

Frank checked the instrument panel one last time.

A light blacked out.

****

"What happened?" Hildi scrutinized the dark indicator as her heart plunged into a deeper dark.

"Don't know," Jasper said in a clipped voice.

"Must have been...the lightning strike." Dan's voice faltered.

Hildi frowned as she turned to him. "Don't talk." She patted his arm.

"Got to. At launch, the instruments went out." Dan paused to wheeze in a breath. "But not for this long."

Hildi's stomach did an I'm-in-the-Vomit-Comet twist.

Jasper took control. "Houston, this is *Valiant*. Still unable to restore the drogue indicator. We could use a little illumination on our problem."

How could the man joke at a time like this?

CAPCOM responded. "This is Houston. We copy your problem and are working on a solution."

Jasper glanced at the other astronauts. "Anything we should try? I'm open to suggestions."

"Reboot...computer." Dan followed his statement with another coughing fit. His lungs should have flown out of his mouth by now.

Hildi's worry pounded on the door of her faith like an obnoxious salesman. "Isn't that dangerous? As in, we might not get the computer back?" No computer, no control, no nothing.

Frank's grim look could have made the bluebird of happiness die of a heart attack. "What choice do we have? If it doesn't work—"

"We'll be in the same boat. Uh, spacecraft." Jasper craned his neck at Dan, who nodded. "Houston, Colonel Stockton feels the situation will resolve itself if we reboot."

"Negative, *Valiant*. We'll let you know what we determine is your best course of action."

Hildi willed her heart rate to slow as they waited. And waited. Frank death-gripped the controls. Dan moaned. Even Jasper looked nervous. Nervous? Hildi was ready to bolt and leave her skin behind.

Jasper keyed his mic. "Uh, Houston, all our indicators are GO except for the drogue. Please advise."

Hildi's breath caught in her throat. If the small parachute failed, it wouldn't drag the main ones out to slow the capsule's descent. If they hit at terminal velocity...

The astronauts waited as Mission Control apparently had a long conversation about the problem. Maybe they were taking bets on where the spacecraft would splat.

"*Valiant*, this is Houston. We think it's the indicator light that's malfunctioned."

Think? Hildi gulped.

Jasper spoke to the crew. "They're not telling us everything."

"Great. Just great." Frank echoed Hildi's frustration and fear. Astronauts were supposed to be fearless. If the public only knew...

CAPCOM continued. "Flight says you have two options. You can return to ISS, or you can start reentry procedure and hope we're right about the parachute light."

"Hope? Is that the best you can do?" Frank strangled the joystick.

"*Valiant*, we believe the drogue will open. Splashdown site remains at the new coordinates."

Jasper took a vote. "How many want to reenter the atmosphere and possibly become a five-inch pancake? I vote GO."

Frank paused then raised his hand, thumb up. "GO."

Dan mimicked the gesture. "GO."

"Hildi?"

She hesitated. Returning to the station held some appeal. But one glance at Dan stiffened her resolve. "Dan needs hospitalization, and I need to get my findings to the CDC. I say GO."

"Houston, this is *Valiant*. Request permission to begin landing procedure."

"Roger, *Valiant*. You are GO for landing. Godspeed."

Speed wouldn't be the problem.

****

Dan watched the gauges through bleary eyes. He was too sick to care about hiding his symptoms. Couldn't fool Hildi, anyway. His protests that he felt fine bounced off a woman with a selective hearing problem. She held a stethoscope to his chest and slapped his hand when he tried to remove it. "Your pneumonia's worsening. I'm ordering immediate admittance to ICU once we splash down. The aircraft carrier has a well-equipped hospital on board."

He stuck out his tongue at her. She pointed at it. "Yes, and I should make a note that you have a case of chronic tongue spasms. Looks serious."

Dan grimaced. He tried strapping down but couldn't cinch the straps tight. He had no strength left, and that was *before* reentry. Then he felt a strong tug.

"Don't want you to fall out." Frank gripped his shoulder before floating back to his seat and pulling his own harness taut.

"Thanks." Dan smiled at his renewed friendship with Frank.

He still needed to fix things with Hildi. This time he'd do it right. Assuming they survived. If they didn't, they'd still be together, although he'd rather confess his true feelings before then. Like now. He squeezed Hildi's hand. She squeezed back.

"I love you." Finally, he'd said it. Long overdue.

"I want that in writing." Her eyes filled with tears. "I love you, too."

I've been a fool to wait so long. Her smile warmed him. So did the worsening fever.

Jasper craned his neck and grinned. "I hate to interrupt such a tender moment, but we have a spacecraft to land." He turned to Frank. "Fire engines on my mark."

Reentry procedure whipped all musings from Dan's mind. Frank fired the retro rockets. The capsule slowed then tipped into an end-first position, the view of Earth shifting to the black of space. Gravity gripped them as they flew backward toward Earth. Jasper grasped his own throttle, ready to help Frank fight the bucking from the thickening atmosphere.

"Houston, this is *Valiant*. Entering ionization blackout."

CAPCOM's voice crackled. "Roger, Jasper. Will pick up your signal in two minutes."

"Elevator to Earth, going down."

Dan rolled his eyes at Jasper's jaunty tone. Same old Jasper.

Gravity sat on Dan's constricted lungs. The spacecraft pitched, rolled, yawed, and seemed determined to do everything but line up its rear end to the required orientation. Once they emerged from blackout, they'd try to deploy the drogue. If it worked as designed, they'd splash down safely. If it failed, the spacecraft would hurtle toward death.

In two minutes, they'd know.

****

Frank's muscles hardened in concentration as he fought to control *Valiant*'s descent. Superheated gases glowed red through the window, thrust away by the capsule's blunt end. He called out speed and altitude, but it seemed unnecessary. They were plunging toward Earth for splashdown or destruction. They'd return as heroes, dead or alive. Frank shook his head. At least three of them would be heroes. The jury was still out on his own status. He clung to the hope that God would intervene.

Jasper glanced his way. "Hold her steady."

Two minutes passed. The red glow dimmed. Still no radio contact. Frank tensed as Jasper keyed his mic. "Houston, this is *Valiant*, do you read? Houston, this is *Valiant*, do you read?"

"*Valiant*, this is Houston." Pete's whoop shattered Frank's eardrums. The clapping in Mission Control drowned out the crew's cheers.

The mood shifted as tension crowded the capsule. The astronauts held their collective breath.

Jasper's confident-commander voice slipped a little. "Deploy drogue on my mark." The change from his usual tone jolted Frank's insides as much as the pull of the parachutes would. Or should. Frank lifted the cover for the parachute toggle and poised one finger over it.

"Three…two…one…mark."

Frank flipped the toggle. "Drogue deployed." *This is it.* He whispered a prayer. "Please let the parachutes open." Amens echoed from the astronauts and Houston.

Frank's muscles clamped his bones. Now they'd find out if those parachutes were worth the millions NASA spent on them. Then he chuckled. Mission

Control couldn't do anything and neither could they. Their survival depended on a billow of cloth and the breath of God.

A tug pushed Frank deeper into his seat as the drogue caught the air, followed by a violent jerk as the main parachutes opened. A porch-swing sway welcomed *Valiant* back to Earth. Relief flooded him.

Jasper merely shrugged. "Hardly even exciting." He cued the mic. "Houston, this is *Valiant*. Drogue and main parachutes open. Coming down on a wing and a prayer." He sang a few bars of a song Frank didn't recognize but he hummed anyway.

"Copy that, *Valiant*. You're headed for a perfect splashdown, so just sit back and enjoy the ride. We'll take it from here."

The capsule splashed into the Pacific and bobbed to the surface.

Valiant was home.

****

Hildi unbuckled her harness before *Valiant*'s second bob in the water. Dan had turned gray. As grins split the astronauts' faces, she felt his forehead and checked his breathing, now labored. The pressure of normal gravity made every movement an effort for her, but Dan's struggle wrenched her gut into Gordian knots.

Jasper keyed the mic. "*Valiant*, this is Houston. When can we expect those choppers? We have a sick man here." Jasper caught Hildi's eye and quirked a question.

"He needs ICU stat." She adjusted the oxygen mask over Dan's face mask and unstrapped his restraints. His body sagged.

"*Valiant*, this is Chopper One from *George W. Bush*." A female voice wavered with vibration. "ETA five minutes. Welcome home."

"Acknowledged, Chopper One. Glad to be home and in one piece." Jasper turned to his crewmates. "We'll take Dan off first. Help him." His eyes reflected his compassionate soul before he turned back to the instruments and initiated shutdown procedure.

Frank and Hildi moved in slow motion, grunting as they fought to maintain their balance in the pitching capsule. Each of them donned orange life vests retrieved from a compartment. Hildi wrestled Dan into a vest and cinched it tight.

Jasper turned off the ventilation system. "Somebody want to roll down a window?"

"*Valiant*, this is Chopper One. Divers are in the water. Stand by."

"Acknowledged."

Hildi and Frank lifted Dan out of his chair then maneuvered him toward the hatch. His legs didn't support him. Jasper keyed the mic. "Request Colonel Stockton be airlifted to carrier, emergency priority."

"Acknowledged."

The spacecraft rocked as divers secured buoyancy devices around the spacecraft. *Valiant* seemed to sit higher in the water, rocking in the slight Pacific swells.

Someone banged on the capsule.

"Come in," Jasper quipped.

Divers removed the hatch. Hildi squinted at the bright sun.

Frank shifted so he supported Dan around the waist, with Dan's arm around his shoulder. Frank grunted. "You've put on some weight, haven't you?"

"The borscht." Dan's humor *tha-thumped* Hildi's heart, but his hoarse whisper made her want to breathe for him. *He'll make it. He has to. I love him.*

A diver peered into the capsule, pulled the scuba regulator out of his mouth, and grinned. "Ready?"

Frank nodded. "We were born ready."

"This is *Valiant*, signing off." Jasper's last words for the mission weighed on Hildi's heart more than the gravity. She'd never see this little spacecraft again. She turned her back on the instrument panel as she helped Frank push Dan out, her legs shaking from muscle atrophy. Strong divers in neoprene wetsuits lifted him out.

Frank exited. Hildi grabbed the case containing the vaccine and followed after one last gaze around. She emerged from the hatch, blinked in the sun, and patted *Valiant*'s metal skin. "Thank you."

The fresh tang of the sea replaced the stale odor that *whooshed* from the spacecraft's interior, something she hadn't noticed until now. If she looked as bad as it smelled...

Divers dragged Frank over the lip of the waiting orange lifeboat. Dan lay at the bow, additional divers bending over him. Hildi allowed the Navy men to grab her under her armpits and lift her into the boat. Jasper emerged last.

She stared at the capsule, remembering the last heroic act of Commander Larry.

Frank read her thoughts and whispered, "Larry should have been here."

Her eyes misted.

The nuclear super aircraft carrier was a blur on the horizon. One gray helicopter circled them at a respectful distance as another thumped overhead.

"Get that litter down here stat," Hildi bellowed.

Orange-suited men leaned over the chopper's side and pushed out a Stokes litter. The two rescuers in the lifeboat signaled them to lower the wire stretcher, but it took forever before they could grab and guide it. The men strapped Dan into the litter. Hildi shivered as she saw the man in her life lying inert, wrapped like a mummy. She kissed his forehead. He smiled but didn't open his eyes.

One of the divers turned to Hildi. "Give me the vaccine."

She hugged the case to her heart then realized how ridiculous her response was. She handed it over. He secured the case to the litter then gave a thumbs-up signal. "Take him up."

The winch drew the cable taut and lifted its burden into Chopper One. Hildi recognized IV bags and other equipment in the helicopter's dark interior before Dan disappeared into its gaping maw.

"I'm going with him," Hildi shouted in her Level 4 voice above the chopper's roar.

The nearest diver winced and held his ear. He grasped her shoulder. "They'll take him immediately to the carrier's ICU unit. Military jets will deliver the vaccine to the CDC."

Hildi fumed. Dan would receive great care on the carrier. But now that he'd confessed his love, she didn't want him out of her sight.

The first helicopter closed its door and hovered for a moment. The pilot saluted then turned the craft toward the approaching carrier and thumped away. Her prayers for Dan followed on swift wings.

The remaining copter moved into position and lowered an orange collar. Gray, orange, gray, orange—

Hildi shook her head. Francine would itch to change the Navy's color scheme.

The divers hooked her into the collar that fit under her armpits then signaled. She lifted from the raft. The sensation of swinging on the line reminded her of the gentle floating on the capsule's parachutes. God had rescued them, and Dan couldn't be in better hands. Her tension drained.

****

Frank shielded his eyes as a chopper lifted from the aircraft carrier, carrying Dan to a waiting hospital on Oahu.

The doctors had pumped Dan full of antibiotics and put him on monitors the moment they had their hands on him. ICU at the top naval hospital in Hawaii would take over now.

Frank's ears pounded. The copter's thumping faded as he lost sight of it. He squeezed Hildi's shoulder before he turned to the crew crowding around them. After the usual greeting by the ship's captain as he welcomed them aboard, Frank collapsed into a wheelchair. Exhaustion from unrelenting stress overpowered him. Dan's flu-weakened body would struggle for every breath, hospital or no hospital. Gravity must be sitting on his lungs like a heavyweight wrestler.

The ship's medical staff checked their vital signs before assigning Frank, Jasper, and Hildi to bunks for a few hours of shuteye. He exchanged handclasps with the doctors before he fell into bed.

51

"I" Plus Thirty-six Days

Frank skidded to a halt inside the entrance to the Houston hospital. Reporters jammed the waiting area. Fortunately, he knew another way to Dan's room, and no one saw him. At Dan's open door, a military policeman nodded permission for Frank to enter. Unless Frank missed his guess, his friends were having one of those mushy conversations. Hildi leaned over Dan with her lips puckered.

"Ahem."

The lovebirds startled, blushing. Frank gave Hildi a friendly hug and grasped Dan's shoulder then plopped into a nearby chair.

"Hi. So, how was *your* week?" Dan's steady voice contrasted with his raspy one after splashdown. The doctors in Oahu had held him for five long days in ICU before they deemed him recovered enough to earn a regular room and be transferred here.

Frank grimaced. "Paperwork. And more paperwork. NASA must have deforested a mountain."

Dan pointed to the IV stretched between his hand and a monitor. "At least you're not chained to a bed." A healthy tone had replaced the grayness on his face, though some of that could be due to his lingering blush.

Hildi squeezed Dan's hand. "The doctors weaned him off oxygen this morning, and his white-cell count is returning to normal, but he'll still have to stay a couple more days."

"Two more days?" Frank whistled. "I'd prefer the paperwork."

"Yeah. I'm about to go stir-crazy."

Frank's eyebrows quirked. "Packed into a spacecraft the size of a washing machine, and you're complaining about a spacious—pardon the pun—and beautifully appointed room?" He swept out his arms to take in the white walls, plastered with get-well cards from across the nation.

Jasper barged in, wearing his NASA togs and badge. The MP closed the door, a look of amusement on his face. Jasper gave hugs to all then jerked his thumb at the door. "Hey, what's with the media in the lobby?"

"The usual. Waiting for the next big story while driving us all nuts." Hildi shrugged.

The telephone rang. Dan rolled his eyes. "Probably my grandmother again. She checks on me every hour, on the hour." He picked up the handset. "Hi, Grandma."

Dan stiffened. He stage-whispered, "I'm holding for the President." He pressed the speaker button.

"This is Reginald Benchley." The President's tenor voice held a smile.

"Mr. President, sir. This is Colonel Dan Stockton." If Dan made his greeting any more formal, he would have bowed. Frank barely kept himself from standing at attention.

"At ease, Colonel."

"Hildi, Frank, and Jasper are here. I've put the

phone on speaker."

"Excellent. I'm glad you're all there. Just wanted to call and convey the hope of the nation for your speedy recovery. You've been in the country's thoughts and prayers, and we're all glad you landed safely." He lowered his voice. "You had me worried."

"You weren't the only one," Jasper quipped. He ducked his head. "Mr. President."

Their commander-in-chief chuckled. "I'm planning a little presentation on the White House lawn on the seventeenth. Think you can make it?"

"Yes, sir." Four voices spoke in unison.

"Good. My chief of staff will be in touch. Thanks again."

Dan hung up, daze clouding his eyes.

Barry Stokes, NASA's public affairs officer, walked in. He nodded at the astronauts. Then he started moving chairs against a far wall and reached for Jasper's.

"Hey. I was using that." Jasper surrendered his chair after a brief tug of war.

"Sorry. We need the extra space." Barry continued to rearrange the furniture. Frank had a bad feeling about this.

A few moments later, men and women crowded the room, brandishing video cameras and microphones. American and NASA flags magically appeared as a patriotic backdrop. Barry fussed the astronauts into position like mannequins in a department-store window. Plastering on an engaging smile, standard attire for photo ops, Frank fought to keep his eyes open with every camera flash. The reporters grinned through every moment of the clamor, but Dan tucked himself further into the sheets until Barry scowled. *Here we go again.* As Frank expected, the media aimed their volleys at him first.

"Frank, what really happened up there?"

"Colonel Schotenheimer, do you think NASA will clear you?"

Frank stuck to protocol. "I'm sorry, I'm not at liberty to say. No comment."

"Hey, hotshot, getting the moon shot?" The silky voice cut through the chatter. His brain hiccupped. *Nancy.* He stared past the first ring of journalists to an attractive brunette with diamond stud earrings. His last would-be affair. The star reporter of the *Houston Herald* had shown too much class to succumb to his charms. Surprise widened his smile.

"Well, Nancy, I'd sure like to. Got a lot of competition, though." He gestured at Jasper and Dan. "But they'll have to catch me first."

The members of the press laughed. Nancy gave him a Girl Scout's salute and a warm smile. The media trained their rifles on other prey.

"Dan, will the doctors release you soon?"

"Hildi, will you return to the CDC?"

"Jasper, do you think we'll beat China to Mars?"

Frank continued to pose for the cameras as Nancy aimed a surreptitious wink at him.

After a long few minutes, Barry held up his hand. He opened the door, eyebrows raised. Murmuring among themselves, the reporters filed out.

The NASA PAO saluted the astronauts. "Good day, gentlemen. And lady." After grabbing the flags, he strode out.

Frank stared at the door, wondering what Nancy was thinking.

****

Dan took a deep breath. It felt so good to breathe on his own. He pinched his nose, still itching from the things they'd inserted up his nostrils. At least he hadn't been wearing them when the media visited. The brief encounter reminded him of old dreams in which he showed up naked for launch. Dan squeezed the hand of the woman he loved before turning his head toward Jasper. "What's the word from the station?"

"Joe says he's fit as a fiddle and happy as a hog in slop." Jasper grinned. "The old cowboy is determined to beat his record for days in space. Looks like he'll do it, too. The Soyuz launch's been delayed for another month."

"Where's Joe from, anyway? What part of Texas?" Hildi cocked her head. "I never had the chance to ask him."

"Milwaukee."

Frank twisted the lanyard of his NASA badge. "Leonid's still coughing, but Shorty and Maria are fine."

"And the pandemic?" Jasper turned to Hildi with serious eyes.

"We're winning the war." Hildi's smile warmed Dan down to his toes. They'd barely had time to talk with all the interruptions. Now her focus was back to her work. Would he ever have a chance to tell her what was on his mind?

He turned wistful, his mind still centered on the mission. He gazed at his fellow astronauts. "We made a good team." He glanced at Hildi. *We'll make a good team.*

Jasper quirked his eyebrow. "Well, next time, I

hope it's not quite as exciting. I'd hate to play another game of catch-the-water with such competition. You guys play rough."

"NASA grilled me within an inch of my life." Frank grimaced. "I've been suspended pending an investigation. NASA's still not convinced I didn't cause the accident. Right now, neither am I."

Jasper laid a hand on his shoulder and tightened his grip. "We've been through this before, Frank. Just drop it."

"I'm having a hard time doing that." Frank glanced at his watch. "I'm due back at the ranch. Another round of questions from the NASA director, no doubt." His chair scraped as he stood and walked over to the bed.

Dan wrapped him in an awkward hug. Why did Frank keep harping on this? Dan wished he had some relax juice for his friend. "I know you'll be vindicated."

"I wish I had your confidence." Frank left, head bowed as if he carried a heavy-lift rocket on his shoulders. Jasper followed hot on his heels.

Dan squeezed Hildi's hand "Where were we before we were so rudely interrupted?"

"Discussing our dangerous jobs, if I recall."

That wasn't what they were discussing. Or at least not what Dan wanted to discuss. He stroked her cheek.

Hildi stepped back. "Dan, we can't keep up like this. It's not just the danger. It's our schedules. You could be gone for months on the next mission—"

"And you could be working in the Congo for weeks, tracking down some new germ."

Hildi inclined her head. "Touché."

Dan cringed. It was a stale argument that started early in their relationship and apparently wasn't going

away anytime soon. Shorty had told him, "Go get her."
How?

52

"I" Plus Forty Days

Frank shuffled into the room like a zombie and faced the jackals. He sat down at a table already crowded with Steve, Hildi, Jasper, and a geek named Nick. The scene seemed surreal after yesterday's meeting with his boss.

The camera flashes blinded him and made him wish for dark sunglasses. He hated press conferences under any circumstances, but this crowd was primed for an inquisition. They expected a beheading.

Barry Stokes presided from the podium and glared everyone into his seat. "All right, people, let's settle down. This is a press conference, not a circus. You all know Steve Walters, flight director for the *Reconciliation* and *Valiant* missions."

The PAO stepped aside as Steve commandeered the lectern. "Six weeks ago, we recovered the damaged *Reconciliation* after a hard-fought effort to control reentry. We transported her here to the Johnson Space Center. Our scientists examined every bit of information from our telemetry and transcripts as well as the spacecraft itself. We made a startling discovery. Allow me to introduce Nick Crane, chief of instrumentation. Nick?"

The geek opened his laptop. His fingers danced

over the keyboard as the screen behind him flashed his PowerPoint presentation. "In examining the system, we discovered a flaw in the controls. It appears a foreign object lodged itself in the mechanism."

Frank's attention wandered from the droning analysis to the sea of reporters, his would-be executioners. He startled as he spotted Nancy, front row center. She winked. He hoped his face wasn't radiating an embarrassing flush. Maybe the press would think it was sunburn.

"Thanks, Nick." Steve nodded him silent.

Nick blinked at the interruption, a frown showing he wasn't done. He opened and closed his mouth like a tuna.

"That's all we need at the moment, Nick. Good job."

Geek blanked the PowerPoint screen, closed his laptop, and sat without another word.

Steve resumed command. "Nick's team of investigators tore apart the instrument panel and found the foreign object. A screw. This one." He held up a small plastic bag containing the small silvery item. Cameras clicked and telephoto lenses whirred as journalists yelled their questions. Stokes's upraised hand silenced them.

The flight director continued after nodding to the press. "This screw caused erratic behavior of *Reconciliation*'s thrusters and resulted in the crash with the International Space Station. Colonel Schotenheimer slowed the capsule and prevented total failure of the station's integrity. When it was determined the spacecraft and ISS were locked together, he performed a rather unorthodox maneuver that separated the two without further damage."

Frank quirked half a smile. Steve had forgotten to mention that he acted without orders. Steve had given him a tongue-lashing before telling him about the screw.

"Our analysis shows that without Colonel Schotenheimer's extraordinary piloting ability, both the capsule and the station could have been damaged or destroyed, along with the catastrophic loss of all astronauts."

Gasps escaped into the room. Apparently, the news hadn't leaked out. Frank's composure slipped as the journalists' faces morphed from condemnation to respect.

Steve motioned Frank to the podium and grabbed his shoulder. He felt momentary stage fright as he stared into the crowd of correspondents, but he needn't have worried about speaking. Everyone stood and applauded. Heat rose up his neck. Frank succeeded in diverting some of the ovation to the others but had to repeat "thank you" uncounted times.

From villain to hero in sixty seconds.

"Ahem." Stokes quieted the reporters.

Frank swallowed a billiard ball and turned to the flight director. "Steve, I appreciate your faith in me and your confidence that never wavered. All the crew at Mission Control were phenomenal in their support." He glanced at his notes although he knew his prepared speech by heart. "I'm happy to report that Dan is doing fine and wishes he could have been here. As for the ISS crew, Shorty, Leonid, Joe, and Maria are all continuing their work." He smiled. "And it appears Joe will beat his own record for total number of days in space."

Applause rang again, with Nancy clapping hardest of all.

Frank's billiard ball swelled to a basketball. "But the real hero of this mission was Larry Gomez, whose last act was to save my life."

He stepped from the podium as Steve motioned everyone to stand. "Ladies and gentlemen of the press, may we have a moment of silence to honor one of our fallen heroes, Lawrence Gomez."

All heads bowed. The press corps was silent for the moment, a calm before the storm. As soon as Stokes signaled the end of the conference, reporters jammed the door, eager to be the first to break the news.

Frank caught Nancy's eyes as she stuffed her iPad into her purse. She grinned at him.

He would definitely give her an exclusive.

53

"I" Plus Forty-one Days

Hildi resisted the urge to scream. Being an astronaut—or ex-astronaut—didn't give her any special privileges with British customs. Finally, she escaped. She spotted her mom and gave her a bear hug that would have put Francine's to shame.

Mom sniffled. "Oh, honey. I've missed you so much."

Hildi hugged her again, not trusting her voice. They walked through the airport, Hildi's carry-on trailing her as they hailed a cab and headed for the hotel.

"I wish you could stay longer, honey."

"So do I. Alan would only give me three days." Strain showed on Mom's usually peaceful face. Yesterday had taken its toll. "Did you see Chet? How is he?"

"Oh, fine. How was your flight?"

"Mom. I hate it when you change the subject." Hildi smiled to take the sting out of her words.

Her mother stared into the distance. "I thought your brother had changed. His e-mails sounded so positive. But when I saw him—"

"Same old Chet?"

"Only even more bitter." Mom sighed. "He's

turned his back on God again. He even refused to accept Dad's red tie."

"I don't understand. Red tie?"

"I guess we never told you about that, did we?" Mom's tone turned wistful. "It was something I gave your dad after we reconciled. Just a birthday gift, or so I thought." She leaned forward. "According to some website we stumbled across, a red tie represents both sin and forgiveness. Your father wanted him to have it." She choked on her words.

Hildi hugged her a long time. Grief and anger bounced around her heart with equal force. She missed her dad. Mom didn't deserve this. Chet caused it all. Another thought intruded. What about Dan? Would they ever get past the roadblock in their relationship?

Hildi turned to safer subjects—London's Big Ben, the Thames, and the Tube they'd take for a little sightseeing the next afternoon. Dan was never far from Hildi's mind. Neither was her brother.

****

Hildi drank her morning tea in silence, staring over her cup at the London skyline. She just wanted to get this over with. "I'd better get going. I don't want to be late for visiting hours."

Mom nodded as tears filled her eyes. "I'll be praying."

Hildi took a taxi to the prison. As she paid the chatty driver, his face showed sympathy. If he only knew…

She endured the indignity of being questioned, frisked, sign-here-pleased, and greeted with indifference by the guards. She stuffed her purse into a locker. Finally, she entered the visitor's room and took a seat.

Prisoners shuffled in. Hildi craned her neck for the first sight of her brother. He emerged, head down. Her heart sank. He'd lost weight. His curly red hair—so much like Dad's—was cropped close. His haggard face haunted her. She tensed as he plopped in front of her. What could she say to this stranger? They picked up the handsets.

"Hi." She tried to smile.

"Hi. I heard you found the key to the vaccine."

"Yes. Because of your help."

Chet snorted.

Hildi's words of affirmation stuck in her throat. Here she was, finally talking to Chet after all these years, and all she could dredge out of herself was a discussion about the virus. The virus he'd unleashed. Her blood pressure rose. Mom's usual tactic suddenly seemed a very good idea. "Heard you'll be arraigned soon."

"Yeah. Domestic bioterrorism."

Hildi cringed. It was one thing to hear the press coverage *ad nauseum*, another to hear it from her brother in such a dead voice.

"So what will you do now, astro-sister?" He spat the question.

Hildi bit back hot words. He was baiting her. "Go back to Level 4, I guess."

"Ever see Francine?"

"Yeah."

"Give her my love. And say hi to old Danny-boy." Chet's sarcastic tone brought Hildi's mama-bear defensiveness to the front. She throttled the handset.

"OK." She'd hoped his change from bitterness to

peace had been the real thing, not jail-induced salvation that would evaporate in the desert of confinement. Tears formed behind her eyes.

Chet scowled. "So that's it, huh?"

"No, it isn't." Hildi took a deep breath. "I'll always love you. You know that."

"Tell it to the judge." Chet slammed down the receiver, whirled out of his chair, and stomped back through the door. Back into prison. A prison of his own making.

Hildi sat and put her head in her hands. It was all up to God now. It always had been.

54

"I" Plus Sixty Days

Hildi's nose itched.

She ignored it as she gave the rhesus monkey a treat and placed her back in her cage. Smiley still showed no symptoms of the virus. The vaccine was still viable. She turned to Francine and grinned.

Any conversation in Level 4 resembled a shouting match, so Hildi yelled, "Done. Finally I can escape and scratch my nose."

"Last time to worry about that." Francine chuckled as she strode to the airlock.

Hildi followed, scrambled out of her blue suit, and scratched her patient nose with ferocity.

"Same old Hildi," Francine muttered. She headed for the showers.

As Hildi hung her suit, she reached up to caress a sleeve. "Thanks, old friend."

Francine cocked her head as they dressed. "Did you say Dan's meeting you in Houston? I thought he was still training in Alabama."

"He promised." Hildi stared into space, lost in the swirl of her thoughts.

"Earth to Hildi, Earth to Hildi."

Hildi smiled. "Just thinking."

"About what? No, don't tell me. You're thinking

about that infuriating man of yours." Francine strangled her tiny purse as she yanked it out of the locker.

"Among other things."

Francine wisely dropped the subject and hugged her. "I'm missing you already. I can't believe you're giving up Level 4 to work in Houston."

"I *will* be back for visits, you know."

"You'd better be."

They walked through the final airlock. The burning, moist smell of giant autoclaves bid Hildi a pungent, final farewell.

****

Hildi spent most of the flight staring out the window. Her clenched stomach had nothing to do with the plane's turbulence. She had enough turbulence of her own to deal with. Quitting Level 4, moving away from Atlanta, moving closer to Dan...Was she giving up everything for nothing? Whiskers sensed her mood and meowed, the one comment from the feline for the whole flight. She scratched behind his ear. "Yeah, I don't like it, either."

She'd hired a small moving company to pack her things and deliver them to her new condo in Houston. She'd sort it out later. Like her feelings.

Hildi deplaned and stretched her legs on the way to baggage claim. She piled two heavy pieces of luggage onto a cart along with Whiskers and wheeled her life toward the exit.

As she emerged into Houston's record heat wave, she spied a sign. It obscured the holder's face, but Hildi recognized the handwriting.

Dan dropped the sign and handed her a bouquet of wilted carnations. He kissed her and whirled her around before placing her gently on the ground. "Hi."

"Hi." Her stomach voiced an empty complaint. Loudly.

"Hungry?"

"What do you think?" She grinned up at him, still a bit dizzy.

"Texas Roadhouse OK?"

Hildi would have preferred a candlelit dinner at someplace romantic, but *romantic* wasn't in Dan's vocabulary. "Sounds great. But let's drop Whiskers off first."

The cat hissed as Dan peered into the cage. "We'll get you to your new home soon, pal."

They drove to her new condo. The walls were lined with boxes. Hildi wondered if she'd ever feel at home. She rubbed her arms as a sudden chill seized her.

Hildi placed the carnations on the counter then took Whiskers out of his prison and hugged him until she'd squeezed out all the purrs. Dan dragged in her suitcases. "What do you have in here, moon rocks?"

Whiskers ran figure eights around her legs as she set out food and water. She showed him the litter box and his cat bed. He immediately started exploring his new domain. "I'll be back soon," she promised, reaching to scratch him behind his ears. Hildi glanced at her cat one more time before shutting the door. He always settled into a new place as if he owned it. Would she ever feel that settled with Dan? She gripped his hand as they returned to the car.

They drove to a Roadhouse close to her condo. Hildi was grateful that Dan hadn't picked something closer to the space center. It reduced the possibility of running into astronauts with awkward questions.

She kept the conversation to pleasantries over dinner, the real issue dangling over her head like Damocles's sword. As they shared the Big 'Ole Brownie, Hildi updated him on the virus. She still felt exhausted from days and nights of fine-tuning the vaccine and supervising the inoculation of dozens of volunteers at Grady Hospital. And her eloquent prayer throughout that anxious time? *Please, Lord.*

"Chet really helped me in developing the vaccine."

Dan smile turned into a snarl. "Chet caused the outbreak. His help doesn't negate his criminal behavior. I hope he's locked away forever." His expression softened. "I know he's your brother."

Guilt tinged her weary sigh. "I blew him off for years. I should have talked to him, listened more. Maybe I could have done *something—*"

"You are *not* responsible, Hildi. Chet made his choice."

Her guilt persisted. Had that Nobel Prize really been so important? If she'd set her ambition aside and reached out to her bitter brother, could she have made a difference? She'd never know.

"What did the World Health Organization say about the loss of life?"

She jerked her mind back to the present. "Fewer died than I'd feared. WHO estimates about 50,000 worldwide. But with the slow distribution to undeveloped countries, the death toll is sure to rise." She shook her head. "You'd think even the insurgents would let the vaccine through instead of demanding bribes."

Hildi gazed into Dan's eyes. His big, blue eyes.

"I'll enjoy setting up the new CDC office. Nabbing the directorship was a big career move for me, and Hunt gave me a great recommendation. I owe him."

Dan nodded. "It'll be nice to have you close to me." He reached for her hand.

She squeezed it and uttered the four words men dreaded. "Let's talk about us."

He fed her a spoonful of vanilla ice cream, effectively keeping her mouth occupied. She swallowed. "Dan, please. I'm serious."

He stroked her hand, but she withdrew it. She waited.

"Things are a bit crazy at the rocket ranch right now. I need to head back to Alabama in the morning, but I'll be back next weekend." He cocked his head. "Why are you frowning?"

"Tired, I guess. I've been at a dead run for the last two weeks—training another scientist to replace me, saying good-bye to so many friends, packing." *And wanting your undivided attention.* Would she ever have it?

Dan smiled. "Well, you're here now. That's all that matters to me."

Is it?

"I'm on the short list for the moon mission."

"That's wonderful." Her heart screamed that it was anything but.

55

"I" Plus Sixty-seven Days

Dan sighed as Hildi snuggled into his shoulder. Warm sand tickled his toes as they sat on a blanket, admiring a pumpkin-colored moon rising from the sea. Stars twinkled their welcome. The surf *shooshed* in a comforting rhythm. Ahh...

Picnic on the beach with his favorite person. A week away from her was too long. The perfect setting for that special question. And this time, Dan wouldn't let it go to waste.

He wrapped protective arms around her, inhaling the citrusy scent of her hair. He pointed. "Full moon."

"Nice." Disappointment tinged Hildi's voice.

"That's not where I'm going."

"Huh?" She swiveled her head.

Dan dropped his arm and held her hands between his. "I talked to the NASA director today. He wants me to take over as CAPCOM when Pete retires."

"I'm so sorry." Hildi touched his cheek. "I know how much the moon mission meant to you."

Too much. "It's OK. I asked for the job."

Her brow furrowed. "Why?"

"I like being CAPCOM. I like working with Steve and the rest of the personnel at Mission Control. I'd planned to do it after I finished my astronaut work, but now…"

Time to take the plunge. Dan scooted to face her. "On the space station, I almost lost you. I can't go through that again. I can't lose you." Dan drew in a deep breath and gazed into her beautiful green eyes. "I…" His tongue knotted.

She smiled. "I love you, too."

He placed a cube the size of a softball in her hand, wrapped in NASA paper from the souvenir shop. Her face fell, but she seemed to put up a brave front. Maybe hoping for something else? His heart thudded to a halt.

She tore off the paper and held up his gift. The clear cube glinted in the moonlight. "It's beautiful."

"It's a paperweight." *I'm really blowing this.* "The image inside was actually laser engraved right through the glass."

"Of the moon." Her flat voice conveyed no emotion. She turned it in her hands.

"Take a good look. It's really detailed." *This is not going well.*

She did, but the thin line of her lovely lips was beginning to assume anger mode.

"You see that spot right there? That's the Sea of Tranquility."

"Uh-huh." Hildi squinted. "There's something on the surface." She peered more closely. "It looks like writing."

Dan faked a puzzled frown. "Where?"

"There. Can't you see it?" She deciphered the words. "I…love…you?" She gazed up at him.

"Well, you did say you wanted it in writing." His mouth quirked. He pulled a black velvet box from his pocket and opened it.

Hildi gasped.

Dan rose to one knee, ignoring the tears pooling in his eyes. "Will you marry me?"

"Yes." She dropped the paperweight and launched herself at him. They kissed and laughed and added more saltwater to the sand.

He placed the ring on her finger. A moonstone surrounded by diamonds flashed in the waning light. She wrapped her arms around his neck and leaned into his embrace. For the first time in his life, Dan felt content. Complete. He held her a long time.

Lifting his head, Dan admired the moon's reflection on the glass cube, on the foaming waves, and on the precious stones of Hildi's ring.

Hildi shifted on the towel. "Talked to Frank lately?"

Dan chuckled. His girl—*fiancée*—had picked up her mother's funny habit of changing subjects at the speed of reentry. "He's dating a reporter named Nancy. I think she's good for him." *And you're good for me.*

Hildi's expression turned wistful. Did she still have feelings for Frank? Return-to-him feelings? Worry pricked at Dan's happiness balloon. Then she grinned at him, and all his nettlesome doubts shriveled like thorns in a flame.

He squeezed her close. "He's training hard, waiting for the next mission."

"Think he'll get the moon?"

He pointed at the orb rising in the dusk. "He's welcome to that one." He picked up the moon cube and placed it in her hands. "This one is yours."